ALL MY SINS REMEMBERED

BLOODY JOE MANNION BOOK FIVE

PETER BRANDVOLD

WOLFPACK
PUBLISHING

All My Sins Remembered
Paperback Edition
Copyright © 2022 Peter Brandvold

Wolfpack Publishing
9850 S. Maryland Parkway, Suite A-5 #323
Las Vegas, Nevada 89183

wolfpackpublishing.com

This book is a work of fiction. Any references to historical events, real people or real places are used fictitiously. Other names, characters, places and events are products of the author's imagination, and any resemblance to actual events, places or persons, living or dead, is entirely coincidental.

All rights reserved. No part of this book may be reproduced by any means without the prior written consent of the publisher, other than brief quotes for reviews.

Paperback ISBN 978-1-63977-875-1
Large Print Hardcover ISBN 978-1-63977-874-4
eBook ISBN 978-1-63977-876-8

ALL MY SINS REMEMBERED

CHAPTER 1

"Bloody" Joe Mannion tied his big bay to the hitchrack at which eight other saddled horses stood hang-headed, and turned to his stocky, middle-aged deputy, and said, "Those five horses are theirs, Rio. See the lather on 'em? They rode hard all night and are wettin' their whistles and partaking of a mattress dance or two, I would suspect."

Rio Waite, in his early sixties, a good fifteen years older than Bloody Joe's forty-seven, broke open his double-barreled scattergun, checked to make sure both tubes were loaded, then closed the gun with a resolute click. "I would suspect you're right, Joe." He took a long look at the decrepit old, mud-brick, two-story building, formerly an overnight stage relay station that had been turned into a road ranch saloon and brothel here in the remote foothills of southwestern Colorado's San Juan Mountains. "How do you want to play it?"

"Careful like."

Rio grinned at his boss, who at six foot four inches tall, stood nearly a full head taller than his middle-aged deputy. "Why, Joe—that ain't like you."

Mannion chuckled as he shucked his prized '66 Winchester Yellowboy repeater from his saddle boot. "Gettin' soft in my later years."

"Pshaw."

"Nah," Bloody Joe admitted. "I'd like to take at least one of these lobos alive, is all, for my own selfish reasons." He flared an angry nostril as he jacked a live round into his Winchester's action. "I'd like to watch one of 'em—especially Bronco Lewis—do the midair two-step at the end of a hangman's rope for putting that bullet into that young teller's chest."

The day before, the five riders and known cutthroat outlaws led by Bronco Lewis, had taken advantage of Mannion and Waite having ridden out chasing rustlers by robbing the Del Norte Bank & Trust, absconding with thirty-six thousand dollars in scrip, specie, and gold coins, and leaving one young teller—Herman Ramos—dead on the floor of his cage. The gang, including Lewis, Willie Casper, Syd Bryant, Sandy "Hoot" Hardeman, and the half-breed, Mordecai Three Fingers—had ridden out whooping, hollering, and shooting.

The only lawman who'd been on duty at the time was Mannion's newest deputy, Cletus Booker. Mannion's youngest deputy, Henry McCallister, had been off fishing. Booker at six six and nearly three hundred pounds, not an ounce of it tallow, was extraordinarily adept at breaking heads but when it came to tracking, he was still taking baby steps.

Maybe one day Bloody Joe would teach him.

As it was, Booker had given up the chase only a few miles out of town. Bloody Joe and Rio Waite had gotten back into Del Norte after dark and had waited till first light to get after the bank-robbing killers. They'd caught up to them now after two days' hard riding, as the five had stopped in two mining towns along the way to kill a few hours spending the money that had apparently been burning holes in their saddlebags, unaware or not caring, it had seemed until a few hours ago, when they'd picked up their speed, that they were being shadowed by the two Del Norte town lawmen.

Bloody Joe's deputy sheriff's commission gave him jurisdiction to pursue outlaws into the rough country beyond Del Norte. Around Del Norte, surrounded by three mountain ranges—the Sawatch in the north, the Sangre de Cristos in the southeast, and the San Juans in the west—it was pretty much all rough country. Rough country filled with outlaws on the dodge...

"I'm pretty sure they realize now they've acquired shadows, Rio," Mannion said as he stepped up onto the roadhouse's rickety front stoop. A player piano was pattering away inside, beyond the batwings. "They may very well be waiting for us."

"I'll keep my eyes skinned."

"Let's go in and have a drink. Let 'em make the first move."

"All right."

Mannion pushed through the batwings and stepped to the left, quickly surveying the drinking hall before him. Rio walked in behind him and stepped to the right of the batwings clattering back into place. He held the shotgun straight out from his right hip, ready for trouble. There were only three customers in view—two men in prospectors' dusty, worn, canvas and wool garb playing two-handed poker near the bar—and a man in a cheap suit and bowler hat, likely a drummer, chatting and chuckling with a scantily clad half-breed whore at a table just ahead and right of the door.

All faces turned to the newcomers and instantly acquired serious casts.

That the place was further occupied was apparent by the groans and sighs of lovemaking—if you could call it love—in the second story, up the stairs running along the wall to Mannion's right. A bed was slamming metronomically and roughly enough against a wall up there to make the entire building shake. A balcony in the main drinking hall's upper right showed four closed doors and some shabby furniture on which three more girls, as scantily clad as the half-breed girl sitting with the drummer, lounged around, smoking what smelled like opium and passing a bottle.

It was behind those doors that the festivities were taking place.

If you could call it festive...

All three doxies turned to regard the newcomers, their own painted faces acquiring instantly serious expressions, as well. Their eyes were glassy from the effects of the midnight oil.

Mannion wasn't normally a patient man. But he didn't want to get anyone killed except the men he was after. He and Rio would take their time, let the outlaws come to them, which they would eventually do when they'd slaked their lust in the rooms on the balcony.

Joe turned to Rio then canted his head toward the plankboard bar running along the wall to his left and behind which an old former prospector, Leo Tollefson—short, bald, and long-faced—stood looking a little constipated.

The player piano, abutting the rear wall straight out away from Mannion and Rio, under a giant, snarling grizzly head, continued pattering away, its tinny, off-key notes echoing around the cave-like room.

Mannion headed for the bar, Rio falling into step behind him.

"Why, Joe Mannion, as I live and breathe," Tollefson said, fashioning a brittle smile on his thin-lipped mouth. His long face was sandwiched by shaggy muttonchops. "What brings you to this canker on the devil's behind?"

The stiff smile told Mannion the apron knew exactly what had brought him and Rio out here.

Mannion fashioned a smile of his own and chuckled, playing along. "Oh, you know how it goes, Leo. The hustle and bustle and endless consarned traffic of town wears on a man's nerves. We decided to ride out and partake of the peace and quiet of the San Juans—Rio and me."

"I know how it goes, Joe," Tollefson said, plucking two shot glasses off a near pyramid and setting one in front of Mannion and one in front of Rio, who laid his big barn blaster across the bar to his right. "I know how it goes. Nothing like the peace and quiet of the country. Not a city man myself." He filled Mannion's glass and then Rio's. "Don't quite know how you can take it, day in and day out."

"Me?" Rio said, lifting his shot glass to his lips and smiling over it at Mannion and then cutting his eyes at the apron, "I think I'll move out here when I retire. Just fish an' hunt and maybe trundle over here for a drink and a mattress dance at Leo's fine establishment."

He looked around the room as though admiring the fine furnishings of one of Denver or Colorado Springs's more tonier establishments rather than the San Juans' notoriously more violent buckets of blood.

"Who're you kidding, Rio?" Mannion said. "You'll never be able to retire. Not the way you go through money." He looked at Tollefson. "Never knew a man to spend money on flowers for whores."

He and the barman laughed.

Rio flushed, then grinned. "I'm an old romantic, gentlemen. Just an old romantic."

Mannion was leaning forward with his elbows on the bar, on either side of his half-finished drink. To Tollefson, he said, "Five of 'em, right?"

Tollefson sobered and gave a single nod.

The player piano was starting to wind down, nearing the end of "Little Brown Jug."

"They all upstairs?" Mannion said, loudly enough to be heard above the piano's final notes.

"One's out back." Tollefson jerked his chin in the direction of the piano. "Been in the privy for the past fifteen minutes."

"Which one?"

"Hardeman. Claimed my beans was bad." Tollefson hooked his thumb to indicate the big, cast-iron pot simmering on the small range behind him. "It ain't my beans is bad. It's his insides is bad."

Standing to Mannion's right, Rio plucked his own half-remaining whiskey shot off the bar. "Everything about that scum bucket is bad. His wick shoulda been snuffed a long time ago." He tossed back the rest of the shot and smacked his lips together in appreciation.

"Watch for him," Mannion told Rio out the side of his mouth just as the piano fell silent. Even more quietly, he said, "I'll keep an eye on the…"

He let his voice trail off. He'd just spied movement in the backbar mirror atop the balcony behind him, where a big man in longhandles had just stepped out of one of the rooms up there, wielding a long, double-barreled shotgun and a wolfish smile. He was large and dark and hairy as a grizzly bear. "Figured you'd catch up to us sooner or later, Bloody Joe!" the man's voice thundered around the drinking hall.

The doves leaped off the shabby furniture and scattered like chickens before a storm.

"*Down!*" Mannion shouted as the big half-breed, Mordecai Three Fingers, snapped the barn blaster to his shoulder.

Mannion, Rio, and Tollefson all ducked at once, an eye blink before the shotgun roared, sending a boom like two boulders crashing together around the saloon, both barrels blossoming smoke and rose-colored flames and blasting out the backbar mirror in a screech of breaking glass.

Mannion shucked both of his silver-chased Russian .44s with seven-and-a-half-inch barrels—one from the cross-draw holster on his left hip, the other from the holster tied down low on his right thigh. Straightening, he aimed hastily and fired first his right-hand gun then the left-hand gun and watched in satisfaction as each slug in turn punched through the half-breed's broad chest.

Three Fingers roared like the bear he so much resembled and stumbled backward, dropping the gut-shredder to the floor at his bare feet. He got both feet settled beneath him, glanced at the blood welling from the two holes in his broad chest, and stumbled forward, lifting his head to send another grating roar at the rafters. He stumbled up against the railing, which buckled precariously against the big man's weight before the entire wooden balustrade bent outward and broke and tumbled toward the floor of the main drinking hall along with the big bear of a man who'd knocked it free.

Both struck the first-story floor with a crashing *boom!*

The din's echo hadn't died before two more second-floor doors opened and two more men ran out onto the balcony, each loudly jacking rounds into the rifles they were wielding—the little, blond-headed Syd Bryant with his Winchester carbine and the tall, skinny, redheaded, Willie Casper, with a brass-breeched Henry .44. At nearly the same time, the back door to the right of the player piano and the snarling grizzly head opened, and Sandy "Hoot" Hardeman—clad in longhandles, boots, and trademark straw sombrero with the image of a naked lady stitched into the front of the crown—ran in wielding two forty-fours and bellowing like a poleaxed bull.

"Rio, take Hardeman!" Mannion shouted as he ran forward to avoid the slugs raining down from Bryant's and Casper's long guns.

In the corner of his left eye, he saw Rio dive to his left across a table and, striking the floor on the other side, cut loose with one barrel of his twelve-gauge. Mannion didn't see the effect of the shotgun on Hoot Hardeman; he only heard the agonized howl. Joe was distracted by the two men cutting down on him from the balcony as he slid across the table and landed in the sour-smelling sawdust on the other side, rising to one knee, raising both Russians, and going to work, shooting at first Bryant and then Casper.

His first shot took Bryant through the dead center of his forehead.

His second shot caromed slightly wide of Casper to plunk into the wall behind him, just inches beneath a bracket lamp. Casper laughed crazily and cut down on Mannion with a bullet that sizzled across Joe's left cheek. That caused Mannion to pull his next shot wide, as well.

And then Casper was aiming at him again. A stone dropped in Joe's belly. Casper had him dead to rights and between shots.

Casper grinned as he took up the slack in his right index finger, squeezing the trigger.

The bullet that would have cleaned Mannion's clock did not come. No smoke nor flames roiled from the Henry's barrel.

There was only a benign *click!*

Casper's dung-brown eyes widened in shock, lower jaw dropping nearly to his longhandle-clad chest.

It appeared that in his haste to bed the so-called "ladies" here at Tollefson's road ranch, he hadn't remembered to load his Henry, which he'd likely nearly emptied on his and his fellow devils' wild ride out of Del Norte.

He switched his exasperated gaze to the rifle of topic, as though it were a good friend who'd let him down in his moment of need, gave an enraged wail and, rising from a knee, threw the Henry at Mannion. Joe deflected the rifle with his raised left arm and then stared up to see Willie Casper himself flying toward him, the outlaw's long, pale, redheaded, longhandle-clad body appearing like some large, deformed bird in attack mode, eyes wide and bright with savagery.

Mannion raised both Russians and shot the skinny killer twice through the chest. Casper's face crumpled in agony a half-second before he slammed into Bloody Joe, and they both hit the floor with a *boom!*, Casper on top of Joe, writhing and bleeding.

"Good God!" Mannion cried, tossing the dying outlaw off him.

Casper lay belly up in the sawdust beside Joe, shivering and hiccupping.

His blue-eyed, liquid gaze found Mannion. He said, "Ah, hell—I'm just another notch on Bloody Joe's Russians!"

He turned his head to one side and half closed his eyes. His skinny chest fell still.

Silence descended on the drinking hall.

Mannion looked around.

The other three customers and the half-breed whore were cowering under their tables.

To Joe's left, Rio slowly gained his feet. He'd broken open his shotgun and was replacing the spent wad with a fresh one from his cartridge belt.

Breaking the room's heavy silence, Mannion said, "Where's Bronco Lewis?"

Rio snapped his shotgun closed. "If I had to guess, I'd say he's still up there."

Mannion followed his deputy's gaze to the rail-less balcony. Three doors were open—one to the left and two to the right of the only remaining closed one.

Whoever was in there was as quiet as a church mouse on the night before Easter.

CHAPTER 2

Behind Mannion and Rio Waite, the barman, Tollefson said, "He's got my best whore up there. Bonnie."

Mannion and Rio looked at him, and he said, "She's my best moneymaker. Makes real good money fer me."

Tollefson looked a little paler and longer faced than before, on the heels of the lead swap and the destruction of his backbar mirror, which would likely cost him a pretty penny to replace. He was likely calculating the cost of his replacing his best whore, Bonnie, as well. Mannion could see the cold calculations occurring behind his eyes.

Joe gave a wry snort then turned to Rio. There were two stairs rising to the balcony. One at the rear of the room, to the right of the door through which the now-dead Hoot Hardeman had run in, howling, and one running up the front wall, ahead and to Mannion's right. He jerked his chin to indicate to Rio the stairs near the back door and where Hardeman now lay in a bloody heap. Holding both of his Russians straight down at his sides, Joe headed for the stairs running up along the front wall.

He gained the stairs and climbed slowly, quietly.

At the rear of the room, Rio did the same. He winced, as did Mannion, as the risers creaked beneath the shifting weight of their ascent.

Mannion and his deputy gained the top of their respective stairs at the same time, turned, and began walking toward the only closed door, roughly in the center of the balcony. Joe stepped over the outstretched legs of Syd Bryant, who sat with his back up against the wall of the room he'd surfaced from, shooting. His eyes were open and opaque in death as he stared out across the main drinking hall below. Mannion's .44 round had drilled a puckered, blue hole in the middle of his lightly freckled forehead.

Sobbing sounded in the room flanking the dead man.

As Mannion passed the open doorway, he glanced into the room to see a girl quivering under a sheet and a blanket on the small room's lone bed. Only her eyes and the top of her head were visible as she stared out fearfully toward the Russian-wielding lawman.

Joe pressed two fingers to his lips and continued toward where Rio was approaching the lone, closed balcony door.

They reached the door at the same time. They stood on each side of it, regarding each other fatefully. Mannion tipped his head toward the door. Inside, he could hear more female sobbing.

"Shut up," said a deep, ominous man's voice, just above a whisper. "Just shut up, dammit!"

Mannion reached for the doorknob, rattled it then pulled his hand away quickly. Good thing he did, too. Just then a revolver thundered once, twice, three times, the bullets forming three points of a rough triangle in the door's upper panel.

Mannion stepped in front of the door and rammed his right foot against the upper panel, just left of the knob.

He lurched back to his right as the revolver crashed three more times, one bullet screeching through the opening and the next two drilling the door again as it bounced off the inside wall and into the frame, adding two more holes to the three already there.

As the last belch of the revolver still echoed, Mannion cast an incredulous glance at Rio, who shrugged. Joe rammed the flat of his right foot against the door once more, slamming it back against the wall to his right. He stepped into the room and stopped another bounce back of the door with his right foot and aimed both silver-chased Russians straight out in front of him.

Bronco Lewis stood before him, his back to the window in the room's far wall. The killer was as naked as the day he was born but a whole lot uglier. He was tall and rail-thin, and long, greasy black hair hung to his pale shoulders. He stretched his lips back from gritted teeth, showing his two silver front ones, as he held the plump, heavy-breasted, redheaded whore in front of him, like a shield. He had his left arm snaked around her neck and he was holding his cocked Army Colt .44 to her right temple.

She stared at Mannion through tear-filled, brown eyes.

Her lips fluttered as she sobbed.

"Drop the irons, Bloody Joe!" Lewis yelled in his thick Texan accent. He'd once been a shooter for the bigger cattle outfits down Texas way. Or so Mannion had heard. "Or I'll blow this girl's head clean off her shoulders!"

Mannion grinned over the barrels of his outstretched .44s. "Go ahead and try, you damn fool."

Lewis's single, black brow stitched in the middle, over his long, crooked, hawk-like nose. "Huh?"

Mannion chuckled. "You fired off all six shots, you dunderhead."

Lewis's jaw loosened and that stitch in his brow tightened as he looked at the cocked Colt in his hand. He shifted his weight from one bare foot to the other, considering the Colt and then Mannion and then the Colt again.

Rio Waite stepped into the room behind Mannion. "Hah!" he said.

Mannion knew his deputy was grinning broadly behind him, shaking his head.

Lewis turned to Mannion again, hardening his jaws in defiance. "No, I didn't never! I still got one load in the wheel!"

The girl glanced at the pistol aimed at her head and then at Mannion, hope growing in her eyes. "He did, didn't he?" she said. "He fired off all six rounds." She rolled her eyes up to glance over her shoulder at her captor and said with saucy confidence, "Even I can count to six, Bronco, you moron!"

Still shifting his weight from one bare foot to the other, Lewis made a frustrated sound through his gritted teeth. He glared at Mannion then shifted his gaze to his six-gun, suddenly jerked the barrel toward Joe, and squeezed the trigger.

Ping!

He looked at the gun in horror.

"*Ach!*" he screeched.

He threw the gun at Mannion, sissy-like.

Mannion ducked and the gun smacked Rio in the head. The middle-aged deputy yowled and cursed.

"Sorry, Rio!" Mannion said.

Cursing the Fates for having let him unknowingly empty all six of the Colt's chambers, Lewis threw the girl at Mannion then twisted around and leaped through the window behind him in a screech of breaking glass. He ran down the sloping roof, hesitated at the edge for just a second, glancing back over his shoulder toward where Mannion shoved the girl aside and strode to the broken window.

"Don't do it, Lewis!" Joe warned.

The naked outlaw grinned then dropped down over the edge of the roof and out of sight. Mannion winced at the sickening snapping sound of breaking bone and the following scream.

Mannion cursed and turned to Rio, who'd taken his hat off and was rubbing his head just beneath his dramatically retreating and thinning hairline. "How's your head?"

"It hurts!"

"Sorry about that."

"I shoulda ducked. Gettin' slow in my old age."

"That son of a bitch is turning out to be far more trouble than he's worth, trying to keep him alive."

"You can say that again!" Rio said, indignantly rubbing the growing goose egg on his temple.

Mannion canted his head toward the girl, who sat on the bed, arms crossed on her breasts, head lowered, sobbing. "Stay with her, will you? I'm gonna see to Bronco."

"Yeah, yeah—all right."

Mannion quickly gathered up Bronco Lewis's strewn clothing including the man's boots and battered, tan Stetson. Clutching the gear in one arm against his chest, he headed out the door. He went downstairs, where the three customers and the whore were beginning to lift their heads above their tables, wary looks remaining in their wide eyes.

"How's Bonnie?" Tollefson called from behind the bar.

"Fair to middlin', but I'm sure she'll be raking in the jingle again in no time," Mannion said as he pushed out through the batwings.

He strode around the road ranch's left front corner to find Bronco Lewis in the sage and brush that had grown up along the base of the building, clutching his left ankle, which had an unnatural bulge in it, and howling. The soles of his bare feet were cut and bleeding from the broken glass he'd walked through as he'd descended the roof.

Mannion scowled down at the naked devil and said, "Are you stupid or drunk or *both*?"

Lewis cast his pain-racked gaze up at Mannion and said, "I reckon...maybe a little...maybe a little o' both. Oh, God, it hurts. I need a sawbones bad!"

"After what you did to Herman Ramos, you don't deserve no sawbones. You deserve a bullet." Mannion crouched to brusquely plant his right index finger against the middle of the killer's single, black brow. "Right there!"

Lewis narrowed his cow-stupid eyes at Mannion as he snapped out, "He was a Mex and he smirked at me an' said we wouldn't get far before Bloody Joe ran us down and kicked us all out with cold shovels!"

"He was right, wasn't he? Least, as far as the other four go, an' I'm reconsidering taking you back to Del Norte riding upright!"

"He was a Mex and I will not abide a Mex smirking at me!"

Mannion chocked down his fury. For the life of him,

he didn't know how he was able to resist the urge to pull one of his Russians and drill a hole through the dead center of the crazy, cow-stupid killer's single, black brow. A few years ago, he would have done just that, no questions asked. Against his reputation, he really was getting soft in his later years.

He tossed the clothes and boots down at Lewis. "Get dressed."

"How can I get dressed? My ankles grievin' me somethin' awful! Look at my feet!"

"Get dressed," Mannion repeated. "I'm gonna go in and wet my whistle. By the time I'm done, you'd better be dressed and ready to ride, or I'm gonna drill you that third eye."

With that, Joe swung around and strode back around the corner of the road ranch to the front. The two miners and the drummer appeared to have had enough excitement for one day. The miners were mounting their horses at the hitchrack, and the drummer was hanging his sample case from his saddle horn.

All three cast wary looks at Bloody Joe.

Inside, Joe found Rio Waite just then setting two shot glasses on the table at which the half-breed whore now sat, comforting the redheaded whore, Bonnie, who'd shrugged into a sheer, lime-green wrap. Bonnie was still sobbing, lips quivering, but she looked angry now, too, as she and the half-breed whore conversed in hushed tones, the half-breed whore tenderly rubbing the redhead's back.

"There ya are, ladies," Rio said. "On ol' Rio. Sure sorry about the trouble."

He turned as Mannion walked into the room. "How's Bronco?"

"He's been better," Mannion said as he headed for the bar.

Tollefson was sweeping up the glass from his shattered, backbar mirror.

"You got him cuffed?" Rio asked as he sidled up to the bar beside Joe.

"Nah," Mannion said.

"Won't he get away?"

"Not with that bulge in his ankle."

Mannion ordered two whiskeys. Shaking his head and muttering about how much it was gonna cost him to get another mirror freighted up here from Colorado Springs, Tollefson set him and Rio up with a fresh whiskey apiece.

Rio looked at Mannion and thumbed his battered Stetson up off his forehead, showing the growing goose egg on his temple. "I kept waiting for the pistol shot."

"Pistol shot?" Mannion said, lifting the shot glass to his lips.

"Yeah," Rio said. "The one I usually hear when an outlaw becomes more trouble than he's worth. You know —like the old days?"

Mannion grimaced then sipped down half the whiskey in his shot glass. He leaned forward, resting his elbows on the bar.

He stared pensively at what remained of the backbar mirror, and shook his head, as puzzled as his deputy by his recent restraint. "I know. I can't figure it, myself." He grinned and turned to Rio. "But, hey, the hangman needs to make a living, too, and what a sight it will be to watch Bronco Lewis dance the midair two-step on Main Street of Del Norte, broken ankle an' all!"

"Hah!" Rio said, slamming his open right hand down against the bar. "Won't the kids and dogs and pious spinsters of the Sobriety League have a ball, though!"

Both men laughed.
Sobering, Mannion said, "How's your head?"
"It hurts!"
"Sorry about that."
"That's all right. I shoulda ducked."

CHAPTER 3

Bounty hunter Ulysses Xavier Lodge rode into Del Norte, southwestern Colorado Territory, around ten thirty the next morning.

The main street running north and south between a good eight blocks of tall, false-fronted business establishments, including the new, three-story Del Norte Opera House boasting tall, arched windows on all three floors, was already busy, a nearly steady stream of ranch, mining, and lumber wagons bouncing and clattering over the street's considerable ruts, which were filled with water after a recent mountain rainstorm.

Rains came often and violent to the high country in the fall.

Ulysses knew that well enough. On the trail up from Pueblo the night before, he'd had to take cover in a notch cave and sit by his coffee fire, brooding out into the rainy night. That was all right. Sitting out there alone wasn't nearly as lonely as it usually was—not with visions of Miss Jacqueline dancing around inside the big bounty hunter's square, bearded, granite-like head.

He smiled now as his gaze slid from the opera house

on the street's right side, to the equally impressive San Juan Hotel & Saloon standing tall, broad, and downright impressive on the opposite end of the block. The San Juan was also three stories, constructed of wood-framed clapboard painted white with spruce green trim and a big red sign with ornate black letters stretching across the top of its third story. No, sir—there was no missing the San Juan—likely the finest, most well-appointed saloon and hotel in the mountains of southern Colorado. It was at least as impressive as the finest hotels in Leadville, another two- or three-day pull, depending on which route you took, to the north.

Yessir, Miss Jane Ford had really outdone herself when she'd built that place. She ran the place, too, with the help of a manager. But she'd likely be on duty this morning, hovering around her "girls." Ulysses had to assume so, anyway. She usually was—all hours of the day and night.

Ulysses Lodge had taken note of that. He'd have to somehow slip inside and avoid the lady's scrutinizing gaze. Avoid Miss Jane and her bouncers, that was. Last time Ulysses had pulled through Del Norte, she'd had three big toughs in fancy suits patrolling the place, wielding hide-wrapped clubs.

Lodge and Miss Jane Ford had had a little misunderstanding the last time Ulysses was in town. Lodge had to admit the fault had been his own. He'd drunk a little too much whiskey and gotten out of line—a little too *passionate*, you might say--with one of the girls.

Miss Jacqueline Hayes, to be exact.

Yessir, the fault had been all Lodge's. He knew better than to overdrink. He knew what happened when he did. He lost all control of himself, and his emotions took over. Well, it wasn't really *all* his fault. He was an *emotional* man, was Ulysses Lodge. He felt things more deeply than most men did. It was just the way he was. He couldn't help it any more than he could help the color of his eyes. Why, his soul was a damn near bottomless fount of feelings, especially when it came to the female sex.

When Ulysses Lodge tumbled for a gal, he tumbled hard.

And he'd tumbled oh-so-hard for Miss Jacqueline Hayes. She'd tumbled for him, too. He could see it in her eyes. Of course, she was a professional. She didn't let on. But she'd tumbled for him, all right.

Ha!

"Hey, look where you're goin', ya damn fool!"

The man's indignant cry jerked Lodge out of his blissful reverie with a start. He stiffened in the saddle and then hauled back on Beast's reins, curveting the horse lest he should run over the gray-bearded little man in the dark-green three-piece suit crossing the street via wooden boards laid through the ankle-deep mud. The popinjay glared up at the bounty hunter, pointing his silver-capped walking stick like a rifle, and said, "You should watch where you're going, you big ape, or you and that big ugly horse are gonna run someone over like you damn near did me!"

Instantly, fury burning up behind the bounty hunter's eyeballs, he reached under his buffalo coat for his big Colt Navy conversion .44, clicked the hammer back, and aimed at the little, gray-bearded man, and said, "What'd you call me? Hey, get back here an' face me! What'd you call me, you puny, little privy snipe!"

But the little man had already given a little yelp at seeing the big hogleg pulled on him and fairly run across the street to the opposite boardwalk. Staring in terror over his left shoulder at his assailant, he ducked into the post office on that side of the street and was gone.

Lodge grinned.

Ignoring the indignant stares of the folks around him, on the boardwalks and on the street, he blew across the end of his big hogleg, twirled the gun on his finger, then dropped it back into its holster.

His fury subsiding—and a good thing it did, too, because it didn't always dissipate that fast, and hadn't Lodge had the jail time to show for it too?—the big, bearded man in the buffalo coat and bullet-crowned, floppy-brimmed hat threaded his way through the wagon and horseback traffic to the west side of the street. He reined up at one of the three wrought iron hitchracks fronting the San Juan on the corner of Main Street and Third Avenue, directly across the main drag from the San Juan Stage Line's main depot building.

The San Juan stage must have just pulled into town ahead of Lodge because there it sat in front of the depot building. The muddy, sweat-lathered six-horse hitch was just then being switched out for fresh. The jehu, Bill Kilmer, was palavering in the street, near the coach's right front wheel with the stage line's manager, Bryce Wilkes. Both men glanced at Lodge. Lodge smiled and waved.

Neither man waved back. They returned their gazes to each other and continued their conversation.

That was all right. They must not have seen Lodge, after all. Maybe they hadn't looked at him like he'd thought they had. If they'd seen him, they'd have waved.

Whistling to keep his mood up, Lodge swung down from Beast's back and tied the big steeldust's reins to the center hitchrack at which four other mounts were tied.

All three hitchracks had a good many horses tied to them, even so early in the day.

Yessir, Miss Jane would be busy.

That was good. That was good. He'd get lost in the crowd, he hoped.

Lodge reached into the right pocket of his buffalo coat, wrapped his hand around the little ring box, and felt an encouraging smile tug at his mouth corners.

It was there. Still there. Good. He'd hate to have lost it, since he'd made a special trip way down to Las Cruces to retrieve it from his mother's old steamer trunk housed in his brother-in-law's buggy shed.

Lodge mounted the broad wooden steps and climbed to the broad wooden veranda on which six or seven men, most in business suits, stood with dimpled beer schooners clenched in their fists, some with eggs lolling on the bottom, the sun glinting off the dark-orange yolks. Seeing those beers made Lodge thirsty. Seeing those eggs made him hungry.

Why, he was fairly drooling like an old dog eyeing a bone!

He chuckled and kept whistling to keep his mood up as he pushed through heavy oak batwings, admonishing himself against ordering any beer or whiskey...or any breakfast, for that matter.

He wasn't here to eat or drink. He was here to see the love of his life. He was here to stave off the bone-splintering cold loneliness of his solitary days and nights, of filling his future with the joy of having someone to share it with...of not dying alone...

That wasn't too much to ask, now, was it?

He was a man with a future, after all. He was a damned good bounty hunter. He'd done well for himself. He'd even bought himself a little, wood-frame house in

Pueblo. He could feel the quarter-folded deed in the front pocket of his hickory shirt even now as he stepped into the crowd of drinkers and diners in the San Juan's main drinking hall, crouching a little so his head didn't rise so far above the heads of most of the other standing men in the room, making him, at six foot six and wide as a barn door, conspicuous.

As though he wasn't conspicuous enough in his bloodstained buckskin trousers further stained from the smoke of a thousand remote campfires, his high-topped buckskin moccasins, and molting buffalo coat that smelled like a dead buffalo left to ripen in the sun too long. (Not to him; Lodge was inured to it, having worn it from September to May for the past twenty-plus years, ever since he'd killed and butchered the beast himself and his Crow wife, one of several Indian wives he'd taken over the years, had tanned it. But others within sniffing distance often turned pale and looked faint before hurrying away from the huge, bearded man in the disgusting garment.)

Lodge sidled his way toward the rear of the room, casting cautious glances toward the elaborate, glistening bar and backbar running along the wall far to his left, where as soon as he'd entered, he'd spotted Miss Jane helping the lone barman pour drinks. Lodge suspected a shift must have ended at one of the area mines, for the saloon was filled with bearded miners clad in canvas, wool, denim, and the customary cork-soled, high-topped, lace-up boots. Lodge was glad for the miners' presence. They looked enough like him—and a few were nearly as large as he—that he didn't feel as notable and out of place as he would have had the room been filled with local businessmen and stock buyers, as it often was.

Miss Jane was busy, pouring beers and whiskeys and

laughing with the men crowding up to the bar, hoping to have a few words with the beautiful redheaded woman decked to the nines in one of her many fancily cut gowns, jewels dangling from her ears, encircling her neck, and trimming her fingers.

A beautiful woman, Miss Jane. But, boy, could she read from the Book to a fellow when she got her dander up!

Fortunately, Lodge made his way to the stairs running up the wall opposite the bar—a good, long ways away from Miss Jane, a good hundred milling, laughing, conversing men between her and Lodge—without him being noticed by no more than one or two half-drunk, laughing miners, and only in passing, at that!

He placed his hand on the banister at the bottom of the stairs and, grinning wolfishly, anxiously, heart thudding expectantly, began his quick, crouching ascent, keeping one eye on the bar and Miss Jane.

One step...two steps...three steps...four...

Miss Jane was leaning forward across the bar to listen to what was likely a joke being told by one of her customers, showing her perfect white teeth between ruby-red lips as she laughed along with the man.

Five steps...six steps...seven steps...

Miss Jane glanced toward the stairs.

Shit!

Lodge's heart banged against his breastbone.

But then Jane swung around to answer a call from another customer, and Lodge took the last several steps two at a time. He gained the second-floor landing, laughing into his arm and almost dropping to his knees in nervous exhaustion. He sobered when a girl, one of Miss Jane's doxies, but not Miss Jacqueline Hayes, came down from the third story, looking sleepy and frumpy and dressed in a skimpy corset, bustier, and high-heeled shoes, feathers in her neatly coifed hair.

She moved awkwardly in the shoes, paying very close attention to each step she took, squeezing the banister on her right, as though it were the rail of a ship on choppy seas.

Ulysses cleared his throat, turned away, and brushed his fist across his chin as he continued up the third-story stairs, brushing quickly past the doxie, who gave him a sour look before quickly glancing away. She carefully turned on the second-floor landing and ambled her way down the second-floor hall. She wasn't going down to the main drinking hall but was likely visiting another doxie on the second floor.

Good.

Lodge didn't have to worry about her reporting to Miss Jane the odd-looking stranger she'd just seen on the stairs, laughing into his arm...

Lodge gained the third floor and quickened his pace, glancing at the closed doors passing on each side of him and behind which Miss Jane's whores were either asleep or preparing themselves for the lunch crowd. He knew Miss Jacqueline's door by heart. He'd been up there five times. Well, four and a half times, actually, since his fifth time had been cut short by a loud knock by Miss Jane herself and a reading from the Book about being too loud and, well...*passionate*.

Lodge's word, not Miss Jane's, of course.

The thing was, when it came to Miss Jacqueline, Ulysses Lodge just couldn't help himself. He honestly didn't think she could help it either. No, not really!

Her door slid toward him, closer and closer, the second to the last on the hall's right side.

Lodge's heart hammered his breastbone not so anxiously now as eagerly.

He stopped at her door—oh, her precious door. The door she opened and closed herself and passed through maybe fifty times every day! Standing there, fingering the little box in his coat pocket, conscious of the quarter-folded deed in his shirt pocket, he sniffed the air, smelling the rarefied, very particular smell of her.

No other girl smelled like Miss Jacqueline. She smelled like...well, like what heaven probably smelled like if there really was such a place. Yeah, that's how Miss Jacqueline smelled. She smelled like heaven in the springtime, if heaven were in the mountains.

Lodge removed his right hand from his coat pocket. He looked at it. It was so big and brown, dirt ground into the tiny grooves and fissures around the knuckles, that he suddenly wished he'd taken a bath before visiting his bride to be.

Ulysses, you damn fool! You've been out on the trail for over two weeks, and you've only bathed once or twice in creeks between here and Las Cruces!

He gritted his teeth against his silent self-castigation.

You didn't even bring flowers!

He shook his head. No, no, no. Don't start in on that. You're just scared. You go ahead and knock on that door, Ulysses Lodge, you chicken-hearted cuss.

He lifted his chin and drew a deep breath, whistled under his breath to get his mood back up. His mood could really drop into the cellar. A really deep cellar, at that. But here he was only a few feet from his gal.

Oh, joy!

Lodge drew another breath and shoved his big, brown, dirty fist toward the door and knocked twice, softly, on the oak panel.

CHAPTER 4

THE OH-SO-FAMILIAR VOICE SOUNDED ON THE OTHER side of the door, wilting the big man's heart. "Come, Frankie!"

Ulysses stared at the door, frowning curiously. He cleared his throat, about to speak, but then nixed the idea and decided to just go ahead and open the door, which he did. He leaned forward, poking his head into the small room, a rumpled bed ahead and to the left, a mirrored dresser abutting the wall ahead and to Lodge's right.

She sat on a small stool before the dresser, gazing into the mirror while she did something to her eyelashes. She was dressed in a white silk chemise and pantalettes, and that was all. Her legs were oh-so-long and creamy. One pale, tender foot rested atop the other as she worked in the mirror.

She chuckled and said, "Frankie, you know you don't have to— "

Just then she turned toward Ulysses, saw the big, bearded, granite-like head with sun-leathered face poking into her room, and gasped with a start. She rose from the stool so quickly that she knocked it over and almost fell as she tripped over it and backed away on her pale, tender bare feet.

"No!" she said, shrilly, fearfully, color rising in her pale cheeks that still showed a few sleep lines from her pillow. "I'm not open for business. Didn't Miss Jane tell you?"

"Shh! Shh!" Lodge said, grinning and pressing two fingers to his lips as he stepped into the room and quickly closed the door behind him. Just as quickly, only half-conscious of doing so, he twisted the key in the lock. "Miss Jackie—it's me. Ulysses!"

He thrust up his two big hands and opened them in supplication, his oily grin in place.

She thrust an angry finger at the door. "Get out of here! Didn't Miss Jane tell you we're not yet open for business—"

"No, no, no, no," Lodge said. "I'm not here for business, Miss Jackie." He moved slowly forward—the room seemed so small with his big bulk in it, but he tried not to think about that; he tried to feel comfortable here, with her—and poked his right hand into the right pocket of his buffalo coat. "Remember how I said wouldn't it be nice if we could be together—you know, like always? And you said it would be nice, too, if only somethin' about the Fates or some such. I can't remember what you said exactly, but I could tell by your eyes you felt the same way I did."

"Listen, you—get out of my room this instant!" she intoned, hardening her jaws and twisting her otherwise beautiful face into an ugly mask. She stomped one of her pretty, pale, tender feet, wrinkling her brows, and again thrust a pointing finger toward the door. "Get out of my room before I scream for Miss Jane!"

"Oh, no, no, no, no," Lodge beseeched her, continuing forward. "Please, don't do that, Miss Jackie. I just wanted to show you what I rode all the way down to Las Cruces to fetch ya! It's right here in my pock—!"

"Get out!" she fairly screamed. "Get out this instant!"

The verbal assault so astonished and exasperated Lodge that he dropped the small, black, velvet-lined ring box to the floor. It rolled under the dresser and came partway open so that he could see his mother's gold wedding ring, set with two small rubies around a single small diamond, residing on a bed of dyed burlap. Lodge's dear mother had bequeathed the ring to him on her deathbed nearly twenty years ago now.

"Here, Ulysses," she'd said, breathless and sweating from sickness. "You find yourself a good, sweet girl who'll make you a good home and give you a passel of strong sons. You need a good, sweet girl to settle you down, keep you from ridin' here an' there, blowin' around like a blame tumbleweed! No more of those rock-worshippin' wimmen! You give up the bottle an' your reckless an' lonely way. You put that ring on her finger, an' you make a good life for yourself!"

That had been his mother's last wish for him, and here he was, only trying to make good on the promise he'd made her. In twenty years, he'd never met the girl his mother had described...until he'd met Miss Jackie here at Miss Jane's San Juan Hotel & Saloon.

Ulysses stopped five feet away from the girl who had backed up against the room's rear wall. Again, he raised his hands, palm out, and said as sweetly as he could, "Miss Jackie, you don't understand. I fetched that ring from my dear ol' ma's steamer trunk in Las Cruces. She given it to me when she was dyin'. In twenty years, I never met the girl I wanted to give it to until I met you." Lodge broadened his grin as he pressed his thumb to the buffalo coat over the shirt pocket in which resided the quarter-folded deed for the neat, little, wood-frame house in Pueblo. "I even bought us a house. You know—to live in after we're married."

The scrunched her face up again and it turned beet red as she opened her pretty mouth that was suddenly not pretty anymore and cut loose with such a loud, shrill scream that it made the big bounty hunter's eardrums rattle.

"Help!" she cried. "Someone, come—"

She didn't get the rest out for just then Lodge lunged forward, instantly closing the gap between himself and Miss Jackie, and wrapped his big hands around her head, closing the right one over her mouth, choking off the infernal screaming that purely had his blood boiling in sudden anger.

Sudden rage.

How could she treat him like this? He'd come here with his hat in his hands, so to speak. He'd been about to gift this girl with his dearly departed mother's own wedding ring—the one his young pa must have worked overtime to afford, mucking out stalls in the livery barn he'd worked in in Mesilla until, when he'd been Lodge's age now, he was kicked so hard in the gut by a mule that he'd died after three long, miserable days of howling—long after Lodge had considered putting a bullet through his head to shut him up.

"Miss Jackie!" he wheezed out in frustration, keeping his hand clamped over the girl's mouth. "There's been a tragic misunderstandin' here, you see. I only came to ask for your hand an' to give you my dear ol' ma's ring! You know, liked we talked about. Oh, Miss Jackie, please stop fightin' me. Won't you please just listen to reason. It's your dear sweet Ulysses. Don't you remember tellin' me about the Fates an' such. Well, I done planned it all out, careful like—oh, Jackie, please stop fightin' me. I'll take my hand away, but first you gotta—"

He stopped when he heard running feet growing louder in the hall outside the girl's room. He could feel the reverberations of said feet through the floor beneath his own.

There were three loud knocks on the girl's door.

"Jackie! Jackie—are you all right?"

"Go away, Miss Jane!" Lodge yelled, gritting his teeth in frustration and growing rage. "I come to talk to Miss Jackie—alone! She's just bein' *ornery* today!"

The doorknob rattled violently.

A moment of silence and then the door crashed open, splinters flying from the latch as well as a chunk of steel that flew across the room. A big man in a three-piece suit and muttonchop whiskers filled the doorway. He stepped to one side and Miss Jane herself walked into the room. The expression on her face was stony, ruby-red lips set in a firm line.

Her amber eyes blazed with fury.

"Lodge, I banned you from my establishment for life! Now, you let that girl go and get the hell out or I will throw you out!"

As she'd spoken, another muscular bouncer in a three-piece suit—a red-haired man with a thick, red, walrus mustache—had stepped into the room, so that the angry Miss Jane was flanked by two three-piece suits stuffed with muscle. The two men, each armed with a hide-wrapped club, eyed Lodge benignly, though Lodge recognized the redheaded one as one of two who'd thrown him out last time he was here.

Rage sang in his ears.

"Ah, no," he said, shaking his head. "You ain't gonna

throw me out. I didn't mean no harm. I just wanted to talk to Miss..."

He'd loosened his hold on the girl's head. She took advantage of that by jerking away from him. Giving a high-pitched sob, she ran to stand beside Miss Jane, clinging to the woman's arm like the whore in the high-heeled shoes had clung to the banister.

"He's crazy!" the girl cried, casting her terrified, stricken gaze at Lodge. "The big ape is plum crazy. He thought I was going to *marry* him!"

Incensed, the rage fairly pounding in his ears and burning in his eyes, Lodge raised his left arm and pointed his index finger at her accusingly. "You said...you said that thing about the Fates, Miss Jackie. I rode all the way down to..."

Miss Jane gave Jackie a gentle shove toward the door. Jackie slinked out of the room to stand behind the frame, peering around it into the room, her blue eyes wide and still terror-stricken.

Miss Jane peered at Lodge, narrowing her eyes in anger. "Get out, Lodge," she said quietly but firmly. "I'm sorry if there was a misunderstanding between you and Jackie. But it was just that. A misunderstanding. I understand that. It happens sometimes. Be that as it may, you must leave and you must leave now. I don't want you to ever step foot in the San Juan again. Do you understand? If you do, Joe Mannion will be called. You will be jailed and face a judge."

Lodge drew a breath against the wild stallion of fury galloping inside him. He'd only come to ask the girl to marry him, because she'd led on like she would! She'd looked right into his eyes and said that thing about the Fates! He'd ridden all the way down to Las Cruces to fetch his mother's ring. He'd even bought the girl a house in Pueblo. He'd spent fifteen thousand dollars on it—almost every penny he'd saved from the bounty hunting trails!

"I ain't goin' no damn where," Lodge said, seething. He was staring at the girl staring at him now as though he were some wild circus animal. All he could think about now was closing his hands around her neck and squeezing the life out of her.

Strangling her until her eyes popped out of her head!

Even that was too good for her, having made Ulysses Lodge look the fool in front of Miss Jane and the two brutes flanking her!

As though of its own accord, Lodge's right hand reached inside his unbuttoned buffalo coat. It closed around the worn, walnut grips of his Colt Navy. He'd just started to slide the big popper from its holster when Jane raised her right hand. Lodge saw that she held a gun in it, clenched tightly in her fist.

It was a small, silver-chased Colt Lightning with a three-and-half-inch barrel and gutta percha grips. A ladies' gun. Miss Jane was threatening him with a ladies' gun!

She clicked the little hammer back and aimed down the barrel at Lodge's head. "If that hogleg rises one more inch from that holster, Lodge, I'm going to drill one through your head."

Lodge's right hand froze, the Colt half out of the holster.

Keeping her eyes on Lodge, Miss Jane said crisply, "Gentlemen, take his gun and throw him out."

Lodge stood frozen in fury as the two men converged on him, the redheaded gent pulling his Colt from its holster and tossing it onto the bed.

"Oh, no you don't!" Lodge raged, turning to the redhead and raising his right, clenched fist.

Before he could swing it forward, the other man laid the club across the top of Lodge's head. He gave a great chuff of expelled air as he fell forward. His knees had just struck the floor when the two brutes—shorter than Lodge but younger, more muscular, and armed with those consarned clubs that didn't give a man a chance!—grabbed each arm and pulled him back up.

Lodge heard himself grunt and groan as the world spun around him. He saw two Miss Janes, both blurry, standing to the right of the door. His head lolled on his shoulders. "Ohhh...ohhhh..."

He saw two Miss Jackies, too, as the two brutes half dragged and half carried him out into the hall. The wild stallions of unadulterated rage continued to gallop inside him, frustrating him to no end because he couldn't do a thing about what was so unjustly happening to him.

Oh, how he wanted to wrap his big hands around her neck and squeeze the life out of the little faker!

Make Ulysses Lodge look the fool, will you?

"We'll see about that!" he bellowed as the two brutes half dragged and half carried him down the broad carpeted stairs until he heard his own voice rocketing around the suddenly silent main drinking hall.

"Make Ulysses look the fool, will ya?" he bellowed again, even louder, his deep, guttural voice echoing wildly around the room of drinkers and diners all of whom now had their heads turned toward him.

More than a few were muttering among themselves, grinning and chuckling. They were really enjoying the show!

"Go to hell!" Lodge raged as the two brutes, strong as oxes and not slowing down a damn bit so that Lodge couldn't even try to get his feet set beneath him. "All of yas—*go to hell!*"

Then he was rammed through the heavy batwings, both doors tattooing his head something fiercely and causing the ringing in his ears to grow louder.

"Oh, you bloody bastards!" was the last thing he shouted as they half dragged and half carried him down the veranda's broad steps just before swinging him back, then forward, then farther back, and then farther forward until he found himself hurling straight out into the dung-littered mud of the street.

He landed face down in a pile of fresh horse apples and mud.

Behind him, Miss Jane's voice yelled, "Get out of town, Lodge. Step foot in the San Juan again, an' you'll think today was a Sunday school picnic!"

There was the sound of hands being brushed together and then two sets of footsteps retreated up the veranda steps, fading into the distance.

Distantly, muffled by the ringing in his ears, Lodge heard someone in the street before him chuckle and say, "Don't take it too hard, Lodge. I've been in your shoes—er, the *mud*, shall we say?—my ownself."

Hooves clomped away.

Lodge lifted his face from the dung, and, a toxic hybrid of rage and exasperation oozing from every pore, bellowed as loudly as he could, which wasn't very loudly at all anymore, he'd had too much gas punched out of him—"Oh, you bloody bastards!"

The din of the street drowned out the wail in even his own ears.

And then he just lay there, belly down, head up, looking around at the passing traffic, passersby commenting and pointing at him and laughing as they continued on their way, walking, riding horseback, or rattling along in wagons.

Ulysses Lodge was just a lowly fool in the mud.

Because of her!

Her—whom he'd ridden all the way down to Las Cruces for!

Whom he'd bought a house for!

Her. The high-and-mighty, back-stabbing, fool-making Miss Jackie!

Suddenly, Lodge had his strength back. Filthy and muddy, he heaved himself up onto his knees. He looked around, growling like a wounded bear. A man stepped down off the boardwalk to his left. Ulysses looked up at him. He was an older gent dressed in cowboy garb. He stepped up to a horse tied at the hitchrack to Lodge's left. The man glanced over his shoulder at Lodge and chuckled.

"Takin' a mud bath, are ya, there, bounty hunter?" He looked over his horse's saddle at another man in cowboy gear stepping up to another horse just beyond the first man's.

Lodge heaved himself to his feet. He pulled the revolver out of the holster of the man who'd laughed at him. When the man turned toward Lodge with a start, Lodge gave another, louder snarling growl and clubbed the man over the head with the heel of the six-shooter. Lodge wheeled and climbed the steps, mud and filth dripping off of him onto the painted wood.

"Hey!" yelled the other cowboy. "What the hell you think..."

He let his voice trail off as he hurried over to see to his partner laid out cold in the mud.

Lodge pushed through the batwings.

By God, he was going to ring the neck of that little,

lying, mocking tart if it was the last thing he did on this earth.

He took three steps into the room, growling from down deep in his belly, chin down, jaws hard. He saw a splash of red in the upper periphery of his vision. He lifted his head. Miss Jane had just come down the stairs and was crossing the room toward the bar, passing not ten feet away from Lodge. She must have seen him in the corner of her left eye because she turned toward him suddenly and stopped.

Her eyes widened in shock. She opened her mouth to speak but before she could get any words out, Lodge found himself raising and cocking the six-shooter in his muddy right hand.

He gave a great snarling wail that rocketed around the room just before he put three bullets into Miss Jane's fancy gown. Miss Jane screamed as the bullets hurled her straight back and onto a table, scattering playing cards, whiskey bottles, shot glasses, and beer schooners.

"Miss Jane!" one of the men fairly screamed.

Lodge looked at the smoking gun in his hand, shocked to see it there.

He looked at Miss Jane laid out on the card players' table.

He was shocked to see her there, blood blossoming like three red flowers on her chest.

"Oh, God!" Ulysses bellowed, suddenly realizing what he'd done. "Oh, Gawd!"

But then he couldn't help chuckling, suddenly amused by what he'd done. Laughing and grunting, he swung around and ran out through the batwings. The second cowboy was just helping the first cowboy to his feet. Both men regarded the big, muddy giant incredulously as

Lodge ripped Beast's reins from the rack and swung up into the leather.

They swung their heads around, the man who'd been clubbed blinking groggily, and watched the big, muddy giant, Ulysses Lodge, gallop hell-for-leather straight north out of Del Norte while a man ran out of the San Juan Saloon behind him, and bellowed, "Someone fetch Doc Bohannon! Miss Jane's been *shot*!"

CHAPTER 5

Joe Mannion, Rio Waite, and the ailing Bronco Lewis—fully clothed though he'd needed help with the delicate process since he was in so much pain and all—rode into Del Norte around ten forty-five the day after the dustup at Leo Tollefson's road ranch.

Bronco's left foot was bare, as the oak-like knot in that ankle had made it impossible for him to pull his boot on. That foot and knotted up ankle were the color of a ripe plum. Before they'd left the road ranch, Mannion had bought the bank-robbing killer a bottle of cheap whiskey, and that had served to keep him from complaining overmuch about how the horseback ride through rough country was really making that rabid dog in his ankle bark. Joe would be glad to get him into his cell in the basement of his jailhouse and office. The killer was so glum he was depressing to be around.

More than once Mannion had cursed himself for not drilling a pill through the killer's head, putting him out of his own and everyone else's misery. He wasn't sure keeping him alive to watch him dance at the end of a noose had been worth the trouble. Too late now, however. The jailhouse, locally and whimsically known as Hotel de Mannion, lay straight ahead and on the right side of the main street, which boasted ankle-deep mud and standing water in wheel ruts after a recent rain.

In the late summer and early fall, this high country wedged in a bowl abutted on three sides by dramatic mountain ranges, was often pummeled by hard rains and hail that lay so white it resembled snow.

Mannion, Rio, and their glum charge, riding without being tied because he wasn't going anywhere on that bum ankle, and with Joe leading his horse by its bridle reins, took regular pulls from the bottle he held in his right hand on his right thigh. They were just then passing the new, impressive opera house on the street's left side.

Joe's gaze automatically slid on up that same block to the San Juan Hotel & Saloon sitting at the block's opposite end. He lifted his gaze to the second-floor balcony, looking at Jane Ford's office. She'd been Jane Ford Mannion all of seven months before she'd served him with divorce papers for his thick-headedness and general, all-round inability to be a good husband. Jane often stood out there in one of her customary stylishly cut gowns, the low-cut bodice showing the deep, freckled allure of ample cleavage, red hair piled in rich coils atop her head, a cigarette holder protruding from between the first two fingers of her right hand as she surveyed the boisterous, burgeoning frontier town before her, like a redheaded, amber-eyed, ruby-lipped, full-bosomed, insouciant queen appraising her grand domain with its unwashed minions.

If Del Norte belonged to any one person, it belonged to the former Jane Ford Mannion, for everyone— including her incredulous ex-husband, Mannion had to grudgingly admit—was at her beck and call. Joe just hadn't quite realized it before he'd married her, which was not, he also grudgingly admitted, had not been a mistake.

His mistake had been letting her divorce him.

He fully understood now what a mistake that had been as well as the errors—yes, multiple errors—of his married ways. He should have subjugated himself to her. A woman of Miss Jane Ford's quality did not come often to a man of Bloody Joe Mannion's ilk way out here on the high-and-rocky and still mostly untamed western frontier.

She was not, however, at her customary place on her balcony this midmorning. Probably working inside. But, no—he just then caught the splash of rust-red on the broad veranda fronting the San Juan. There she was, standing at the top of the steps while two muscular bouncers, apes in suits, threw a shaggy-headed and bearded man even bigger than they were and clad in a long buffalo coat out into the street beyond the veranda's bottom step.

The man bellowed as he flew through the air to land with a splash in the ankle-deep mud and finely ground dung of Del Norte's main drag, between two hitchracks crowded with saddled horses even this early in the day.

Jane glared down at the man as she said, "Get out of town, Lodge. Step foot in the San Juan again, an' you'll think today was a Sunday school picnic!"

Mannion stopped Red in the street, roughly ten feet from where the big man he recognized as the bounty hunter, Ulysses Lodge, lifted his bearded face from the mire. Joe chuckled and said, "Don't take it too hard, Ulysses. I've been in your shoes—er, in the *mud*, shall we say?—my ownself."

He glanced at Jane. She looked back at him.

The former Mrs. Mannion.

"You still got it, I see, Jane," Mannion said, giving a dry chuckle and glancing at the bounty hunter, who was blinking and looking around, dazed.

Jane glanced at the bare left-footed Bronco Lewis then returned her own hard stare to her former husband. "You do, too, I see, Marshal."

She swung around and followed her bouncers through the batwings.

Mannion glanced at Rio sitting his horse to Joe's right. The deputy gave a wan half smile. Joe chuckled, shook his head, then booted Red on down the street toward the jailhouse.

Jane...

Get her out of your head, he told himself. *It's done. It's over.*

Water under the bridge.

He turned Red toward one of the two well-worn hitchracks fronting Hotel de Mannion, tugging Bronco Lewis's mount along by its bridle reins. He'd just stopped Red when a gun thundered somewhere behind him.

It thundered again.

Then one more time.

Mannion looked back in the direction from which he and Rio and their prisoner had just come, hearing shouting and yelling. It seemed to be coming from the San Juan. A big man just then ran out through the San Juan's batwings. It was the mud-soaked Ulysses Lodge. He ran down the steps in his heavy, lumbering way then ripped the reins of his big steeldust from one of the hitchracks. Lodge clambered into the saddle, turned the horse out into the street, and batted the heels of his high-topped moccasins against its sides.

The horse lunged into an instant gallop, horse and rider galloping toward where Mannion and Rio and their prisoner sat their horses, staring incredulously toward the San Juan.

As Lodge galloped past the jailhouse, crouched low in his saddle and casting wary glances behind him, a man ran out onto the porch of the San Juan, shouting, "Someone fetch Doc Bohannon. Miss Jane's been *shot!*"

Mannion's heart leaped into his throat. He turned to Rio and jerked his chin at Bronco. "Get him inside, Rio!"

He swung Red around sharply and booted the bay into a gallop back toward the San Juan a block away to the south and on the opposite side of the street from the jailhouse. He leaped out of the saddle while Red was skidding to a halt. In his haste, Joe lost his footing, dropped to one knee, and then he was back up again, running, taking the San Juan's veranda steps two at a time. He ran across the porch, pushed through the batwings, and stopped, frozen in place, unable to move.

Every man in the room was on his feet, staring in hang-jawed, wide-eyed shock toward where Jane Ford lay belly up on a table roughly halfway between the batwings and the Bear Den gambling parlor at the back of the main drinking hall. She was surrounded by men, one hunched closely over her, pressing a cloth against her chest and squeezing her left hand in his right one. This was Jane's manager, Bart Simms—a small, slender, gray-haired man with tobacco-brown eyes. He rarely made an appearance in the drinking hall but was glued to his account books and ledgers and product order forms in his third-story office.

Because of Simms and the rest of the men around Jane, Mannion couldn't see much of her, but he could see enough—the stylishly cut cream gown with brown trim that complemented her hair, and her hair itself, fairly glowing fire red in the light angling in through the front windows to either side of him.

Joe finally got his feet to move. Each felt as heavy as lead.

He nudged two men aside and stepped up to the table and looked down at Jane, who lay unmoving, head turned to one side. Her hair had partly come out of the large bun she'd been wearing atop her head and lay in loose coils on scattered coins and playing cards. Blood matted the corset of her dress and over her chest and belly. Three neckerchiefs had been stuffed into the wounds to try to stop the blood, but blood still oozed out around the blood-soaked cloths.

The room was filled with a low, shocked hum.

Mannion cleared his throat, looked from Jane to Simms, and said, "Is...is she dead?"

Simms looked up at Mannion, his eyes bright with shock and worry. "I can feel a pulse but it's very weak."

Mannion swept the room around the table with his gaze. "Did someone send for Bohannon?"

"Merle Swiper ran to fetch him," one of them said—Ed Chessman, a longtime clerk at the local mercantile.

Mannion moved to the right side of the table. Jane's right hand hung down over it, rings glistening on three of her long, pale, tapering fingers. Joe picked it up and held it between his, absently fingering her rings, brushing his thumbs against her palms. He didn't like the chill he felt there.

She appeared to be breathing weakly, her chest rising and falling shallowly. Blood continued running down over her flat belly. He pressed his left hand over one of the wounds, trying to get the bleeding to stop.

She'd been shot three times in the chest, and she'd already lost a lot of blood...

Christ!

"Jane," Mannion said, feeling sick to his stomach and weak in his knees. "God, Jane...no. It can't end like this. Not like this."

Running footsteps sounded on the street. Boots pounded the porch steps and then the porch itself, growing quickly louder. The batwings parted as the runner ran into the room, breathless. "I heard!"

Mannion glanced over to see his junior deputy, Henry "Stringbean" McCallister, slow his frantic pace halfway between Joe and the batwings still clattering back into place behind him. Henry had lost the nickname over the past couple of months, ever since he had returned from Arizona, where he'd escorted a Mexican outlaw princess known as La Stiletta, who'd been set to testify against Diego Hidalgo, her boyfriend and a formidable border bandito and revolutionario, who'd robbed three Gatling guns from the U.S. military. It had been a hellish trip for both Henry and the girl, but they'd survived it and had even killed Hidalgo's savage gang including Hidalgo himself.

Henry, formerly known as "Stringbean," had kept La Stiletta out of the hands of Hidalgo, who'd intended to kill her to keep her from testifying against him and for running out on him when he'd been arrested by the army and U.S. marshals. Henry had come back a changed man—a man, indeed. Thus, it had only seemed natural that he lose the nickname and become known only as Henry McCallister, deputy town marshal of Del Norte.

The young man had even filled out some in the months since his return from Arizona, was no longer nearly as lanky as he'd been, and the former soot-smudge mustache he'd been trying to grow was no longer a smudge but a thickening and downright impressive blond lip mantler.

"I heard," Henry said again as he approached the table where Jane continued to lay unmoving. His wide-eyed gaze met Mannion's, and he said, "Is she...is she...?"

"Not yet," Joe said, "but she will be if she keeps losing blood." He crouched and swiftly scooped Jane up off the table and turned toward Henry and said, "Open those batwings, Deputy! I'm taking her over to Bohannon before she bleeds dry!"

"Marshal, we shouldn't move her!" protested Simms.

"Not gonna stand here and watch her die!" Joe said as he strode quickly across the room to the batwings held wide by Henry.

Then he was out the door, crossing the porch, and dropping quickly down the steps. He swung to his right and lurched into a jog, heading for Doc Bohannon's office.

"Don't you die on me, woman," Joe wheezed out, his heart hammering his breastbone. "Don't you dare die on me. This isn't finished yet. *We're* not finished yet!"

He didn't know why it had taken something so tragic to make him realize that, but it had.

Dammit, it had.

"Out of the way," he yelled at folks blocking the boardwalks. "Make room! Get the hell out of my way, *goddamn your scurvy hides!*"

CHAPTER 6

Fortunately, Mannion didn't have far to run.

Doc Bohannon had built himself a nice, neat, brick office across the main street from the San Juan and a half a block down the first side street to the east, which was Second Avenue. As Mannion jogged toward the office, he saw that the doctor's black surrey had just pulled up and Bohannon, a middle-aged, slouch-shouldered, slightly pot-gutted man with long, blue-gray hair hanging down from beneath his dusty, brown bowler hat, was just then climbing out. Another man, taller and younger than the sawbones, and dressed in a crisp, black, three-piece suit with a gold vest and red foulard tie, was climbing out of the surrey's opposite side.

Like Bohannon, he was clutching a medical kit in one hand. He had longish, wavy, brown hair and matching mustache he'd likely grown to add a little depth and ruggedness to the otherwise boyish but not unhandsome plumpness of his fair-skinned, recently sunburned features.

Merle Swiper, who'd been sent to fetch the doctor, was just then standing beside the surrey's left front wheel, talking and gesticulating wildly in the direction of the San Juan. Swiper, who was part-owner of a Del Norte livery barn as well as part-owner of a little grog shop down in what was becoming the Mexican part of town, jerked his enervated gaze toward Mannion, looked away, then turned to Joe again. Joe was twenty feet from Bohannon and Swiper and was jogging, wincing against the possible further damage he knew he might be doing to the woman in his arms.

Since he'd set out, Jane's bleeding had gotten worse. He probably should have left her in the San Juan, but he hadn't been able to bring himself to just stand there, watching her bleed out, feeling helpless.

The bullets needed to be dug out of Jane's chest pronto.

"Dear God," Bohannon said, canting his head to indicate his office. "Get her inside.

Mannion hurried up the steps of the brick front porch then had to wait for Bohannon to dig the key out of his pocket. The middle-aged medico, who looked weary—he'd likely been working late out in the country, maybe delivering a baby or tending broken bones at one of the mines or lumber camps—fumbled with the key for precious seconds before he managed to poke it into the lock.

"For chrissakes, Doc!" Mannion carped, impatient. "Turn the damn key!"

Bohannon grunted as he turned the key in the lock. He cursed as he twisted the knob, threw the door wide, and stepped back to let Mannion pass. "Through the door behind my desk," he said, pointing at the partly open, oak door flanking the doctor's cluttered desk. "First examining room on the left."

"Gunshot wounds?" asked the young man—likely in

his mid-to-late twenties, Joe guessed—following the doctor into the office.

"That's what it looks like," the doctor said, following Mannion through the door and into the hall that Joe knew led to two examining rooms facing each other on each side of the hall and three hospital rooms beyond.

"Three bullet wounds to the chest, Doc." Mannion fumbled open the door Bohannon had indicated, carried Jane inside, and laid her out on a leather-padded examining table with a red satin pillow. The room's walls were lined with glass and wood cupboards and cabinets teeming with bottles of all shapes, sizes, and colors.

The smell of camphor and other medicines was heavy in Mannion's nose.

"Good Lord—who would do such a thing to dear Jane?" Bohannon wanted to know, pegging his hat on the wall and running a black-gloved hand through his hair, which was sweat-damp. Dust and weed seeds from the country hung in the straight, gray hair hanging below the indentation made by the man's hat.

Mannion eased his hands out from beneath Jane and turned his hard, angry-eyed gaze to the sawbones. "Ulysses Lodge," he said through gritted teeth.

"Oh, no."

"I haven't figured out why yet, but I have a pretty good idea."

"Likely abusing one of Jane's poor girls again."

"Most likely." Mannion backed away from the examining table, making way for Bohannon and the younger man, both looking down at Jane with professional concern. "He won't live to abuse anymore—I can tell you that," Joe promised, seething. He glanced at the younger man just then removing a wadded neckerchief from one of Jane's wounds. "Who's this?" he asked Bohannon.

"This is Doctor Ben Ellison," Bohannon said. "He's interning with me his last year in medical school." The older doctor turned to Mannion. "Don't worry, Joe. He's good. Very good. He specializes in surgery."

Ellison removed another neckerchief from another wound and looked across the table at the older medico. "She's lost a lot of blood, Doctor. We're going to have to remove those bullets as quickly as possible."

"Agreed," Bohannon said with a nod and, removing his coat, turned to a charcoal brazier in a corner of the examining room. It was cold, but a steel pot of water sat atop it, ready for heating. The doctor glanced at Mannion and said, "Leave us to her, now, Joe. We need all the room we can get. Don't worry—we'll do all we can for her."

Mannion nodded and looked at Jane. She looked so pale and small and vulnerable and bloody, lying there on the cold examining table. The only movement she made was a slight, shallow rising and falling of her chest and an occasional fluttering of her eyelids. Mannion was reluctant to leave her, to remove his eyes from her for even a second. He knew this might very well be the last time he'd ever see her alive.

"Please, Marshal," the young doctor said, placing a hand on Joe's shoulder. "Let us do our work. We'll let you know as soon as we know anything ourselves about her prospects."

Joe nodded and backed out of the room.

The young doctor gave him a gentle, reassuring smile, and closed the door.

Joe wasn't reassured. He had a cold, hard feeling down deep in his belly that he'd seen the last of Jane Ford alive.

He'd just turned to take a seat in the small waiting area furnished with a half dozen Windsor chairs and a couple of tables sporting old catalogs and newspapers, to the right of the doctor's desk. He turned to the door when he heard running footsteps outside. Two sets of feet clomped across the porch and then the door came open and Joe's daughter, Vangie Mannion, poked her auburn-haired head into the room.

She was dressed in her traditional wool shirt, blue jeans, stockmen's boots, and tan Stetson, the chin thong hanging down against her chest. Vangie spent most of her time with her horses and dressed accordingly. The rustic garb took nothing away from her beauty; in fact, Joe thought the contrast only accentuated it.

She wore her hair in a neat French braid behind her head, the way she'd seen her mother wearing her own hair, of the same color, in the few tintypes Vangie and Joe had of Sarah.

The eighteen-year-old girl moved slowly toward her father. "Pa, my God—I was in Tillman's Grocery when I saw Henry run by!"

As if on cue, Henry McCallister stepped into the office behind Vangie and quickly doffed his hat. Vangie glanced over her shoulder at the young deputy and said, "He said Jane's been *shot!*" Vangie regarded her father in disbelief, slowly shaking her head. "But how? *Why?*"

"Haven't gotten to the bottom of it yet," Joe said. "All I know is right after I heard shooting in the San Juan, Ulysses Lodge went galloping out of town like that big steeldust of his had tin cans tied to its tail."

"Lodge," Vangie said, making a sour look.

"Yeah."

Henry stepped slowly forward behind Vangie, worrying the brim of his hat with his gloved hands. "Want me to go after him, Marshal?"

"No," Mannion said, flaring his nostrils in barely

bridled rage. "I'm going after him. As soon as I hear about Jane."

"Oh, Pa!" Vangie had been moving steadily toward her father and now she wrapped her arms around his waist and pressed her cheek to his chest. "Why Jane? Why her of all people?"

"I don't know, honey," Mannion said, wrapping his arms around her and rubbing her back consolingly. "Some things don't make any sense, and this is one of 'em. I reckon Jane got crossways with Lodge. I don't even know what he was doing in the San Juan. She'd kicked him out for life months ago!"

Vangie looked up at her father from beneath the brim of her Stetson. "I never told you this, but I once caught Lodge ogling me through some bushes when I was working Cochise in the breaking corral. I called him out and he galloped off."

Mannion gritted his teeth and shook his head. "Damn, his loco hide!" He smashed his right fist into his left palm. "I'll find him. I'll find him and I'll kill him if it's the last thing I do! I just have to know that Jane's going to be all right first."

Vangie placed her hand on her father's arm. "Come over here and sit down, Pa. You're getting yourself all worked up. Sit down and I'll bring you some water."

"I don't want any water," Mannion said. No, what he really wanted was a nice, tall glass of whiskey. He didn't say as much to his daughter, of course. He'd been trying to cut back for the past year or more. He and the firewater didn't mix. At least, not without Joe going off half cocked and laying a room and everyone in it to waste.

To please Vangie, he sat down in a Windsor chair and accepted the water she fetched from a covered porcelain bucket sitting on a stand beside the front door. He'd just taken a sip when he realized he'd heard a soft tread on the porch. Now he looked up to see another girl step into the door that Henry had left standing half open behind him when he'd entered.

Molly Hurdstrom, Henry's former girl, who'd broken up with the junior deputy when he'd accepted Mannion's task of leading the beautiful and dangerous Mexican bandita, La Stiletta, down to Arizona. Henry had been back for several months—in fact an entire summer had passed—but as far as he knew, he and the pretty, delicate, gray-eyed girl, estranged from her wealthy parents because she'd once promised her hand to Henry, then known as Stringbean and whom her parents had thought beneath her. There'd been much more to it than that, including the girl having killed a former suitor, whom her parents *had* approved of—as he'd been from a wealthy albeit corrupt family—when the young man, visiting the Hurdstrom family with his father, had tried to kill Stringbean and thus pave the way for his own marriage to Molly.

They'd had a complicated past, those two—Henry and Molly. Mannion knew from his own experience that complicated pasts were difficult to get over. He was only now realizing how important it was to do just that.

The gray-eyed brunette, pale and delicate but also pretty and clad in a black skirt and purple blouse that became her lovely figure, cleared her throat and knocked tentatively on the door. She held a black knit shawl about her shoulders, against the autumn chill in the mountain air.

Henry gave a slight start and swung around. "Molly!" he said in surprise.

Pleasant surprise, Joe thought.

It was, indeed, a pleasant surprise for Henry McCallister, despite the reason he knew Molly had come.

"Hello, Henry," Molly said, softly, tentatively. She looked at Mannion and then at his daughter, who'd taken a seat beside him. "Marshal…Miss Vangie."

Mannion nodded to her.

Vangie said, "Hello, Molly. I take it you heard?"

Molly pursed her lips and nodded. "Everyone in town has heard about it by now. It's all everyone's talking about." She looked at Mannion. "I'm so sorry, Marshal. How is she?"

"Thank you, Molly. We don't know yet. I have a feeling it's going to be a while."

She turned to Henry, who didn't seem to know what else to say. But then it must have come to him. He gave a little jerk of his shoulders and walked toward Molly, ushering her out through the door then pulling it closed behind him.

CHAPTER 7

On Doc Bohannon's front stoop, Henry McCallister turned to Molly, feeling more than a little awkward. He hadn't talked to the girl, whom he'd once intended to marry, since he'd gotten back from his Arizona adventure, as he secretly called his trip with the notorious Mathilda Calderon, the half-Mexican, half-Italian young woman also known as La Stiletta.

It had been one hell of an adventure. Henry had nearly been killed countless times, and so had she, but he'd do it all over again in a heartbeat. It had changed him. He didn't think it was being too maudlin or dramatic to say that it had made a man of him at long last. He certainly had grown calmer and more confident, having survived such a harrowing trek—outlaws of every stripe and, in one case, even a wildcat, coming out of the proverbial woodwork to do him and La Stiletta in.

Including her savage bandito boyfriend, Diego Hidalgo, and his entire gang, which had numbered nearly a dozen.

Deputy Henry McCallister had killed them all, including Diego Hidalgo himself!

With La Stiletta's help, that was. In fact, she'd saved him from being killed by the barbaric killer by stabbing the man in the back and then nearly blowing his head off with his own gun. But Henry had saved her from near-certain death at the hands of her former boyfriend, so they had both called it even steven, and grinned.

No, he hadn't seen Molly except in passing since he'd returned from that adventure or misadventure, or whatever you wanted to call it, and, truth be told, he hadn't really wanted to. She'd taken umbrage with his having accepted the job of escorting La Stiletta down to Tucson, assigned to him by his boss, Marshal Joe Mannion, and, deep down, he really hadn't forgiven her for that.

It had been childish and petty. He'd only been doing his job, after all. True, La Stiletta was one beautiful young woman. Sexy, fiery, and deadly. What more could a man want?! But Henry, who'd been known as "Stringbean" by everyone except Molly back in those days not all that long ago, had been nothing but professional when it had come to his prisoner, and he had and still did resent Molly believing that he would be anything else.

Besides, a certain other woman had come into his life since he'd returned from Arizona...

"How've you been, Molly?" he asked now, trying unsuccessfully to keep the stiffness out of his voice.

"I've been well, Henry. When I heard about Miss Jane, I had to come see how she was doing. I work at Miss Goldstein's dress shop these days. She pays me ten more cents a day than I was making... Well, I just wanted to come see how Miss Jane is doing."

"It's a terrible thing." Henry held his hat before him, still worrying the brim with his fingers. "She's such a good lady. I know the marshal is awful broke up about it."

"They're divorced, aren't they?"

"Yeah." Henry sighed. "I think the marshal made a mistake when he signed that paper, and I think he knows it, too. Truth be told, I don't really think Miss Jane wanted him to sign it. But who am I to say?"

"Well, you know them both. You love them both. They're like family to you, Henry. If anyone would know, you would."

He gave another sigh and tapped his fingers against his hat brim. "I reckon you're right, Molly."

An awkward silence followed.

Henry stared down at his hat.

Molly stared down at the toes of her ankle boots sticking out from beneath the hem of her skirt.

"Henry?" she said finally, glancing up from beneath the brim of the little, black felt hat she wore, one eye narrowed.

"Yes, Molly?" Henry said, returning her gaze with one of his own eyes narrowed.

She winced and said, "I'm awful sorry about being so jealous about you and that Mexican woman. What was her name?" She gave a wan, sheepish smile. "La Stiletta?"

"Oh, that's all right, Molly." Henry carefully, briefly considered what he would say next. "We all make mistakes."

Because she *had* made a mistake and he was no longer the sort of boy...er, *man*...who would not call her out on it.

"Henry?" Again, she looked up at him, squinting one eye.

"Yes, Molly?"

"Could I...well, could I apologize to you? You know, for that? For how I was about you and her, and..."

"And me just doing my job?"

She hesitated, wrinkling the skin above the bridge of her nose. "Well...yes."

"No need, Molly," Henry said, holding up his left hand, palm out, and spreading the fingers of the hand holding the hat. He smiled. "Water under the bridge."

Her frown grew more severe. "Really?"

"Yes, of course."

"Henry, I thought that...I thought that maybe we—"

"I best go back into the doc's office, now, Molly. In case Bohannan has any news about Miss Jane. And then my shift starts at noon, so..." He cocked an eye toward the sun edging toward its zenith.

She studied him closely for a moment, still frowning up at him, curious, maybe a little perplexed. Finally, she said, "Well...okay, Henry."

He smiled at her, feeling a little guilty but fighting it off. Why should he? She'd underestimated him. And now...well, now he'd moved on. There was another woman on his mind now. And he didn't feel at all guilty about that.

Why should he?

"Goodbye, Molly. Be seein' you around."

"All right, Henry. Goodbye," she said, scowling maybe a little indignantly up at him.

No, maybe not just a little indignantly at all. Maybe downright angrily.

Suspiciously.

Jealously.

A faint flush rose in her cheeks.

As she turned to walk down the steps to the street, Henry opened the door and stepped back into the cool, sullen shadows of the doctor's office.

That evening, just before seven, when the autumn shadows were growing long across Del Norte's main drag, Henry walked up to the jailhouse to see Rio Waite sitting in his customary chair on the front stoop, to the right of the door, his black-and-white cat, Buster, sitting on one thigh, eyes half closed, dozing.

"What're you doing here, Rio?" Henry asked, setting one foot on the bottom step and closing one hand around the porch's roof support post on his left. He held his Winchester carbine on his shoulder and squinted up at the craggy-faced, middle-aged deputy. "You're shift doesn't start till eight."

"I came to relieve you early," Rio said. "I figure me and Cletus can keep the lid on the town for the rest of the night."

Cletus Booker was Marshal Mannion's most recent hire—a big head-buster who'd been a deputy town marshal in the rough-hewn mountain mining town of Forsythe until the man's boss had had to fire him because the town's mucky-mucks hadn't liked how Booker had gotten things done. Mannion had liked how Booker had gotten things done, and still did. When big Cletus—six foot six and nearly two hundred and fifty pounds—walked into a saloon, he cast a long shadow.

Silence usually accompanied that shadow. Silence and good behavior.

That was the kind of man a man like Bloody Joe Mannion thought he needed to keep a lid on Del Norte, still growing in spite of the fact that two rival railroads had not made it to the high-country town due to corruption at the heads of both businesses and right here in Del

Norte which Bloody Joe himself had exposed. The incident had played out in the sending of Del Norte's former mayor, Charlie McQueen, to the gallows for the defrauding of two sets of railroad investors as well as murder and the attempted murder of Bloody Joe himself as well as conspiring to kidnap Joe's daughter, Vangie.

Quite a crowd had showed up for the hanging of Charlie McQueen, a little popinjay in a spotless three-piece suit, trimmed beard, and small, round, silver-framed spectacles. McQueen had been a thorn in Marshal Mannion's side for a good many years. He'd always taken umbrage with the marshal's hard ways, had claimed they were antithetical to progress. But then it had turned out he was as corrupt or even more so than most of the men Joe had shot or whose heads he had broken or whom he had sent to the territorial pen or the gallows. For that reason, Marshal Mannion had taken special delight in the snapping of the little hypocrite's neck at the end of that long fall from the gallows' trapdoor.

Del Norte was still fighting over who would be its next mayor.

A special election was to be held at the beginning of the next month, October, the two most likely candidates being a businessman from New York who now operated a lumber yard in town, and a longtime resident of Del Norte who'd been one of its unofficial founding fathers—an old, gray-headed, gray-bearded former mountain man, Richard Northly, who lived with a half-breed woman in a one-room cabin on the outskirts of the Mexican side of town.

Northly was a hometown favorite. Too bad he was drunk most of the time...

"Truth be told," Rio continued now, absently watching the dwindling wagon and horseback traffic on

Main Street behind Henry, "I ain't been able to rest, thinkin' about Miss Jane and the hell ol' Joe's been goin' through." He turned his head to look in the direction, south along Main, where Jane was holed up with Doc Bohannon and the young intern, Dr. Ben Ellison, who was doing his last year's college work under Doc Bohannon's counsel.

So far, there had been no word regarding Miss Jane's condition, and that had both Henry and Rio deeply concerned.

They hadn't realized before what a grace note Jane had been in the otherwise dusty, loud, and violent town they called their own.

Ever since Joe had carried Jane over to the doctor's new office, the entire town had been quieter, somehow, more on edge than ever before. And Del Norte had been through quite a lot in its recent history.

If it lost Miss Jane, well, it just seemed anything could happen...

"I know what you mean," Henry said, following Rio's gaze along Main to the south. "That's all I've been able to think about, too. Most everyone's been able to think about. It's been as quiet today as Mondays usually are. I haven't had to break up one fight even on the Mexican side of town." He continued up the porch steps and strode past Rio and Buster as he headed through the office's partly open door.

"Where you off to?" Rio called as Henry poured tepid water from a large, porcelain pitcher into a wash basin standing atop the washstand at the room's rear, just beyond the stout oak door that led to the cellblock below.

"Oh, here and there," Henry said, giving a thin little smile despite his concern for Miss Jane. He knew that

Rio suspected he was up to something he, Henry, wanted to keep to himself. He didn't know how Rio knew about his secretive outings, but the older man knew, all right. And he was dying to know what Henry was up to.

Henry wouldn't tell. Not even Rio despite their being as close as a close uncle and nephew. Henry loved Rio dearly, but Rio wasn't the best at keeping secrets. This was one secret that must not get out. At least not until the lady Henry was going to see wanted it out.

"Here and there, eh?" Rio said from the stoop while Henry unbuttoned and shrugged out of his shirt. "Here and there," the older man muttered to himself in frustration. "Here...and...there, Buster. What do you think about that?"

Henry hung the shirt from a wall peg then went to work, washing first his face and then his chest and under his arms. When he had a good lather worked up, he scrubbed it in good. Despite the weather having cooled off, he still worked up a sweat making his rounds about the town, and the dust of Main Street after the mud from storms had dried, which was usually quickly, had a way of seeping under your clothes and working its way into your skin when you were milling around in it for hours on end.

Those big mine and logging drays were the worst for kicking up the dust.

As he washed, Henry couldn't help feeling guilty about the fond anticipation he felt at the thought of the lady he was going to see. She was older than him by seven years, and wiser. Maybe he shouldn't go; maybe he should wait around here with Rio for news about Miss Jane.

Ah, heck, that wasn't going to help Miss Jane's condition any. Besides, he had chores to tend. That was their agreement. He tended chores for the pretty, new schoolteacher in town, Grace Hastings, and in return Miss

Hastings taught Henry how to read. Theirs was a platonic relationship though Henry couldn't help wanting it to be more than that. Miss Hastings was pretty, sweet, cultivated, and she'd read more books than Henry had ever even laid eyes on. In his twenty-three years, he'd rarely had much access to books and, since he hadn't been able to read much more than wanted circulars until Miss Hastings had started teaching him a little over a month ago, it wouldn't have done him much good if he'd had.

She wanted to keep their relationship secret because, even though they were just friends, their being together, alone, would have the look of impropriety—a single, thirty-year-old schoolteacher and a single, young deputy town marshal. At the very least, rumors would fly.

When he'd washed and toweled off, Henry grabbed the clean shirt hanging from a wall peg beside the dirty one, shrugged into it, then took his time combing his hair in the chipped mirror hanging from a nail over the washstand.

Henry heard the chair on the stoop creak and a couple of shuffling foot thuds. In the mirror, he saw Rio step into the doorway, holding Buster and scowling in at the younger man. "Oh, hell—anyone can see you're gettin' yourself gussied up to see a girl. I take it it's not Miss Hurdstrom...?"

"Ain't sayin', Rio." Henry shoved his comb in his back pocket then grabbed his saddlebags hanging off another wall peg. He opened a flap to make sure the book Miss Hastings had lent him, as well as the hinge he'd bought for her schoolhouse's front door, were still there then buckled the strap and hung the bags from his left shoulder. He was young, but he was an experienced enough lawman—especially under the much-experienced Bloody

Joe Mannion's tutelage—to always keep his right hand free in case he needed to make a quick grab for the old Remington revolver jutting from the holster tied down on his right thigh.

He walked toward Rio, giving a crooked smile. "It ain't what you think." He winked at the older man then pressed his hand over Rio's left shoulder as he sidled past him onto the stoop.

"Hmmm," Rio said, turning to watch Henry walk down the porch steps and into the street. "You're just full of puzzles these days, ain't you? Ever since you came back from Arizona, you been—I don't know—different somehow. More sure of yourself."

"Chalk it up to experience, I reckon."

Feeling a flush of pride rise in his face, Henry untied his reins from the hitchrack fronting the jailhouse and swung up into the saddle. Rio was right. He did feel surer of himself these days. And that felt good. What felt even better was most folks having cleansed his nickname of "Stringbean" from their vocabularies. Nowadays, he was known as Henry or, in some cases, Hank. But hardly ever Stringbean.

He liked it that folks saw him as a Henry now and not as a Stringbean. It made him feel more of a man, which, pushing twenty-four and having considerable lawdogging experience under his belt, he was.

"I'll be back this afternoon to check on Miss Jane." He cast Rio a grave look. "It sure looked bad. Powerful bad, Rio." He shook his head.

"Yeah, but Miss Jane's a tough woman. I'm sure we'll hear something shortly." Rio dropped Buster to the porch floor, hitched his baggy denims higher on his broad hips, and said, "Well, I'd better start makin' my rounds. I'm sure I'll turn up Cletus eventually. He's probably over bustin' heads to the Wooden Nickel."

"All right," Henry said, swinging his coyote dun out into the street. "Later, Rio."

"Later, kid. Behave yourself." Rio winked.

CHAPTER 8

Henry grinned as he booted the dun into a spanking trot along Del Norte's main street, heading north.

He turned down the next cross street then, looking behind him to make sure no one was following—someone might have seen him riding well off his beaten path several times a week over the past weeks, and gotten suspicious and decided to follow him—he cut across a wooded lot behind a pig farm, crossed a gully that was dry this time of the year and then, avoiding the main trail, passed through still more woods and rode up behind Miss Hastings's cabin.

He felt a little silly as well as guilty for taking such elaborate precautions, but if anyone saw him visiting Miss Hastings's cabin unattended, as it were, he and the teacher would be ripe fodder for scandal.

Besides, at thirty, Miss Hastings was seven years older than he, and it was unusual to have an older woman in the company of a younger man—especially when that younger man wasn't even her student.

The cabin, originally an old prospector's hovel, sat at

the edge of the woods. The neat, white-frame, clapboarded school with obligatory bell tower sat beyond it, facing Del Norte to the west. No school was currently in session, as there were enough ranch kids in attendance that Miss Hastings had postponed school until the fall gather was over. Henry booted the dun between a clothesline sagging with a colorful, still-wet wash, and the privy and keeper shed. He'd just stopped the dun outside the teacher's back door, believing she'd be in the cabin, but then he heard the thuds of what sounded like wood being split coming from the opposite side.

He reined the dun around the cabin's right side, heading toward the school. Sure enough, Miss Hastings was splitting wood outside the school's back door, taking logs down off the pile that Henry had neatly cut and stacked against the school's back wall, near an overturned washtub she'd probably used to wash clothes. A small fire was still burning beneath an iron tripod standing over it, to the right of the teacher and the chopping block.

She just then set another log on the chopping block around which a considerable amount of split wood lay, hefted the splitting mallet high, then brought it down with a grunt, her red-blond hair blowing in the cool breeze that shepherded yellow aspen leaves around the hem of the woman's dark-green wool skirt and black ankle boots. She wore a white blouse with a ruffled front, and a tan leather waistcoat. The ruffles of the blouse blew in the wind.

A pretty woman was Miss Hastings. Often as Henry stole admiring looks at her while she sat close beside him in the school, helping him make letters or standing at the chalkboard, demonstrating, he felt a lump grow in his throat.

"Hey, hey, hey!" Henry said, booting the dun into a trot. "That's my job!"

Miss Hastings had just driven the mallet down through the log, cleaving it neatly in two. Now she turned toward her visitor and jerked with a start, lowering the mallet, slapping a long, pale hand to her chest, and taking one stumbling step backward. "Oh, Henry!" she said, laughing. "You gave me such a start!"

"I'm sorry!" Henry reined the dun to a stop. "I reckon I should've called out, but when I saw you out here doing my job for me, I reckon I got a little excited!" He swung down from the saddle and dropped the reins. "You should've told me yesterday you needed wood split. I would've been happy to do it."

Miss Hastings stuck the mallet in the chopping block with another soft grunt then stooped to gather the wood she'd split. She was breathless and beautifully flushed from exertion, ringlets of her piled hair jostling against her cheeks. Her brown eyes sparkled in the crisp autumn sunshine.

"Oh, Henry, you've split more than enough wood for me this week. Besides, I like coming out and wielding the mallet now and then." She started walking toward the cabin with her arms heaped with wood. "Nothing like a little fresh air and exercise to keep a woman feeling young!"

She laughed. Henry loved her laugh. It was deep and sort of husky, not the kind of laugh you'd expect from a woman so pretty and rather delicately put together.

She stopped suddenly and wheeled to face him. "Oh, Henry!" she exclaimed, a look of astonishment and sorrow passing like a cloud over her face. "I heard about Jane Ford in town! You must be so worried. Isn't she a good friend of yours?"

Henry wagged his head and hung his shoulders. "Yes, she sure is. Shot down in her own saloon! I offered to go after that varmint, Ulysses Lodge, who shot her, but the marshal wants to go after him himself. I'm gonna check on Miss Jane as soon as I ride back into town. There's not much I could do for her, though. Except worry, of course. Worry never does much good. Besides, I thought riding out here and having a lesson with you would get my mind off it."

"Is it really bad?"

"I'm afraid it didn't look too good to me. He shot her three times. But like Rio says, Miss Jane's a strong woman."

"I certainly hope she pulls through. She's so widely loved and respected around here."

"Yes, ma'am. She really is. No one else quite like Miss Jane." Except for the woman standing before him, Henry did not respond aloud.

"Just awful," said Miss Hastings as she continued walking toward the cabin.

Henry crouched to pile a load of split wood in his arms then hurried to catch up with the pretty teacher as she approached the cabin. "I'll get to working on the school's front door first thing. I brought a new hinge from the mercantile. After that I'll sand those two desks you…"

He let his voice trail off when she turned to him suddenly, laughing. "Oh, Henry. Dear Henry! I hope you brought an appetite. I made a very hardy stew. After we eat, we'll get to your lesson, and then you can fix the door, but the other stuff can wait till tomorrow. You need to see to your friend, Miss Jane."

"Yeah, I suppose you're right."

She fumbled the door open, and Henry followed her

inside.

"How are you enjoying *Ivanhoe?*" she asked him.

Henry made a pained expression as he followed her across the dyed hemp rug to the firebox that sat to the right of the potbelly stove. "I gotta admit—I mean, *I have to admit*," he corrected himself, conscious about his English around this learned woman. "It's a might puzzling in places. In fact, a *lot* of places. Way too many high-dollar words for this old horse breaker!"

He laughed as he dropped the wood into the box.

She laughed as she straightened and touched fingers to her hair that had come partway loose from the large bun atop her head. "We'll stick with *McGuffey's* for a while. You're doing so well, though, improving so fast, that I thought it might give you something to look forward to. I have a feeling you'll be reading it...and understanding it...before you know it. And it is *such* a wonderful novel. Pure romance with beautiful women and knights in shining armor!"

"Well, then, if you say so, I look forward to getting back to it and understanding it."

She headed into the kitchen part of the cabin and used the pump to fill a porcelain pan. "Let's wash and eat. I'm starving!"

"That stew sure smells good," Henry said, walking to the door, pegging his hat, and smoothing his hair into place. "I could smell it a hundred yards away before I got here!" He turned to where she was washing her hands in the pan. "You don't need to feed me, though, Miss Hastings. The lessons you give me are more than enough."

She cast him a winning smile over her shoulder. "Nonsense. The work you put in?! Besides, I like cooking for you. And I like having someone to eat with. Truth be told," she added, turning her head forward, a forlorn note entering her voice, "It gets lonely eating alone all the time. Doing everything alone except teaching, I guess you could say."

Suddenly, he felt sorry for this lonely, beautiful woman. He'd heard that sad note in her tone before and had wondered at it. He decided after a few minutes of quiet contemplation, as he washed at the pan, to say, "Do you mind if I ask you a question, Miss Hastings?"

She'd just finished drying her own hands, and now she put one of them on his shoulder. "Only if you promise not to call me Miss Hastings anymore. We're friends, Henry. Student and teacher but friends first and foremost. Please, won't you call me Grace?"

He looked at her hand on his shoulder, and felt heat rise in his cheeks. He just realized she'd never touched him before. Maybe just in passing but never with any sign of affection. He liked it. He liked the feel of her hand just fine.

"I'm sorry," she said, flushing now herself and removing her hand from his shoulder. "I didn't mean to embarrass you."

"Oh, no, no," Henry said, turning toward her as he toweled his hands. "Grace it is. Yes." His smile broadened and he was feeling just fine about getting to know Grace Hastings better. "I like the sound of that just fine...Grace."

"All right then—it's settled. Now, let's eat!"

THE STEW COOKED WITH LIGHTLY CHARRED AND tender beef and vegetables from Grace's garden—potatoes, peas, onions, and carrots—was rich and delicious. So was Grace's crusty, brown homemade bread which

Henry slathered with butter and homemade wild plum preserves. Grace got her milk, which she cooled in her springhouse, from the same farm from which she got her beef, and that washed the rest of the meal down to Henry's pure, unadulterated satisfaction.

His mother back in Oklahoma had been a good cook, but he hadn't had much home cooking since he'd left home nearly ten years ago, though he did like the surroundings Miss Ida here in Del Norte served up in her simple but appropriately named Good Food Café.

After lunch, Henry helped Grace clear the table and wash the dishes. Then they sat down to an hour's worth of vocabulary and spelling lessons and Henry reading, albeit haltingly, several passages from a story about a boy and a dog on a fishing trip to their favorite creek and the big fish the boy finally landed after two summers of trying.

Henry liked that story. It reminded him of his own boyhood in Oklahoma. It gave him a vague longing for a proper home again instead of the boardinghouse he lived in with eight old, glum retired folks and the persnickety woman who ran the place.

To end the lesson, Grace read to Henry a few passages from *Ivanhoe*—an exciting one, at that, about two knights fighting fiercely over a girl. That wet Henry's appetite for reading the entire book himself though he wasn't sure he'd be able to as quickly as Grace thought he would.

He might have felt more confident as a lawman now and walked around town with his head up and shoulders squared, but when it came to book learning, he still felt a hind-tit calf, though, thanks to Grace, he was feeling even more confident about that. He was feeling more and more like a better-rounded person.

More and more, too, he felt himself falling in love with Grace. He wondered if she felt the same way about him. She was so naturally nice and reserved in that nice sort of way that he just couldn't tell.

When Grace had finished reading to him from *Ivanhoe* and the lesson was officially over, Grace got busy weeding her garden while Henry fixed the schoolhouse's front door. It didn't take him long. He was right handy with fixing things. As soon as he was done, against her objections, which she voiced from her garden to the south of her cabin, he split nearly an entire cord of wood and stacked it against the school's rear wall.

Afterwards, he rolled his shirtsleeves down and buttoned them, donned his hat, and returned to the cabin, where Grace was scrubbing her windowsills.

Henry was reluctant to leave. But Miss Jane and the marshal had been in the back of his mind all day, with a sharp pang of dread of what he might learn when he returned to the heart of town.

"I'd best be leaving, I reckon," he said now from the open doorway. "I'll be back in a few days to sand those desks. I'll get 'em done before the kids return, don't you worry."

"No hurry, Henry," Grace said, looking up from her work, moisture from her toil showing in the west-angling light on her forehead. "It's getting late, isn't it?" She dropped her scrub brush in the bucket of soapy water on the table and moved to a kitchen cupboard. "Just you wait, now, Henry."

She opened a cabin door and pulled out a small canvas pouch. She brought it over to where Henry stood with his hat in his hands. "I want you to take this. It's two sandwiches I made from the beef I bought from the Fagerlands. I can't eat all of it alone, so I want you to take it. When you get back to the boardinghouse, stick it in Mrs. Graham's icebox and it should make you a good lunch tomorrow. There's a pickled egg in there, too."

She extended the bag to him, and he said, "Oh, you don't need to do that Gra—"

All thumbs, he dropped the pouch. He and she both stooped to pick it up at the same time and ended up butting heads. They each gave a laughing exclamation and straightened, rubbing their foreheads. Their eyes met. Their gazes held. They stopped laughing and grew very sober. Instantly, Henry felt something very real between them. A warm longing, maybe even a sexual desire.

It was in her eyes, and he knew it was in his eyes, too, and that she recognized it for what it was.

Suddenly, without realizing what he was doing until he was doing it, he reached out, grabbed her arms, and drew her to him. She gasped with a start but did not resist. And then his mouth was closing over hers and he was kissing her with a passion he hadn't felt before. Maybe a few times with Molly, but not even that was like this.

It was overriding and all-encompassing.

When Grace made no move to withdraw her mouth from his, Henry intensified the kiss, wrapping her in his arms and tipping her head back and to one side. She groaned deep in her throat, and he felt her shiver with hunger. He dropped his hat and the sandwiches she'd made. She wrapped her arms around his neck and drew him toward her with as much passion as he drew her to him.

She parted her lips; he parted his. She tasted just how he'd thought she'd taste—like wild cherries and cinnamon.

Her lips were swollen and heavenly, smooth and silky against his, her tongue sliding against his.

Suddenly, Henry realized he'd been hearing the approach of horses. She must have, too, because she pulled away from him with a startled gasp. They both turned to the two kitchen windows above the plywood counter and saw four riders angling toward the cabin from the direction of the school.

From this vantage, they appeared a hard-bitten, ragged-looking lot.

Frozen in place, Henry and Grace swung their heads to peer out the doorway behind Henry. The riders were just coming around the corner of the cabin, moving slowly, rolling their hips and shoulders with the sway of their mounts.

Henry and Grace stood awkwardly, still facing each other from a foot away, heads turned to the open doorway. Their hands hung straight down against their sides. They were both still breathless from the sudden passion, dazed, disoriented, both wondering if they were just imaging the riders, like a bad, waking dream.

The four riders reined up in a stirrup-to-stirrup line in front of the cabin.

From close-up, they appeared even more hard-bitten than they had from farther away—unshaven, well-armed, dusty trail clothes, battered Stetsons. Their horses were dusty, sweat-lathered, and flecked with weed seeds.

The man sitting his horse second from left of the group—a lean, sandy-haired man wearing three- or four-days' growth of beard stubble on his bony, hard-jawed, heavy-browed face, canted his head slightly to one side and hooked a wolfish smile.

"Hello, Grace. Been awhile."

CHAPTER 9

In Doctor Bohannon's office in Del Norte, a door latch clicked.

Joe Mannion, who'd been sitting in a waiting room chair beside Vangie and had been half dozing with his head tipped against hers, opened his eyes and lifted his head with a start. Vangie did, as well, blinking sleepily and casting her gaze, as did her father, toward the door behind the doctor's desk which led to the two examining rooms and three hospital rooms.

Two sets of footsteps sounded in the hall beyond the door.

Mannion rose as the door opened and the two doctors walked into the office, the short, gray Bohannon first, who had the mildly seedy air of a drummer, and the young, tall, handsome Dr. Ben Ellison, who appeared the epitome of Eastern professionalism. Mannion's heart thudded hard against his breastbone when he saw the grim looks on the medicos' faces.

"Doc," Joe said, "don't tell me..."

"She's alive, Joe," Bohannon said as he and Ellison both came around to the front of the desk and leaned back against it, arms folded. "Ben here got the bullets out." He glanced at the younger man and said, "Well, he can tell you better than I can."

"One was lodged very close to her heart," Ellison said. "One nicked a lung but the other missed any major organs. The one I'm mainly concerned about ricocheted off her sternum and snugged up against the aorta, which is the main artery leading to the heart. I got most of it out, but it had broken apart and I couldn't get some of it out. I had to leave it in there."

"What does that mean?" Vangie had risen to face both medical men gravely.

"It means she's going to be a very sick woman," Ellison said. "The blood loss was significant."

Mannion said tensely, "Is she...is she going to...?"

"Impossible to tell," Ellison said. "For now, she's stable. But she's in a coma. For how long that will last, we won't know until she comes out of it. That could be..." He sighed, shrugged his shoulders, and cast his sympathetic gaze to each Mannion in turn. "That could be tomorrow...the next day...in two weeks, or..."

"Never," Mannion finished for him.

The mustached younger man drew his mouth corners down. "I'm afraid that's right. I'm sorry, Marshal. You have to know that Doctor Bohannon and I did everything we could."

Bohannon said, "Ben here specializes in cardiac surgeries. Uh, *heart* surgeries. We're very lucky he's here. I never would have been able to perform the delicate procedure he performed, and without hesitation, too, I might add. Quite actually"—here again Bohannon glanced at his younger colleague—"I was more than a little impressed. And that the patient could survive the sort of procedure he had to perform on her."

"I've done it before, when I was working with another doctor in St. Louis," Ellison said. "Not quite as complicated a procedure as this one, but I knew what had to be done. I can tell you that with confidence, Marshal Mannion, Miss Mannion. Now, I'm afraid it's going to be a waiting game," he added with another weary sigh. "Every patient is different. Each one reacts to the shock of a bullet wound and blood loss differently."

"Can we see her?" Joe asked.

"Briefly," Bohannon said.

Mannion started forward. Behind him, Vangie said, "I'll leave you and Jane alone, Pa. I'll see her tomorrow"—she glanced at the younger doctor—"if that's allowed."

"Depending on her condition tomorrow," Ellison said and gave a gentle smile.

Vangie nodded.

"Okay, honey."

Mannion continued around the desk and into the second door down the hall on its left. He sucked a sharp breath through gritted teeth when he saw Jane lying there against the snow-white sheets, covered by a snow-white blanket, looking herself so awfully small and pale, eyes closed, her lips fluttering slightly. They were usually ruby red but now they had a pale blue death pallor. Her lusterless, rust-red hair was fanned against the pillow beneath her head.

Her pale hands lay down against her side, as limp as small, dead birds. One of the doctors had removed her rings. Mannion had never seen her without her rings.

"Dammit, Jane," Joe said. He dropped to his knees beside the bed, picked up one of her hands, and held it firmly between both of his, which dwarfed it. "You come back to me—you hear? This isn't finished. What we had isn't finished. I think we both knew it. It was pride, all pride that broke us up. Dammit, woman, I want a second chance. You owe me that. We meant something to each other!"

He looked at her, hoping, half expecting her to awaken.

Her eyelids, delicate as moth wings, fluttered a little but did not open.

"Ah, hell," Mannion said, rising but keeping her hand between his.

He stared down at her. "I'm gonna get him, honey. There isn't much I can do for you, but I can do that!"

He leaned down, doffed his hat, and planted a very light kiss on her lips.

"I'm going after Lodge. Don't worry—Vangie will be here. Hell, the whole town is praying for you, pulling for you. Don't let us down, goddammit, Jane!"

He hadn't realized how loudly he'd said that last until footsteps sounded in the hall. The door opened and Doc Bohannon took one step into the room and said, "That's enough, now, Joe. You and Vangie better go on home and get some rest."

Mannion stared down at Jane, anger burning deep within him. He could feel it rising behind his eyes. He gritted his teeth and shook his head. "No, it's not, Doc. It's not near enough." He turned to the doctor and donned his hat. He glanced once more at Jane and then brushed past Bohannon as he stepped into the hall. "It's not near enough—but soon, when Ulysses Lodge is wolf bait, it will be!"

———

As Mannion and Vangie stepped out onto the porch fronting the doctor's office, looking at the late-day shadows stretching across this side street and across Main Street just beyond, on their left, Vangie said, "Are you really going to set out after Lodge so late in the day, Pa? How are you going to track him? It'll be dark in a couple of hours."

"There'll be a moon," Mannion said, glancing to the east, at the high, long, thin clouds turning the pinks and greens of the early evening. "Besides, I know where he's going."

"Where?" Vangie asked as they set out on foot back in the direction of Hotel de Mannion. Vangie had ridden one of her three horses to Bohannon's office but, knowing she and her father would likely be there for most of the day, she'd had the local, young, odd-job boy, Harmon Haufenthistle, stable the horse at Morrison's Livery & Feed along with her father's big bay, whom Mannion had left at the jailhouse.

They'd fetch both horses on their way home.

"He's headed for the Sawatch," Joe said. "That's where he's been hunting outlaws for the past twenty years, taking most up to Gunnison or Crested Butte to claim the reward money. Used to have a squaw up there. No, that's his home country, his feeding ground. He's on his way to try to get lost up there. He likely shot Jane in a fit of mindless rage and now, having thought over what he'd done, he's likely— pardon my French, honey, but I know you're used to it— pissing down his leg, knowing that I'll be after him."

They were walking along the boardwalks on the east side of Main, the wagon and horseback traffic on their left gradually dwindling, the stoops fronting the saloons and hurdy-gurdy houses gradually filling. Several people called out queries regarding Jane and Joe answered briefly but mostly just shrugging and throwing up his hands.

Bart Simms, Jane's manager, had sent folks over to the doctor's office several times earlier to inquire about Jane's condition, as well. Rio had checked on her, too.

"You know a spooked dog's a dangerous dog, Pa," Vangie reminded her father.

"So's a mad one, honey."

"I'd like to ride with you, Pa. I'd take Cochise, and we could help you track. Besides, I'd like to have a go at that vermin myself!"

Joe wagged his head as they approached the jailhouse. "No, no. It would be nice to have a second pair of eyes, and I know you got the bark on, my once-little girl." He chuckled dryly. "But I need you here to look after Jane. If she wakes, I want you here."

Vangie stopped and touched her father's arm, stopping Joe, who turned to face her, his gray-brown brows arched over his wolfish, gray eyes, inquiringly. "Any particular message you'd like me to give her?"

Mannion winced, frowned, massaged his chin between thumb and index finger as he gazed off speculatively. "Uh...well..."

"How 'bout that you love her?"

Joe winced and looked around again, embarrassed, wondering if anyone had heard.

Vangie crossed her arms on her chest clad in a blue and white wool shirt and tapped one boot toe against the dirt at the bottom of the jailhouse's porch steps. "It's not a cuss word—you know, Pa? Love? There's nothing wrong with saying it."

"Okay, all right," Mannion said, quickly. "Tell her I love her." He'd started up the porch steps but then stopped and turned back to Vangie, his expression again pensive, grave. "Tell her I'll be back for her."

Vangie canted her head to one side and gave a lopsided grin. "No better medicine than that, Pa."

"Speaking of which, that young doctor—I think he fancies you."

"A young doctor, fancying *me*? Pshaw!" But Joe saw the high flush in the girl's cheeks.

He smiled back at her then turned to start up the porch steps again. "I'm gonna grab my rifle and saddlebags."

"All right. Then ride on home with me and I'll fill the war sack with the usual trail supplies."

"You spoil me, girl."

"I know—and you don't deserve it a bit!"

Mannion laughed as he walked into the jailhouse.

CHAPTER 10

"Vince?" Grace Hastings said, stepping onto the patch of hard-packed dirt outside the door of her cabin. "What...what are you doing here? How did you find me?"

Henry followed her out and stood beside her, finding it more than a little hard to believe that the Grace Hastings he knew—beautiful, sweet, and cultivated—could know the four men sitting their horses ten feet from the cabin, all four regarding her and Henry with flinty eyes and wolfish grins.

"You're hard a woman to find," the lean, hard-jawed, sandy-haired Vince said from where he sat a black gelding second from left of the group. "But you look long and hard enough, you can find anyone. If you want to bad enough." He narrowed one eye with sudden shrewdness and anger. "And we very much wanted to find you. And you know why."

"Vince, I..."

"Who's this?" Vince's eyes slid to Henry, and the hardness grew in them. Then his own lips twisted a leering, insinuating smile. "Or ain't it none of my business?"

Henry took one step forward, tucking his thumbs

behind his pistol belt, and regarded Vince and the others with authority. "Who are you and what's your business with Miss Hastings?"

"Does he know?" Vince asked, his eyes returning to the woman who stood regarding him with a mottled red-and-white flush in her cheeks, more than a little apprehension in her brown eyes.

"Vince, I...I..." Frowning curiously, she shook her head, glanced at the ground. "No, he doesn't." She returned her apprehensive gaze to Vince. "When did you get out?"

"Last month. After seven long years," Vince said coldly. "But we all had lots of time to *think*, Grace."

"Listen," Henry said, "I'm Henry McCallister, deputy town marshal here in Del Norte." He wasn't wearing his badge, he rarely did when he wasn't on duty and wanted to feel like just another citizen. He suddenly didn't want to feel like just another citizen. "You don't seem to be wanted here, so why don't you—"

"No, Henry, please," Grace said, glancing at him, touching his shoulder. "I can handle this."

"Yeah, let her handle it, Deputy," Vince said.

"Grace," Henry said, "if you don't want these men here..."

"What're you gonna do about it, Deputy?" said the man on the far right of the group. He had mean, dark eyes set below the brim of his black, low-crowned hat. Curly, black sideburns crawled down both sides of his sun-seasoned face. Leaning forward in his saddle, jutting his chin and hardening his anvil jaws, he closed his gloved right hand around the grips of the pistol jutting from the holster positioned for the cross-draw on his left hip. "There's four of us and only—"

"Now, now, now, Shane," Vince said, grinning and

keeping his eyes on Henry. "We don't want any trouble." He spoke with exaggerated and feigned equanimity. "We just wanna have us a little sit-down chat with the lady. If she *is* a lady." Suddenly, his voice hardened, and he slid his gaze back to Henry. "Somehow, I'm beginning to doubt that."

"All right, mister," Stringbean said, taking one step forward and closing his own hand around the grips of his own holstered six-shooter. "You can't ride in here talking like that!"

"Like I said," Shane said, raising his voice. "There's four of us and only one of you, and none of us gives a good holy damn your *law*!"

The two other men in the group—one short and blond, the other older, stocky, and bull-chested—shook their heads, chuckling. Apparently, Shane's temper was well known to them and a source of amusement.

"Now, now, now," Vince said, again his voice softening and that feigned smile quirking his mouth corners, showing the ends of his teeth. "Let's not let this get out of hand—shall we, boys? The lady knows why we're here." He looked at Grace again. "We're gonna follow the deputy's orders and ride on out of here, give you some time to think it over. We'll be back."

Vince started to rein his horse away, returning his gaze to Henry. "Be seein' you around, *Deputy*."

He booted his horse back in the direction from which he'd come, as did the others except Shane who, turning his own horse, fired his mean, black gaze back at Grace and said, "You think it over, Grace. About Casey. You think it over *real good*. Hi-yahh!"

He raked his spurs against his gray's flanks. The horse whinnied and leaped off its rear hooves and lunged into a hard run, heading after the others.

Henry found himself staring after them with Grace in awkward silence.

For a long time, a full two minutes after the riders had disappeared, likely heading for a saloon in the heart of Del Norte, Henry stood beside Grace, both staring in awkward silence.

Finally, she turned to him. "Henry, I..."

"Who are they, Grace?" he asked. "What do they want? Who's Casey?"

"Come inside," she said quietly, turning toward the open cabin door, suddenly seeming unable to meet Henry's gaze with the suddenly timid one of her own.

She went inside, pulled two stone mugs down from a shelf above the kitchen counter, and set them on the freshly scrubbed table. A coffeepot sat on the warming rack of the potbelly stove. She went to it, used a leather mitt to remove it from the rack and to fill each mug with the steaming, black brew. She returned the pot to the stove, set the bucket filled with soapy water on the floor, then slid a chair out from the table and sank into it.

She looked up at Henry who stood on the other side of the table from her, regarding her in incredulous silence.

"Sit," she said, still not meeting his gaze directly.

Slowly, she lifted her mug, blew on the steaming coffee, and took a small sip.

Henry slid out the chair before him and sank into it. He placed his hands flat on the table, on either side of his own smoking mug, and said, "Look, Grace, you don't owe me any explanations. We can just...we can just..."

"Don't be ridiculous," she said with a dry chuckle, lifting her gaze now to his. "After what happened before they came means I do. Maybe it shouldn't, but what happened means something to me." She studied him briefly, wrinkling the skin above the bridge of her nose. "Does it to you?"

"Of course, it does," he said quietly. "It means a lot to me."

"Did you expect it to happen?"

"No." That was true though he'd wanted it to happen many times before.

"I didn't either." Grace smiled and took another small sip of her coffee. "Getting to Casey," she said with a sigh. "He was my brother. My younger, *outlaw* brother. When our folks died in a Sioux raid in Nebraska, I took Casey and my younger sister, Bethel, to Denver. An aunt and uncle had invited us to stay with them. Only, Casey was unmanageable, so our uncle threw him out."

Grace sipped her coffee, swallowed, and shook her head, pursing her lips angrily. "I didn't blame him a bit. Casey got worse and worse with every passing month. Wouldn't go to school or get a job or help out around my uncle's barn and stables. He fell in with the wrong crowd —a crowd like the men you saw ride up here today. He'd disappear for days at a time."

"I'm sorry, Grace," Henry said. "That must have been hard on you and your sister."

"It gets worse," she said, pensively turning her cup around on the table, staring down at it. "Bethel died from a milk fever. The next year, I went to a girl's academy in Council Bluffs then moved into the mountains near Buena Vista to teach school. I'd seen an ad in the *Rocky Mountain News*.

"It was there I ran into Casey again. Or, I should say, *he* ran into *me*. He'd heard about the new teacher in town and called on me to ask for money. He was down on his luck, a gambler with little talent for gambling though he had plenty for the entertaining of improper women. I gave him what I could, and he left without so much as a thank you. Two years later, he showed up at the house I was renting. Like here, it was just a cabin near the school in Buena Vista. He was badly wounded—he'd taken a shotgun blast to his side. It was just awful!"

Grace drew a deep breath and let it out slowly, keeping her sad gaze on her coffee. Absently, she tucked a vagrant strand of hair back behind her left ear and continued. "I didn't know what had happened, who had shot him or why. He wasn't in any condition to tell me anything. He died the next day, and I buried him in the woods behind my house. I didn't want anyone else to know about my brother who'd come to such an awful and disreputable end. I was worried about the stigma that would be attached to the town's young schoolteacher.

"Two days later the four men you just met—Vince Chaney, Shane Nordstrom, Lonnie Russell, and Dutch Deering—paid me a visit. It turned out that they, Casey, and another man—a half-Mexican named Latigo something or other—had robbed the Pueblo Stage. Casey and the Mexican had been shot by the shotgun messenger. Latigo died outright. The others and Casey had ridden into the mountains and holed up in a cave somewhere around Texas Creek.

"The others tended Casey's wound, even fetching medicines from a doctor in Gunnison. Casey paid them back by getting up one night and riding out while the others slept—with the fifty thousand dollars in gold coins they'd taken out of the stage's strongbox. Pay for a local mine. Figuring Casey would come to me, Vince and the others paid me a visit. They'd visited before—they and Casey spending a day or two now and then. I suspected they'd been on the run from the law, though they didn't say as much. Don't ask me why I didn't go to the sheriff, because I really don't know why I didn't. Some strange, misbegotten brother-sister loyalty, I guess."

Grace looked across the table at Henry, wide-eyed with exasperation at herself. "Oh, dear Henry—what you must think of me, having learned all this. My disreputable past!"

Henry reached over and placed his right hand over her left one, gently squeezing. "I'm not judging, only listening. You can stop whenever you want, Grace."

She gave another dry laugh and said, "Oh, no—you haven't heard the grand finale!" She laughed again, pursed her lips, and shook her head. "Vince and the others, learning that Casey had died, thought I had the money or at least knew what Casey had done with it. They thought he would have told me. Well, he hadn't, and I didn't. They were about to get rough with me when a posse showed up. They took the four outlaws by surprise, without firing a single shot, and led them off to Gunnison. Vince and the others spent seven years in the territorial pen. Today was the first time I'd seen them since they were led away."

"And the payroll gold was never recovered, I take it?"

"No. It was generally agreed that Casey took the secret of where he'd stashed it with him to the grave in my backyard." Grace shot Henry a sharp look from the other side of the table. "*Now*, what do you think of my story, Deputy?"

Henry wagged his head, sipped his coffee, tepid by now, and sat back in his chair. "I think it's a heckuva story and that you're in one tight spot. But don't you worry." He narrowed an eye at her. "No harm will come to you. Not if I have anything to do with it, and I will."

Grace offered a weak smile. "Thank you. But like he said, there's four of them. And they're hardened criminals. Likely even harder now after spending the last seven years in the state pen."

"Like I said—don't you worry," Henry said, confidently. "But don't they have any sense? If your brother had given you that loot or told you where it was hid, why would you still be teaching school? Heck, I'd figure you'd be living high on the hog in San Francisco by now!"

"Or I'd have returned it to the mining company it belonged to," Grace said crisply.

"Oh, sure, sure," Henry said with a sheepish smile. "Of course, you'd have given it back."

"I would have, Henry."

"I believe you, Grace."

"Unless..." She looked out at the darkening windows, her expression again pensive.

"Unless what?"

"Unless they think I know where it's hidden but want nothing to do with it, knowing that telling anyone my brother had stolen it would only damage my reputation. You know as well as I do that a schoolteacher, especially as young a woman as I was seven years ago—I was your age, Henry, only twenty-three years old and just building a life for myself—has to maintain her reputation. How many parents would want a teacher with an outlaw brother teaching their children?"

She turned a grave, level look to Henry. "My reputation is worth more to me than fifty thousand dollars, Henry."

"I believe it. And I believe it's a long shot, Grace. Them thinking you know where the money is but want nothing to do with it. I think they're just loco. Loco, greedy, and poison mean. I could see it in their eyes. Especially that one with the black eyes riding the gray horse."

"Shane Nordstrom." Grace shivered and crossed her arms as though chilled.

"You best not stay alone out here, Grace. Maybe you should ride into town, get a room for a few nights in the San Juan. Just until I can run those four out of town. I can, too. You just watch me. I'll get Rio to back me."

She cast him another weak smile. "Thank you, Henry. But I can't afford a room at the San Juan. I'm not being paid now while school is out of session."

"I have a few extra dollars stashed away."

"No, no. I couldn't ask you to do that. I'll stay here. I have that shotgun over there," she said, casting a determined look at the double-bore Greener resting atop pegs over the front door. "If they come again..."

"That only has two barrels." Henry reached into a pouch of the saddlebags he'd draped over the chair to his left. He pulled out a six-shooter, flipped it in the air, and closed his hand around the barrel. "Take this. It's my spare. It has five in the wheel." He thumbed a shell from his pistol belt and set it on the table, bullet end up. "That's six."

Grace considered the gun in the deputy's hand, looked down at the bullet on the table.

"Go ahead," Henry urged. "Leastways, if I hear shooting from this direction, I can come running. If it comes to that. I mean to run those four varmints out of Del Norte pronto, have them out of town before sunup tomorrow. I'll cite them for vagrancy. There'll be no mention of you."

"Oh, Henry, what would I do without you?"

Henry smiled.

She reached across the table and accepted the old Colt Navy conversion revolver.

"Now, I'll say good night." Henry rose, draped his

saddlebags over his shoulder, and moved to the door. He stopped with one hand on the knob, glanced back over his shoulder at Grace. "Makes you wonder, though—doesn't it?"

"What's that?"

"Where your brother might have hidden that loot."

"I have to admit I've wondered about it, of course. I'm only human. I'm guessing somewhere up around Cottonwood Pass, before he rode down to Buena Vista. Plenty of abandoned mine shafts up in that country."

"Plenty of mine shafts around here too," Henry said. "And I reckon..." He let his voice trail off as he stared out a near-dark window, pondering.

"You reckon what, Henry?"

"I reckon Casey might've led Vince an' the others right through here, if he was headin' from Turkey Creek toward Cottonwood Pass."

"Yes, I suppose he would have."

"Talk about lookin' for a needle in a haystack!" Henry laughed.

"Definitely. A needle in a haystack."

"Well, good night, Grace."

"Good night, Henry."

He pinched his hat brim and left.

CHAPTER 11

THE MAN, BEAST-LIKE, LIFTED HIS HEAD AND FLARED his nostrils, sniffing the wind.

He closed his eyes, dreamily, grinned, and opened them.

"Woodsmoke," he grunted.

He reined the big steeldust to a halt along the narrow, rocky trail he'd been following for several hours, and looked up the steep, fir- and pine-carpeted ridge on his left. It was late in the day, the light fading fast from these high climes in the Sawatch. It was the fading, angling light that revealed the woodsmoke lifting like a blue mist from the crowns of the firs and pines roughly halfway up the ridge.

The smoke, touched with the tang of pine resin, flatted out over the forest, drifting down, down over those fur-like, blue-green pines...down, down the steep ridge and onto the rocky trail that followed the crease between that ridge and the equally steep one on his right. It touched Ulysses Xavier Lodge's broad nostrils from which tufts of hair bristled, gray as the grayest streaks in his thick, curly, graying beard.

Most men wouldn't have detected the scent, for most men didn't have Lodge's keen senses. He'd honed those senses over many years of hunting the most dangerous and lucrative animal of all—other men.

Staring at the rising smoke a good hundred yards up the ridge or more, Lodge muttered, "Must be a shelf up there. They're camped up there. Two, maybe three men, judgin' by the size of the fire. One man alone wouldn't need a fire that big. Only calls attention with those with a sniffer and peepers sharp enough to smell an' see it."

He chuckled. To anyone but himself it would have sounded like a bear's deep snort in satisfaction of having found a tree hollow filled with honey.

He booted the steeldust ahead along the trail. He needed an extra horse and trail supplies, as he hadn't laid in fresh before visiting the little gal whom he loved dearly with all his heart and whom he'd thought from what she'd said and how she'd looked at him had returned his affections.

Bitch!

"Come on, Beast," Lodge said, batting the heels of his tall moccasins against the big steeldust's flanks. "Let's find us a way up, invite ourselves to supper. You know, I do believe I can even smell that coffee they're cookin' up yonder!"

He found a switchbacking game trail after another two hundred yards of riding and followed it up the ridge through the cool pines fragrant with the smell of forest duff and rife with the late day piping of birds, chittering squirrels, and the occasional caw-caw-caws of quarreling crows.

A half hour later he found the relatively flat shelf jutting out from the mountain's belly, like a fat man's gut, and followed it southeast, around the mountain's broad shoulder.

Fifteen minutes later, the metallic rasp of a rifle being cocked came to Lodge's ears from ahead and around a slight bend in the trail.

He reined Beast to a halt, grinned, making his beard climb his sun-, wind-, and cold-leathered cheeks, and called jauntily, "Halloo the camp! I'm friendly as a tree full of chickadees if y'all are!"

Again, he chuckled.

Silence, save for the peeping of said chickadees.

A man's voice called out from around the bend in the trail. "Ride in slow."

Lodge could see smoke rising in the trees over that way. The sun had gone down, the shadows were thick and deep, and the smoke swirled lazily up toward the darkening tree crowns.

"Slow ahead, Beast," Lodge said.

The big steeldust continued forward, slowly following the bend in the trail until the fire appeared roughly fifty yards ahead, where the shelf had cut deeper into the belly of the mountain. Another twenty yards beyond the fire, an aspen-sheathed creek flowed straight down the mountain, from Lodge's left to his right. He could hear the soft gurgling of the water dropping down over shelving rocks and knew that earlier in the year, when the snow was melting, it was likely a raging torrent. He'd crossed it below a few minutes earlier, on the main trail—merely a freshet running along the bottom of its six-foot-deep, rocky cut.

Back in the pines near the creek, Lodge's eyes picked out four horses tied to a picket line strung between two trees—two paints, a stocky American, and a dapple-gray.

That big American would suit his packing purposes just fine.

Around the fire sat four men, the firelight flashing bronze against three of the men's faces, filling the hollows of their eyes beneath their broad-brimmed Stetsons with dark shadows. The fourth man sat back against a rock, facing Lodge, away from the fire and several feet to the right of it. He wore a plaid shirt under a striped blanket coat against the building mountain chill, and leather chaps over wash-worn denims. The weathered, cream Stetson was tipped back off his dome-like forehead.

He was a big, stocky man with broad shoulders and bulging gut. He held an old-model Winchester across his thighs, and Lodge could see with his keen eyes even in the fast-fading light that the hammer was drawn back to full cock.

The bounty hunter grinned as he approached the man and the fire behind him. "How do, gents? How do? Smelled your fire from down below and my gut cried out for grub shared with friends around a warm fire." He glanced at the big, speckled coffeepot hanging from a tripod over the dancing flames. "That coffee sure smells good."

One of the men sitting around the fire, on the left side of it, flanking the big man leaning back against the rock, turned to the man to his right and said quietly but loudly enough for Lodge's keen ears to pick it up. "Big son of a bitch, ain't he?"

The man to whom he'd addressed the observation didn't respond but kept his stony face turned toward where the newcomer was reining the big steeldust to a stop.

"Don't see many strangers out this way," said the man

who'd been leaning back against the rock but who straightened now and rested the barrel of the cocked Winchester on his shoulder.

Lodge smiled to himself.

In the stocky gent's own subtle fashion, he was asking Lodge his name and what in hell he was doing out here. Lodge's size had always made him a threat. Even from a fairly early age. Hell, he'd grown to his full six foot six by the time he was seventeen years old.

"The name's McDougal," Lodge said, knowing that his name was likely known in these parts, since this was his hunting ground though he mostly kept to himself. He didn't like strangers because strangers didn't like him for his intimidating size and his, well, *untraditional* appearance. "Jed McDougal." Again, he grinned, trying to set these men at ease. "Call me Mack."

He'd once met a Jed McDougal up in the Sangre de Cristos—a shy, retiring loner who'd fished and trapped and lived in a cabin high up near Wheeler Peak. Lodge didn't care for most other men, but he'd taken a liking for old McDougal mostly, he supposed, because old McDougal had reminded him a lot of himself. Or how he saw himself, anyway, having little understanding of his own off-putting savagery.

"Hello, Mack," said the man with the rifle. "I'm Walt Iris. We ride for the Quarter Circle Six between here and St. Elmo. We're scouting our herds scattered to hell and gone out on here on open range, getting ready for the fall gather. You can tie your horse with ours over yonder then come on over and have a cup of mud. We have beans and bacon leftover, and you're welcome to scrape the pan. Coyote Davis over there makes a mean pot of biscuits, too, and last I checked there were two left."

"Don't mind if I do, don't mind if I do," Lodge said.

"Mind if I drag my gear over and share your fire tonight with you fellas?"

Iris glanced at the other men. All three looked back at him. The same one who'd vocalized his observation regarding Lodge's size hiked a shoulder in the affirmative.

"Sure, why not," Iris said, offering a cordial smile, depressing the Winchester's hammer and lowering the rifle to his side.

"Mighty kind of yas, much obliged." Lodge pinched the brim of his bullet-crowned hat and turned the steel-dust toward the other horses all peering toward the newcomers, twitching their ears. The big American loosed a greeting whinny and stomped a hoof; Lodge's steeldust answered in kind.

Lodge tended his horse, casting several furtive, critical glances toward the four horses around him as well as at the fire. Iris had joined the others, sitting on a rock and sipping a fresh cup of coffee. He'd set an iron fry pan on a rock near the guttering flames, heating the beans and bacon for their visitor. Lodge had seen him add two biscuits to the pan, as well.

"Damn nice of him," Lodge said quietly to himself, the trickle of the creek behind him covering his voice, as he ran a swatch of burlap down Beast's stout left rear leg. "Damn nice of him. Good to be in nice company for a change—ain't it, Beast? That's mountain folks for you..."

He glanced at the big American, a broad-barreled sorrel, peering at him dubiously, and added even more quietly, "Nice horseflesh, too. I hope you two get along. I don't wanna be breakin' up no fights. Hear me, Beast?"

He chuckled deep in his chest.

When he finished watering Beast at the creek and graining him after tying him to the cowboys' picket line, Lodge dragged his gear over to the fire and dropped it down in an open spot on the side of the fire nearest the creek, at the base of a large spruce whose branches didn't start until nearly ten feet up from the base of the trunk. He leaned his sheathed rifle against the tree.

"Help yourself to coffee, and them beans and bacon should be hot by now," Iris told him from where he sat on the opposite side of the fire.

"Don't mind if I do," Lodge said.

While he was pouring coffee and gathering up the pan of beans, bacon, and biscuits, Iris introduced him to the three other cowboys—Coyote Davis sitting to Lodge's immediate left and Pike Payne sitting just beyond Iris. Payne was the one who'd commented on Lodge's size. The man sitting to Lodge's right was Willie Sadler—a loose-limbed, sparkly-eyed kid with long sandy hair curling down over his ears, beneath a low-crowned, narrow-brimmed hat with decorative white stitching running around the crown's edges. A leather thong hung down against his neck. He kept smiling at the others over the rim of his coffee cup as though they all shared a secret, and he was having trouble keeping it.

Or...maybe he found the big stranger amusing...

Lodge found himself glowering at the kid, anger rising in him, as he dug hungrily into his vittles. He glanced away to see Iris staring at him from where he sat on his rock, holding his coffee cup in both his big, rope-burned hands between his knees.

Lodge grinned and continued shoveling the beans and bacon into his mouth and smearing bite-sized pieces of the two biscuits around in the bean juice and grease and shoving those into his mouth, too, not caring that a good bit of the food was clinging to the beard around his mouth.

Every few bites, he took a sip of the coal-black coffee,

which was bitter-strong from having hung so long over the fire.

That was just the way Lodge liked it.

Aside from the anger rising in him because of the lingering, sparkly-eyed grin on Willie Sadler's moist-lipped mouth, he was content.

He'd barely started eating before he was through. He swabbed his plate clean with the last bit of biscuit, belched loudly, set his plate and fork aside, and rose to refill his coffee cup.

"Thankee mighty kindly, gents," he said, moving the pot from the tripod with a leather swatch. "That was right fillin'." He belched again, loudly, and chuckled as he poured the smoking brew into his cup.

He returned the pot to the tripod then went over and sat down against the tree, between Coyote Davis on his left and the kid, Sadler, to his right. Davis was angular-faced, late twenties, and he, like the others, wore a single Colt on his hip, the end of the butt worn a little from long use in grinding coffee beans around fires much like this one.

Lodge blew on his coffee and sipped.

"Say, uh..."

He looked across the dancing flames—they were considerably shorter now since Lodge had ridden into the camp. The night was considerably darker around the fire too—to see Iris staring at him, his broad forehead beneath his shoved-back, cream Stetson rung with deep, long lines of incredulity. He had very blue eyes, and he was clean-shaven, the oldest of the four cow nurses—probably somewhere in his late thirties, early forties.

"Say what?" Lodge grunted.

Iris slid his blue eyes to Lodge's plate and fork. "It's custom in a cow camp—we each tend our own dishes.

Since you were the last one to eat, it's up to you to clean the pan, as well." He looked at the empty, black, cast-iron skillet remaining where Lodge had left it on a flat rock in the fire ring.

He smiled.

CHAPTER 12

Again, anger rose in Lodge.

The kid was really smiling at him now, the fire sparking in his eyes and in the moisture on his lips.

"Well, shit," Lodge said. "Can I finish my coffee first?"

The smile left Iris's face. His eyes went cold. "Sure," he said, but he was riled now. Lodge could see that.

"Oh, hell!" Lodge set his cup down then removed the pan from the rock in the fire with one gloved hand. He picked up his plate and fork; the fork rattled on the tin plate as he stomped angrily past the horses to the creek. The big American sidled away from him, whickering.

Lodge scrubbed the plate and pan out with sand then gave them another cursory scrub in the creek. He did the same with his fork, dropped the fork into the pan, and stomped back into the camp.

"You happy now?" he asked Iris and dropped the gear beside the burlap war sack near Iris's boots, which bulged unevenly from other cooking and eating paraphernalia.

Iris didn't say anything. He stared stonily across the flames and sipped his coffee. The others looked at him and then at each other. The kid, Sadler, had a lopsided grin on his face, his grin directed at Iris now.

Lodge trudged back to his rock, sat down, picked up his cup, and sipped.

"Yep, sure enough—damn near cold." It wasn't cold, just warm. Still, Lodge's dander was up, and it was no easy thing to get it back down.

He sipped his coffee and stared moodily into the flames. He was very aware of the hogleg he'd taken from the cowboy in Del Norte holstered on his right. His buffalo coat was open, the right-side flap pulled back behind that gun.

He could feel Iris staring at him from across the fire, but he ignored the man until Sadler said in his now-flat, dull voice, still holding his cup in both hands between his knees. "I seen you somewhere before."

It almost sounded like an accusation.

Lodge looked over at him. He shook his head, pursed his lips inside his food-stained beard, and shook his head. "Nah, you got it wrong."

The lines cut deeper across Iris's forehead. "I don't think so."

"Sure, sure," Lodge said, and chuckled as he returned his gaze to the fire.

For a long time, Iris stared at him stonily. He didn't move. He didn't even seem to blink. He just stared stonily across the fire at his big guest.

The others shifted their nervous gazes from Lodge to Iris and then to each other, and then they started the rounds all over again.

Slowly, the flames went down...down. Darkness encroached like some mysterious, untamed thing around the camp, moving closer and closer as the flames grew shorter and shorter. No one seemed to want to move, as though they'd become suddenly glued in place.

You've heard "the tension was so thick you could cut it with a knife?"

The tension in the darkening camp was so thick you'd have to use an ax.

"Salida." Lodge's low, even voice rose from the other side of the fire. The silence and stillness had become so complete that it was like a sudden explosion. It made young Sadler jerk his shoulders with a start.

The other three swiveled their heads to Iris. Their gazes held on his for several tense seconds, and then they turned to Lodge.

"Salida," Iris said in that quiet, stony voice. "Ulysses Lodge walked up to Red Miller while Mike Davis was dealing farrow with him. Miller had a girl on his knee. She was singing softly along with her eyes closed to the Mexican, three-piece band. Lodge drew his Colt and shot Miller through the ear, making a mess all over that girl's face." Suddenly, Iris smiled. "Lodge held up a wanted dodger, told everybody to pipe down—Miller was wanted alive *or* dead! Then you proceeded to cut his head off with a bowie knife."

Lodge smiled.

Iris held his gaze on the big bounty hunter. "Ulysses Xavier Lodge is a notorious loner. Rarely shares a camp with anyone but his hoss." He paused, sucked in his lower lip a little, let it out. "My guess is you're on the run...an' you're here for grub...maybe hosses. Am I right?"

Lodge's smile grew a little wider.

The smile on Iris's face disappeared.

He dropped the coffee cup he'd been holding in both hands. It fell to the ground with a tinny thud, coffee sloshing. His right hand slid to his right, chap-clad thigh.

The other three cowboys turned their gazes back to Iris and then back to Lodge, their eyes growing large as 'dobe dollars.

Iris yelled and rose from his stone, sliding his Colt from its holster. It bucked and roared, an orange flash in the near darkness around the fire. The bullet spanged off a rock near Lodge's right boot. An instant later, the bounty hunter was on his feet, and the cowboy's Colt in his right fist stabbed orange flames toward Iris and then at Coyote Davis to his left. He saved the last round for the kid, who'd risen from his own rock and had his Schofield in his hand.

The gun wasn't cocked but it was leveled at Lodge.

The kid just stared, lower jaw hanging. The Schofield shook in his shaking hand. There was a dribbling and a soft thudding sound.

Urine was dribbling down the inside of his denim-clad thigh onto his right boot, glistening softly in the lingering orange glow from the fire's coals. His thumb was on his pistol's hammer, but he seemed unable to cock the piece.

His face was a mask of terror. "No," he quaked. "No... I don't." His high-pitched voice grew plaintive. "We was only...*gatherin' cows!*"

Lodge blinked once, slowly, almost dreamily. He squeezed the trigger of the Colt aimed at the kid's head.

———

MANNION STARED DOWN AT THE TRACKS OF THE HORSE he'd been following for nearly ten hours off and on, having lost them where the trail had become too flinty to betray the passage of its navigators.

There weren't that many trails out here—north of Del Norte on the way toward Salida and the Sawatch

Range—so Mannion had stubbornly clung to the main one, usually picking up the hoofprints again after twenty minutes or a half hour after having lost them.

Now, here in the deep canyons of the Sawatch, the tracks swerved off the main trail onto a game trail that appeared to switchback through the pine forest on the steep ridge to his left. He was relatively certain they were the same horse tracks he'd been following since earlier in the morning, having picked them up north of Del Norte, where the tracks of other saddle horses and those of ironshod wagon wheels had grown sparse, having branched off toward ranches, remote mining towns, and mines.

He believed that the tracks that continued to head straight toward the Sawatch belonged to Ulysses Lodge's big steeldust, Beast

One, the hoofprints were larger than normal. Two, the indentations were deep. They were the prints of a big horse ridden by a big man.

Mannion had followed them across the rolling, sagebrush prairie and into the canyons of the Sawatch Range, the main peaks of which had loomed far ahead and beyond him, the wide-set peaks of a massive range that ran roughly eighty miles from southeast to northwest. The range formed part of the Continental Divide, its eastern side draining into the headwaters of the Arkansas River. Its western drainage fed the headwaters of the Roaring Fork River, the Eagle River, and the Gunnison River, all tributaries of the Colorado River.

Fifteen of the range's peaks rose higher than fourteen thousand feet.

It was a big, bold, massive range—good wilderness country for a man to get lost in. It was familiar territory to Ulysses Lodge. That's why he was riding into them with Mannion believing that, having ridden all night and judging by the age of the man's tracks, he was now only about four hours behind his quarry. He'd been pushing Red hard. Lodge's tracks also revealed that the man had kept a steady, even pace, going easy on his horse.

He must have believed—or had believed, anyway—that he'd had no close shadowers.

Whether he still believed that now, well north of Del Norte, was anyone's guess.

Mannion didn't underestimate the savage giant who was crazier'n a tree full of owls, as the saying went. When it came to wilderness travel, and to tracking and knowing when he was being tracked, Lodge was savvy. And handy with his rifle and pistol, with no qualms whatever about using both. In fact, Mannion believed the man was one of those primal human creatures who took delight in it.

He swung Red off the trail's left side and followed the tracks of the big horse climbing the switchbacking trail into deep forest.

A half hour later he came upon the scene of bloody murder.

He was on Lodge's trail, all right.

———

Mannion stood over one of the four men lying dead around the cold fire. He knew the man he was staring down at—a big man, early forties. Walt Iris, foreman of Norman Waycross's Quarter Circle Six, the headquarters of which lay roughly ten miles northwest, between here and the raucous little mountain mining town of St. Elmo. Lodge's bullet had taken him through the bridge of his nose, right between the eyes.

Mannion grimaced as Iris stared up at him, astonished and horrified even in death by his grisly demise.

Mannion walked around the fire ring heaped with dead ashes, his Yellowboy resting on his shoulder. He didn't recognize the other three dead men—killed as Iris, all with headshots—though he'd run into them before out here on open range when he'd been hunting owlhoots of one stripe or another. All three punchers had been riding with either Iris or Waycross's second lieutenant, Jake Driscoll.

Lodge might know this high-and-rocky country, but Mannion knew it, too. If the big man went farther north, though, up toward Aspen on the ranger's west side and Leadville on its east side, Lodge would gain the upper hand. Mannion needed to run the big man down before the country became more and more unfamiliar to him, which would mean harder tracking for him and the increased possibility of Lodge taking advantage of his better knowledge of the terrain to effect an ambush.

He turned to the three horses tied to the picket line strung between two pines near the creek gurgling behind them—two paints and a dapple-gray. They regarded him warily.

"Didn't even free the saddle stock," Mannion said in disgust. He looked around at the camp gear, strewn carelessly around the camp. Most of the food was gone; only cooking gear remained. Apparently, Lodge had taken Iris's big American sorrel to carry it all on.

Lodge had ridden in here, falsely putting these men at ease. He'd taken advantage of their hospitality—Joe had known Iris to be a right hospitable fella—and rewarded them with bullets while they'd sipped coffee around the previous night's fire.

"Likely gotten himself a good night's sleep after he'd

killed you," he grumbled down at Iris's open eyes, "and woke the next morning feeling fresh as a daisy."

Mannion cursed and spat, thoroughly appalled. He'd seen a lot of depravity in his life, but such senseless, savage killings as those he saw here still revolted him.

He walked back to where Red stood ten feet away, eyeing the dead men dubiously, twitching his ears and flicking his tail, and shoved the Winchester down into the saddle boot. Heading for the picket line, Mannion said, "Least I can do is get you fellas back to the Quarter Circle Six headquarters. I don't have time to give you a proper burial, but I know ol' Norman will want you to have one."

He didn't want to take the time. The detour from the main trail, Lodge's trail, would cost him a good hour, but he had to do it. Not even Bloody Joe Mannion could leave a man like Walt Iris out here to the coyotes and wolves.

He saddled the three remaining horses, wrapped the dead men in their blanket rolls, and hefted two of the younger, lighter men over one of the paints and Iris and the remaining man over the second paint and the dapple-gray, respectively.

He mounted Red and set off back down the mountain toward the main trail, jerking the three pack mounts along behind him by their lead lines. He gained the main trail, picked up Lodge's distinct trail again, where he'd come down off the mountain a little farther north of where he'd gone up, and followed it for nearly an hour into a badlands area below a pass before something whistled ominously just off his right ear to spang off a rock behind him

Ambush!

CHAPTER 13

Joe cursed as he hauled back on Red's reins and looked around wildly.

A loud bear's laugh echoed off the crags around him.

If a bear could laugh, that was.

No, this could only be the bear-*like* laugh of Ulysses Xavier Lodge.

Joe had ridden right into a bushwhack!

Smoke puffed from a dark granite escarpment just ahead and on his right, from about thirty feet down from the crest. The bullet caromed in, whining louder and louder until it ripped Joe's hat off his head.

Mannion managed to shuck the Yellowboy from its sheath before Red whinnied shrilly and rose so quickly up off his front hooves that Joe, stunned, merely brushed the fingers of his left hand across the horn, dropping his reins, before he went tumbling back off the bay's left hip.

The ground came up to slam him hard about the head and shoulders.

"*Damn!*"

He rolled onto his belly and covered his head with the Yellowboy as Red dropped down to all fours and wheeled. The bay's galloping hooves hammered the ground to Joe's right before he and the three packhorses galloped back down the trail in the direction from which they'd come, whinnying and buck kicking, the packhorses' grisly freight jostling stiffly across the three saddles.

Knowing another bullet would be seeking him out soon, Mannion rolled to his right. Sure enough, another slug hammered the ground where he'd been lying a second ago. In fact, he felt the wind of its passing across his left shoulder just before he rolled up against a boulder with a concave base that acted as a relative shield from the escarpment above and beyond him.

Joe shook his head to clear the cobwebs then edged a cautious look out from beneath the shielding thumb of rock. He could see the silhouette of Lodge's bulky head and shoulders, the bullet-shaped crown of his hat, and the barrel of the man's rifle aimed at an angle down the scarp toward Mannion.

Smoke puffed and orange flames stabbed from the barrel.

Mannion drew his head back behind his cover an eye wink before the bullet slammed into it, sending shards flying onto the trail before him.

Joe jacked a round into the Yellowboy's action, snaked the rifle out from under the rock, and aimed up at the escarpment where Lodge was just then raising his rifle in his big, gloved hands to cock it. Mannion hardened his jaws and drew a deep, calming breath, trying to slow his heart and to keep his hands from shaking. He aimed steadily.

Just as Lodge lowered his rifle again, Joe triggered the Yellowboy. Lodge's own hat went flying off his head to bounce back off the escarpment wall behind him.

That made the grizzled, shaggy-headed giant pull his head back sharply. He was not too far away for Mannion to see the man's eyes and mouth open wide, briefly, in astonishment.

Lodge raised his rifle as he grabbed his hat then, stuffing the topper back on his head, cast a wary look over his shoulder at Mannion and then scrambled quickly for a man of his size up a long, crooked fissure in the scarp, heading toward its pine-spiked crest.

Mannion cursed and sent three more bullets hurling toward his fleeing quarry, watching in keen frustration as the bullets merely blew up rock dust to either side of the big man's head, shoulders, and running legs, the narrow fissure somewhat concealing him, making him a damned hard target.

Joe wriggled out from beneath his covering rock, his ankles and knees feeling creaky, his shoulders aching, head still reeling from his unceremonious meeting with the ground beneath Red's hooves. Rage propelled him forward across the narrow cut, an ancient streambed he'd been following up Clayton's Pass, negotiable only on horseback so avoided by wagons other than a few prospectors' nimble, three-wheeled carts pulled by sure-footed mules.

Rage propelled him. So did exasperation and humiliation.

The savage giant had outsmarted him!

Either Lodge had known that Mannion was behind him, or he'd assumed so. He'd laid up to switch his and Mannion's roles—to turn hunter into prey. And he'd done a damned good job of it. Almost too good. If the bullet that had ripped Joe's hat off his head had been an inch lower, it would have drilled him a third eye.

He'd be lying dead up here, wolf bait.

He crossed the old streambed in six long strides and began climbing the scarp near the top of which Lodge had effected his ambush. He moved quickly, mindless of his sundry aches and pains, holding the Yellowboy up high in both hands across his chest. He kept one eye on the stone mountain he was climbing, uneven enough for a relatively easy ascent. But it was steep enough that it wearied his forty-seven-year-old body fast.

As he climbed, leaping from one thumb of rock to another, raking breaths in and out of his lungs until they began to feel like sandpaper, he kept one eye skinned on the crest of the scarp above him.

He knew full well that Lodge might be lying in wait for him up there as he had been just a few feet below.

When he was about twenty feet below Lodge's original perch, he saw what he'd been watching for—the barrel of a rifle sliding out from over the top of the scarp, showing between two large rocks just below it. It angled ominously downward. Lodge's shaggy, bearded head followed, the man's face appearing more animal than human, the two big eyes sunken deep in stony sockets.

Joe had just leaped off one knob of rock to a stone ledge three feet above when he threw himself to his right and wheeled, pressing his back against the face of the scarp, one hand holding the Yellowboy down low in his right, gloved hand and pressing the flat of his open left hand against the scarp.

The bullet whistled past Mannion's right shoulder as he faced out away from the formation to spang loudly off the thumb of rock Joe had just leaped from.

The crash of Lodge's rifle thundered half a second later.

Joe wheeled, took the Yellowboy in his left hand and raised it, pressing the butt plate against that shoulder. He sent two of his own slugs hurling up along the fissure and watched with his lips bunched angrily as both slugs found only open air before caroming off toward the cobalt sky beyond.

Lodge had pulled his head back right after firing his shot.

Fool him once, shame on Mannion. Fool him twice...

Likewise, Joe thought.

Raking another round into the Yellowboy's chamber, he continued climbing, raking his gaze along the crest of the crag, which he was closing on quickly though his lungs and knees were wearying, the knees stiffening, feeling like drying cement.

He was within ten feet near the crest of the crag.

Eight...

Six...

Four...

Instinctively, knowing he was going to see Lodge kneeling a few feet back from the crest of the crag half a second before he actually did, he threw himself hard left. Lodge's savage grin beneath the brim of his bullet-torn hat was blazed on his retinas as the man's rifle crashed loudly, echoing.

Mannion quickly gained his feet and took two more running steps until he was within three feet of the crag's crest and raised the Yellowboy.

He'd just started to squeeze the trigger when the big man bunched his lips and hardened his eyes and jaws and swung his own Winchester back behind his shoulder and forward. The stock came hurling toward Mannion in a blur of fast-arcing motion, the brass butt plate glinting in the sunlight, striking first the Yellowboy just as Mannion squeezed the trigger, throwing the slug wide, and then against Joe's left temple.

Joe yelled as the Yellowboy flew from his hands as he himself was hurled down and sideways by the force of the giant's blow, striking the belly of the scarp and then rolling down it at angle, arms and legs pinwheeling, his head bouncing off the scarp's uneven rock face.

"Goddamn you, Bloody Joe!" he heard the bear-like man roar.

Mannion rolled up against a shelf of rock.

Once again badly dazed, feeling the burn of a large gash in his left temple, blood trickling down around the socket of that eye, he scrambled to his knees as he raked the big Russian from the holster angled for the cross-draw on his left hip. He gritted his teeth against the pain in his right shoulder as he raised that arm, clicking the Russian's hammer back.

Ulysses Xavier Lodge towered atop the scarp, raising his rifle to his shoulder and bellowing, "Goddamn you, Bloody Joe!"

Mannion got the Russian centered on the man's broad chest clad in heavy buffalo hide, but just as he fired, Lodge twisted to one side and hurled himself straight back out of sight.

Joe's slug caromed through the air where the giant had been standing a quarter second before.

Lolling weakly on his knees, the mountain pitching around him, Mannion fired again and then again in frustration, cursing.

He shoved off his knees with his elbows and ran, limping, weak-kneed, to the top of the scarp, now aiming both his Schofields out before him expecting to see Lodge confronting him once more. No, Lodge was running down the opposite side of the scarp, through a natural corridor of stacked boulders and towering pines.

Mannion aimed both Schofields and fired each one in

turn, the bullets blowing dust from the rocks to each side of the giant just before he disappeared around a bend.

"Come back here, Lodge!" Mannion bellowed, and started running unsteadily forward, down the other side of the scarp and into the natural corridor between piled rocks. "Stop running like a damned Nancy-boy! You shot Jane—come get your medicine!"

Joe slowed his pace as he approached the bend in the trail, wary of another ambush. He stopped as blood oozed into the corner of his left eye, burning. He sleeved it away with his coat sleeve then continued striding along the corridor, extending both Schofields straight out before him and clicking their hammers back as he slowly rounded the bend.

His boots clacked, spurs changing softly against the stone floor. The corridor straightened before him.

He was in a ravine now, pine forest rising on both sides of him, beyond the eight-foot embankments. A spring bubbled out of the rocky wall to his right forming a freshet beneath his boots, making the dark rocks glisten in the afternoon sunshine.

It was cool and damp in here, in this ancient stone riverbed that probably still flowed mightily with snowmelt each spring. White flecks of long-dead animals likely killed by the ancient peoples who once dwelled in this reach of the Sawatch, shone in the walls to each side of him, which were also occasionally spotted with the faded but once-bright primitive figures including suns and moons and stick figures throwing bayonets painted by those long-dead ancient ones.

Ahead, the ravine opened as it leveled out slightly.

Beyond lay more rocks and trees giving way to a broad valley tufted with gray mountain sage and running perpendicular to the corridor Mannion was in. Pine forest ran down the valley's opposite side, and a narrow stream meandered through it like a single strand of bright blue thread. Mannion knew that the Quarter Circle Six lay in a secondary canyon offshooting that valley, to the north, on Mannion's left.

Between Mannion and the valley, a good half a mile away or more, lay nothing but rock and pines, many of which had been toppled by the spring floods and which he had to meander and clamber over now, keeping the Schofields aimed and ready.

He stopped suddenly.

The short hairs at the back of his neck were standing straight up.

Ahead, a big, man-figured silhouette wielding a rifle stepped out from a bend in the broad ravine, fifty yards ahead and to Mannion's right. Mannion threw himself down over a fallen spruce to his left as the killer's big rifle flashed and roared. The dead, brown prickly spruce branches poked at Mannion. When he finally made his way out of the thorny bed and gained his feet, he extended both Schofields, but held his fire.

Lodge was riding off down the canyon toward the broad valley below, his big steeldust trailing Walt Iris's sorrel American, burlap bags of trail supplies bouncing against its sides. Mannion lowered the Schofields and depressed the hammers.

He watched as the silhouetted figures of the big, hatted rider and his two horses rode out into the copper-lemon light of the valley, heading straight across the valley toward a feeder canyon beyond, all but lost against the pine-carpeted opposite ridge, which was a conduit to the town of St. Elmo and the higher, lonelier reaches that backed up against the massive, snub-nosed formation of Mount Harvard.

"Damn coward," Mannion said.

He was too tired to holster his pistols.

He turned and like a man who'd had too much to drink and was only looking for a pillow, began retracing his footsteps but more slowly, even more heavily than before.

"Shoot a woman an'...run...like a damn...yellow-livered...dog."

He holstered one pistol and then the other and kept walking, stopping only to brush blood from his eye, wishing the two rocky ravines he saw before him would merge into the single one he was in now.

By sheer force of will, the world dimming around him, the ground slanting up this way and down that way, so that he felt he was on a ship rolling with slow ocean swells, he made it back to the top of the rocky escarpment. He'd just started down the other side when his knees buckled.

Both knees hit the ground and he fell straight forward without even using his hands to break his fall, hearing a man shout down the ridge below him, "*Up there!*"

Gauzy night closed over Bloody Joe Mannion.

CHAPTER 14

Evangeline "Vangie" Mannion sat in a plush-covered armchair in the corner of Jane Ford's room, dimming now as the sun went down and turning a soft, golden rose through the thin, rose-colored curtains.

Vangie had been watching Jane closely for any sign of the life she'd once seen in her. She'd been sitting here in this chair for several hours, watching constantly, hoping and praying that Jane would at least move her eyes or flutter her lips. But there'd been none of that.

None of the Jane that Vangie had once known as a good friend and then, briefly, as a stepmother, made an appearance. Jane was like a waxen doll lying there under the sheets and one white blanket, unmoving except for the very slight rising and falling of her chest.

She reminded Vangie of dreams—nightmares, rather—she'd had of her mother lying dead after she'd hanged herself from the tree in their yard back in Kansas, when Vangie had been only a few months old. Of course, Vangie had no memory of her mother, only memories of *imaginings* of how her mother might have looked after hanging herself—how pale and blue and frail in death, already yielding to the void, nothing at all how she'd appeared in life, especially not how she'd appeared when her father had fallen in love with her and had asked her to marry him.

Had her father really loved her mother?

If so, why hadn't he helped her see her way out of the darkness?

Vangie had asked herself those questions many times over the years.

She'd come to the conclusion that while her father had loved her mother, because Vangie knew he loved *her*, Vangie, and was thus capable of love, and *must* have loved her mother, he was incapable of showing it at times. Or he got so tangled up in other emotions—namely, pride and anger—that love became too far away for him to retrieve.

Vangie knew that he loved Jane. She'd heard it in his words as well as seen it in his eyes. Joe Mannion was not one to bandy words like "love" around lightly, nor was he one to go around revealing his emotions with his eyes or actions.

Vangie only wished it hadn't come to this, Jane on death's doorstep, for him to see the error of his ways, of holding his love back tightly, like a secret he dared not share.

"He does love you, though, Jane. I want you to know that. He wants you to know that. To hear it if you can." Vangie leaned forward in her chair. She had the sleeves of her plaid flannel shirt rolled up to her elbows; she rested her elbows on her spread, denim-clad knees now, and regarded the sleeping Jane at once sadly and desperately, wanting so terribly for her words to get through to her.

"Can you hear me, Jane? I know you're down deep... somewhere. But I hope you can hear me. And I hope my words might help to bring you back to us. Poppa loves you very much. As much as he loved my mother, I think. Maybe more because he's lived long enough to know the value of it, and the horror of not showing it."

Emotion welled in Vangie.

Her throat swelled with it. Tears flooded her eyes. She brushed them away with the back of her hand.

"Won't you please come back to us, Jane? I don't know what it's going to do to Poppa if you go. If you don't come back to us and never know how much we both love and miss you. How much of a mistake Poppa knows now that he ever let you go."

She stopped swabbing the tears from her eyes. It did no good. They kept coming.

She lowered her head and sobbed, letting the tears roll down her cheeks, tanned from working so many hours in the corrals with her horses, especially the bronc her father had caught for her so she could tame its wild heart, like she'd so often tried to tame Bloody Joe's heart.

Cochise, she'd named the blue roan—appropriately, she thought.

She sobbed. She couldn't stop.

All the hurt, all the heartache she felt. Little of it for herself. Most of it for her father—what he'd put himself and Jane through, with his stingy ways with his love. What he'd put himself and his mother, dear Sarah, through with his stingy ways with his love...

He was always the one he hurt most of all.

Vangie felt the saddest for him. How he tortured himself.

Sarah was dead. Jane likely felt nothing where she resided now, neither alive nor dead but somewhere in between. Vangie, a practical girl as well as a well-read one, believed in neither heaven nor hell. She'd seen no sign of either on earth except in a book written by men.

How he must be torturing himself now—Bloody Joe. Riding raging through the mountains looking for the man who'd shot the woman he loved most in this world. Unable to believe what he'd done when he'd signed that divorce decree, knowing full well that neither he nor Jane had wanted him to.

Vangie closed her hands over her face and bawled, shoulders quaking.

She felt as though she was expressing all the heartbreak in the world from the very beginnings of time.

She'd imagined all the people who'd never been able to express their love for each other and what hell it had brought them when they'd realized it was too late. The people they'd loved were gone and would never hear it now if they climbed to the top of the highest mountain in the world and shouted it at the tops of their lungs.

"Oh, God!" she heard herself mewl into her hands. "*Oh...God...Sweet merciless—!*"

A soft knock on the door.

Vangie looked up, choking on another sob and swabbed the tears from her cheeks with her hands.

The door latch clicked. Young Dr. Ben Ellison—he was older by eight years than Vangie but relative to the much older Dr. Bohannon he was young—poked his head in the door. Concern shone in his dark-brown eyes set beneath full, dark-brown brows.

"Miss Mannion, are you all right?" he asked, gently.

Vangie couldn't stop sobbing. Now humiliation as well as great bereavement burned in her. She had enough of her father in her to dislike displaying her emotions to others. It humiliated her. She hadn't meant to display them to Dr. Ellison. Annoyance added to the toxic mix of emotions inside her now.

"I'll be out in a minute," she said, trying without success to keep her voice from quaking.

"Take your time." Dr. Ellison pulled his head back into the hall and drew the door closed with another click.

Pull yourself together, Vangie told herself, placing her hands on the arms of her chair and grunting as she heaved herself to her feet, suddenly feeling as old as a very old woman. *Pull yourself together*, she repeated to herself, stifling the sobs and wiping the last of the tears from her eyes. *You're a Mannion, goddammit!*

She laughed at this. She couldn't help laughing out loud. She clamped a hand to her mouth and widened her eyes in shock at the irony of her behavior. But then she laughed again into the palm of her hand.

You're a Mannion, goddammit!

Dear God—she was her father's daughter, after all!

That almost caused her to start sobbing again. Yes, she was her father's daughter. She was very much like him. He was very much like her. He felt all the things she did, she knew. They thought and felt all the same things and yet they were both still victims of their own pride and stubborn self-restraint, reluctant to reveal themselves to anyone.

What torment!

Vangie leaned down over Jane and placed a light kiss on the woman's cool forehead.

"Goodbye, Jane," she said tenderly. "I will be back first thing in the morning to check on you."

She straightened, drew a deep, stealing breath and moved to the door. She opened it slowly, quietly, and stepped into the hall lit by two candle lamps. Her boots clomped noisily on the wooden floor as she moved to the door at the end, opened it, stepped into Dr. Bohannon's office, and closed the door behind her.

Only Dr. Ellison was in the office lit by a Tiffany lamp on the doctor's desk. Bohannon must have gone home for the evening.

Ellison sat on the opposite side of the desk from Bohannon's, in a chair facing away from the desk. He sat with his broadcloth-clad legs spread, holding a teacup and saucer between them. His long, wavy, dark-brown hair was parted neatly, and curved down over his ears.

He looked up as Vangie glanced at him quickly then just as quickly moved to the outside door, very conscious of the thudding of her stockman's boots on the floor. "I'd like to stop back in the morning and check on Miss Jane, if that's all—"

"Would you like a cup of tea, Miss Mannion?"

She stopped with her hand on the doorknob and turned to him, scowling, a flush of aggravated embarrassment—she was already embarrassed by her display in Jane's room, bawling like a damn baby—rising in her cheeks.

"What's that?" she asked then glanced at the delicate cup and saucer in his pale hands. Attractive hands but rather delicate hands—not the hands of a man who worked outdoors. "Oh, no…I…I don't drink…"

"I can brew a pot of coffee."

"Oh, no…"

"It's no trouble."

Vangie turned her head quickly to the door and opened it. "Oh, no, I should—"

"Really, it's no trouble at all." Ellison rose from his chair and set his teacup and saucer on Bohannon's desk.

She looked back over her shoulder at him again, scowling at him, her heart thudding. She felt as uncomfortable as she'd ever felt in her life. Her hands were sweaty. He seemed so insistent to trap her here that she found herself relenting against her will. She wanted to run away but she'd already made a damned fool of herself in Jane's room, bawling like a moron.

Slowly, stiffly, she turned to him. "Well, I...if you insist...I'll try the...I'll have tea."

Ellison strode to the potbelly stove hunched to the left of the door, under several shelves of cups and small packets of dry goods, one small pouch with the single word TEA stenciled on it.

"You've never had it before, I take it?"

"I don't think I have, no."

Vangie chuckled silently at herself. *Don't think I have. You know you've never had tea, you idjit.* She'd always considered tea the beverage of choice of old, neatly coifed and attired ladies in stuffy parlors with delicate furniture and a clock on the wall, like the clock on the wall here, behind Bohannon's desk, tick-tocking monotonously.

She guessed now that it must also be the beverage of choice of educated, civilized men.

"Maybe it's time to try it," Dr. Ellison said, pulling a delicate cup and saucer down from the shelf above the stove and setting it on the small table to the stove's left. "You might like it, though this is all I can get out here. It's not nearly as good as the stuff I get back East, but it will do." He flashed a rather disarming, toothy smile at Vangie standing stiffly in front of the door. "You never know—it might open a whole new world for you."

Vangie drew a breath, hiked a shoulder. "You never know."

Again, he smiled at her as he pulled the tea sack down from the shelf. He spooned tea from the bag into a delicate teapot on the table then added water from the kettle steaming on the range's warming rack. He picked up the pot, swirled it around a little, and then poured the lightly colored liquid into the cup sitting atop the saucer.

Oh, great, Vangie thought. *I'm going to have to deal not only with that tiny, delicate cup but the tiny delicate saucer it's supposed to sit on. What's the point of the saucer, anyway, other than to make an uncivilized girl's life even more miserable than it already is?*

"Why don't you sit with me over here?" Ellison said, indicating two small, brocade-upholstered chairs with scrolled wooden backs sitting in the room's corner, to his right, with a small table sitting in the *V* between them, covered with a cloth of delicate white lace. Both chairs and table were in semi-darkness now that the night had grown darker outside the room's two curtained windows, beyond the small sphere of light from the Tiffany lamp on Bohannon's desk.

Vangie looked at the chairs. She looked at Dr. Ellison holding the teapot in both his civilized hands—he wore a ring with a square, near-black stone on the ring finger of his right hand—regarding her with what she supposed she should see as a comforting smile.

For some reason, however, she felt as though she were being lured to the gallows by a smiling hangman promising her a cup of some mysterious toxin to ease her passing before the trapdoor dropped.

CHAPTER 15

Again, conscious of the thudding of her boots which seemed inordinately loud in the office's tight, civilized confines, the room's otherwise silence relieved only by the ticking of the clock on the wall and the occasional, distance-muffled hoot or holler of a drunk on the street, Vangie made the crossing to the chairs without stumbling or otherwise making a fool of herself.

It seemed like an awfully long way, however.

She felt too large for the room, somehow, though Ellison was several inches taller than she. Her clothes didn't help her feeling of a bull in a china shop. They were clothes you'd see on a man on any range pushing cattle this way or that, and they were in sharp contrast to Ellison's black, three-piece suit with butterscotch waistcoat, black foulard tie, white silk shirt, and gold-washed chain dangling from the waistcoat's watch pocket.

She wondered if he could smell the shit on her boots. She wasn't certain there was shit on her boots, but there often was, and now she imagined that she herself could smell it so why couldn't he?

He set the teapot on the table, retrieved both their

cups and saucers and, without so much as rattling either cup on its saucer, brought them over to the table and set them down on it. He filled first her cup from the pot and then his own. The tea smelled a little like aspen leaves and cinnamon on a warm summer breeze, Vangie thought.

Nice.

"Please, sit," he said, offering the steaming cup perched delicately on its saucer.

Vangie sat down in the chair and accepted the cup and saucer in both her hands, which suddenly felt much larger than they normally did. She felt as though she were wearing heavy hide mittens. How was she supposed to drink from such a delicate cup wearing mittens?

She thought of using the night tending of her horses as an excuse to take her leave but thought it would only ring hollow. At least, that's why she thought she'd nixed the idea. Or was there something just compelling enough about this learned man to have made her want to stay despite how ill at ease she felt?

Vangie sat stiffly with the cup and saucer on her knees, which she pressed tightly together.

"Please," Ellison said, smiling at the steaming cup on her lap, "sip."

Vangie looked down at the cup as though it were a snake in her lap.

Here we go...

She curled her index finger through the very small handle, raised the cup to her lips, blew on it gently, not wanting to send tea slopping down over the sides, and sipped. "Mmm," she said, swallowing. "Good," she lied.

While it smelled all right, it did not taste good.

He smiled and lifted his own cup to his lips. "It grows on you." He swallowed and set the cup down very delicately onto the saucer resting on his knee. "I take it you prefer coffee."

Vangie raised and lowered a shoulder. "It's what I grew up with. I started drinking coffee almost as soon as I started walking. I'd sit on Pa's lap at the kitchen table after supper while he read the paper and had a smoke and cup of coffee. I liked the smell, so he let me take a few sips at first and soon I was drinking half a cup before graduating to full cups of my own when I was around ten or eleven."

"I take it your father raised you alone?"

"Yes. My mother died when I was very young." Vangie politely, carefully lifted the teacup to her lips again and took another sip. She tried not to make a face—the concoction tasted like weak, sour coffee—before she set it back down onto the saucer without spilling a drop or rattling it overmuch—so far, so good—and said, "She hanged herself."

She squeezed her eyes closed for a second, wincing. Why in hell had she had to go and blab that out so point-blank?

Had she been raised by wolves?

"I'm very sorry to hear that," Dr. Ellison said. "That must have been hard for you—growing up without a mother."

Again, Vangie shrugged. Her cheeks burned with embarrassment. "I didn't really know the difference. Pa was enough for me to handle."

Dr. Ellison laughed. "I see, I see."

She hadn't meant to make the joke. It had just leaped right out of her mouth. She had to admit it was a good one. She smiled, feeling somewhat more at ease.

"I take it Miss Jane," Dr. Ellison said, glancing toward the closed door flanking Bohannon's desk, "was a mother to you for a time. I mean, I heard as much from Dr. Bohannon."

"For a few months," Vangie said with a slow intake and then exhalation of air.

"I see."

Vangie saw no reason to elaborate.

"Tell me, Doctor," Vangie said, "do you—"

"Please, Ben."

Vangie frowned at him, incredulous.

Again, he offered his warm, gentle smile. "I'd like it if you'd call me Ben."

Vangie didn't know what to make of that. It didn't really seem right for her to call Miss Jane's doctor by his first name. She hardly knew the man and doubted she ever would. Of course, there was some reason he'd offered her tea, but the idea of their relationship going beyond anything more than professional was almost too much for her to think about. They were from two different worlds.

Why could he possibly want such a thing?

It *was* too much for her to think about. She quickly shook her head, dismissing the suggestion outright, and started again with: "Do you think Miss Jane will ever wake up?"

Ellison sighed and stared down at his half-empty cup, absently running a pale thumb along the rim. "I honestly don't know. I can tell you from my limited amount of experience that each day that goes by means another day of healing. She's asleep because her consciousness has shut down in order for her body to channel all of its energy into mending itself. At least, that's my theory in Miss Jane's case."

He gave a half-hearted smile and sipped his tea.

"I see," Vangie said, drawing down her mouth corners and nodding.

It wasn't an entirely satisfactory answer, but she could live with it. Really, no answer would satisfy her except the one that Jane would pull out of it for sure and make a full recovery.

She looked down at the teacup on her lap. Dutifully, she closed her index finger through the handle again and began to raise it to her lips before Dr. Ellison reached out, took the cup from her hand, removed the saucer from her lap, and set both on the table before them.

"That's enough of that," he said, chuckling. "I refuse to torture you a minute longer. Next time we'll have coffee."

"Oh, well, I..."

"No, no, it's all right, Miss Mannion." He paused, studied her pensively for a few seconds then said, "Do you mind if I call you Vangie?"

She looked down at her lap, suddenly wishing she had the teacup and saucer to fix her attention on. "I reckon... I reckon..."

Oh, that was good, she castigated herself. How eloquent!

"All right," Dr. Ellison said, chuckling again. "For now, we'll remain Dr. Ellison and Miss Mannion. Does that make you more comfortable?"

Vangie kept her eyes on her knees, heart thudding. "Um..."

"Never mind." Again, he paused. "You know, I find you very fascinating, Miss Mannion. Please, if I'm being inappropriate, tell me."

"Inappropriate how?" Vangie said, frowning at him. She honestly wasn't sure. All she knew was that she felt uncomfortable in his presence but at the same time intrigued. Not in a huge hurry to leave.

What *did* he see in her?

"I understand from Dr. Bohannon that you don't get out too much."

"Umm...well, yep, I guess you could say that."

"Prefer to be with your horses, do you? I mean, prefer them over people?"

"Yes, I guess you could say that," she said with yet another nervous shrug after consciously formulating the response while resolving to strike the words "I reckon" from her vocabulary forevermore.

"Why is that, do you think?" Dr. Ellison asked, beetling the skin above his long, fine nose—neither too narrow nor too wide.

"I guess I really haven't thought about it much," Vangie said. "I guess I am rather odd. Pa keeps trying to get me to let one of the boys in town court me, but..." She let her voice trail off and met the doctor's gaze with a generally puzzled one of her own. "I really don't know why I don't."

"No interest?"

"I guess not."

"You have plenty of prospective suitors, I take it?"

Vangie wasn't sure how to answer that. Several boys had shown up at her and her father's door, but Vangie had rebuffed every one of them except for a young man named Edgar Winters, the son of the local Bank & Trust's loan officer. Vangie had sat out on the porch swing with Edgar a few times, but when he'd wrapped his arms around her shoulders one night and tried to kiss her, she'd elbowed his arm away and leaped to her feet and fairly screamed at him to get away and leave her the hell alone! Who did he think he was, coming over here and pawing her like some puppy worrying a bone!

Inwardly, she snickered at the memory. No wonder everyone in town regarded her skeptically, warily. Of course, it didn't help that she was the daughter of Bloody Joe Mannion.

Again, inwardly, she snickered. She didn't mind being seen as odd. It kept people away, which, she suddenly realized, was what she wanted.

At least, she thought she'd wanted it.

Now in the presence of this cultivated, polite young man who made no move to kiss her but only to get to know her, she found herself possibly detecting some chinking in her armor...

"I reckon I...er, I mean, to be *honest*, I have had prospective suitors," Vangie said.

"I don't doubt that a bit."

Vangie looked down at her knees again, tucking her upper lip over her bottom one, feeling another blush rise in her cheeks.

"You're a good rider *and* horse *breaker*," Dr. Ellison said. "This from Doctor Bohannon, as well."

"Gentler," Vangie said. "I would never break a horse. That means to break its spirit. Why would anyone want to do that to anything?"

"Ah, good point." Dr. Ellison nodded, smiling at her wistfully, admiringly. "Could I watch you ride sometime?"

"What?" she said in surprise. What an odd question. No one had ever asked to watch her ride her horses.

"To be honest," Dr. Ellison said, "I'm a bit of a dandy. I was raised in Philadelphia. My family has money. We never had to ride our own horses nor even drive our own carriages. We had employees who did that. While the wealth with which I was raised opened many doors for me—I'm well-schooled and traveled and I don't mean to boast about it at all, merely stating facts—I'm afraid it closed many doors, as well. I never learned to ride though one of the reasons I decided to practice my internship in the West was because I've always been fascinated by it."

He grinned broadly and for the first time this evening, a flush rose into his broad, handsome face with its warm, intelligent eyes and the high cheekbones and broad forehead of good breeding. At least, if he were a horse, judging by his conformation—the good head and the clean lines of his body, which neither boasted too much nor too little flesh, and betrayed the fact that while he might have worked indoors, he did take at least a little exercise—Vangie would deem his bloodline strong and noble. His upper arms were thick, and his shoulders were broad, his stomach flat. His feet and hands appeared neither too large nor too small for the rest of him.

"When I have time, I distract myself with a dime novel or two of an evening, by such ink spillers as Deadeye Dick!" Again, he smiled then pressed two fingers to his wide, full mouth. "Please, no telling!"

Vangie laughed. She had trouble seeing him sitting in a stately room, armed with a cup of tea in its delicate saucer, reading one of those slender novels with their lurid, pasteboard covers depicting half-dressed women and lantern-jawed men wielding blazing six-shooters and wide-eyed, galloping horses, their tails arched.

"What's so funny?" the doctor wanted to know, feigning indignance.

Vangie laughed harder, covering her mouth.

Her laughter died quickly, and she lowered her hands to her knees, clearing her throat.

"What do you say?" the young doctor prodded her.

Vangie looked up at him. "What do I say about what?"

"Can I watch you ride sometime? While Doctor Bohannon is watching Miss Jane, of course."

"Oh, well..." Vangie ran her hands slowly up from her knees to her thighs and then even more slowly back down again. "I...guess I...don't know why not," she finished with a long exhalation, flushing yet again.

"How about tomorrow afternoon?"

Again, Vangie ran her hands up and down her denim-clad thighs. "I reck...er, I mean...all right." She shrugged. "Why not?"

"Settled!" the doctor said.

"I'd best get my horses settled in for bed," Vangie said, rising, a little reluctant to leave. The dreadful anxiety she'd felt earlier had been replaced by expectation...excitement.

Her heart was still beating quickly, but it was not an altogether bad feeling. She couldn't deny a tingling in her fingers.

"I shall see you to the door," Dr. Ellison said, forthrightly rising from his chair.

"All right, then."

Vangie followed him to the door, no longer so aware of the thudding of her boots on the floor.

CHAPTER 16

Mannion opened his eyes to see a giant crow staring down at him.

CAW! CAW! CAW!

Joe gasped, shuddered, and jerked the sheets and quilts up taut beneath his chin.

The crow stared down at him, turning its head this way and that, those pellet-sized black eyes staring deeply into his own. Its beak, black up closer to the head and turning gradually paler as it tapered to the end, opened and closed, opened and closed, as though the beast were laughing at him.

CAW! CAW! CAW!

"Infernal thing," Joe heard himself wheeze out. "Why do you haunt me so?"

He'd been haunted by the crow back when the old, heretic pastor, Ezekial Storm, whose gypsy daughters had been killed by Frank Lord's gang in the San Juan Mountains, had somehow brought Joe back from death, when Lord's bunch had beaten the stuffing out of both ends of him and hanged him upside down from the stout branch of a cottonwood in a pounding mountain thunderstorm.

Coming back from that dark nadir, being pulled up as though by invisible hands from the chasm of death, Joe had seen his dear wife Sarah turn to him as she'd stood in the fork of the cottonwood she'd hanged herself from. Turning her face toward him looking out at her in horror from the second-story window of their house in Kansas, her head had become that of a crow—a giant crow's head; the very same winged serpent he'd seen just now in the waking dream.

She'd cawed at him three times before turning her crow's head forward and stepping out from that fork in the tree to drop six feet before the rope around her neck drew taut.

Immediately after the rope had snapped her neck with an audible *crack!*, four-month-old Vangie had cried out from her crib.

CAW! CAW! CAW!

Sporadically, the crow had haunted Mannion's dreams, both asleep dreams and waking dreams, ever since Storm had brought him back from the dead and set him on the trail once more of the kill-crazy gang of Frank and Billy Lord. Mannion believed the specter was the earthly manifestation of whatever demon Storm had summoned to help him restore life to Mannion's pummeled carcass.

Storm had exchanged with the demon Joe's soul for his life, so that he could continue helping Storm exact vengeance on the Lord gang, which they'd done though Storm had lost his life in the process.

Of course, Mannion never would have told anyone what he believed about his soul. It sounded plum beehive crazy even to himself. Maybe that's why he'd never given it voice to even himself—neither aloud nor silently. But at the periphery of his consciousness, he was aware he'd never felt the same since Storm had brought him back from the abyss. Something had been missing in him.

His soul?

How did a man feel without a soul?

A strange emptiness around the periphery of his life. A bleakness weighing heavy on his shoulders. A washing out of the days' colors. Or, had Mannion always felt that way but had just never been conscious of it until Storm had laid hands on him and introduced him to the demon, the crow, who'd taken great amusement in restoring his life at such an awful cost.

A cost that no man should ever have to pay.

The crow's head staring down at him suddenly became the brown, wizened face of an old Indian crone. She was waving both hands down around the sides of the bed he found himself on. Smoke was drifting up around him, enshrouding him.

Mannion's nostrils were peppered with the unmistakable smell of sage.

The old woman walked around the bed, smudging him with the smoke from the long braids of sage she clutched in her gnarled, bony hands. She smiled at him, showing her tiny, brown, crooked teeth, chuckling, small, black eyes slitted and drawn upwards at their deeply lined corners. She wore a calico dress and a necklace of porcupine and the round, bleached skulls of small animals—rabbits or squirrels.

Mannion knew that both animals were sacred totems to the Ute, of which this woman was one—the wife of Norman Waycross, owner of the Quarter Circle Six whose house Mannion now realized he was in. A young woman, dressed similarly to the older one, stood in the shadows to the right of the white-painted door.

She stood with her arms crossed on her chest, her

head canted slightly to one side, the sleeves of her dress rolled to her elbows. Her features were rather blunt, her thick, black hair piled sloppily atop her head. She had a slightly bored air.

She was one of several of Waycross's granddaughters, Mannion assumed, though he hadn't paid a visit out here for a couple of years. The last time was when he and Rio had been trying to crack a rustling ring formed by one of Waycross's competitors up here in the mid-high reaches of the south-central Sawatch Range. He'd visited with Waycross's riders, including Walt Iris, whenever they'd ventured to Del Norte for supplies they couldn't get in St. Elmo.

The old woman turned to the younger one, who stepped forward to take the two braids of sage. The old one turned her hawk-like, wizened face with liver spots the size of dimes and nickels toward Mannion and frowned as she probed the bandage wrapped around Joe's head. She touched the area on his left temple that had taken the blow from Lodge's rifle.

"Hurts?" she asked.

A rusty knife of pain spliced into his skull.

He grimaced. "Like holy blazes!"

She cackled, staring down at him and running the tip of her tongue across her thin, cracked lower lip. "He got you good, eh?"

There was a whirring sound in the hall beyond Mannion's closed door. The whirring grew louder and then there was a loud thump on the door.

The girl who'd resumed her place beside the door opened it, and yet another half-breed girl, younger and shorter than the first, and with a stouter body and rounder face, pushed a wheeled chair into the room—a wheeled chair bearing the corpse-like figure of Norman

Waycross himself, a striped blanket draped over his spindly legs.

"Joe, by God, you're up and around!" the rancher said, pulling a fat, half-smoked stogie from his mouth. "I'm glad. Been waitin' around to find who in the hell gunned down my punchers!"

Mannion was taken aback by the old rancher's appearance.

He'd heard in town that Waycross had been diagnosed with cancer. Now he saw it for himself. The man looked as Indian as his wife and granddaughters. Maybe even more so. He'd always been dark, but now he was as dark and wizened as any elder with one foot in the grave. In contrast, however, his thick, wavy hair swept straight back from his sharp widow's peak was as white as the mountain winter's first snow.

Lean and tall, he'd never been a heavy man. Now, however, he looked considerably shorter and smaller. Under all those blankets and with a thick, red bandanna knotted around his neck, inside the collar of his dark, flannel robe, he appeared the size of your average thirteen- or fourteen-year-old boy.

"Yes, yes," Waycross said with a dismissive wave of the hand holding the stogie, drawing smoke circles in the air beside his head, "I'm dying. Not going down without a fight, however. Just hope Sheldon can run the ranch when I'm gone!"

Sheldon was his oldest son who last time Joe was through this neck of the Sawatch had resided in a large log house a quarter mile away from his father. He hadn't been much of a hand a few years ago, as he'd preferred to ride the long coulees. Mannion had had to lock Sheldon up in town a few times, though he'd heard that old Norman was now cultivating him for the job of foreman.

That might have to be stepped up now with Iris's demise.

Old Norman wheeled himself up close to Mannion, took another few puffs from the stogie that couldn't have been doing his ill health any favors, letting the smoke wreathe his raisin-like head with its odd cap of dashing, snow-white hair, and said, "Who killed my boys and tattooed your head like that, Bloody Joe?" He pulled his head back, slackening his lower jaw in a shocked expression. "Who in Sam Hill could get the better of Bloody Joe Mannion? Unless you're getting old, Joe. Are you getting old?"

"If you don't mind, Norman, the subject's a touchy one for me. We'll talk about it later." Mannion tossed his covers back. "I gotta get after him!"

The old woman gave a startled "*Ay-eeee!*" while the younger woman standing by the door formed a concerned expression and, with a grunt, took two steps forward, extending her hands as though to shove the lawman back down against his pillow.

The younger girl stood stoically behind her grandfather's chair, regarding Mannion without expression. She had a round, cherubic, Indian-dark face but with clear hazel eyes. The eyes of her grandfather.

Mannion dropped his legs, still clad in his denims, over the side of the bed and sat there, sucking air sharply through his teeth, pressing the heels of his hands against his temples. He was still wearing his red balbriggan top, as well. Lodge's tattoo felt like a rusty railroad spike rammed none-so-gently through his temple and into his brain plate.

"There!" Waycross crowed. "Now, see there? You ain't goin' nowhere, Joe. Let my boys go after him. Sheldon's already gotta crew saddled and ready to ride. They all ride for the brand dammit—the Waycross Quarter Circle Six—and they're sworn to defend it and avenge those who would attack our own!"

Mannion almost chuckled. Waycross had always been the dramatic sort. If he hadn't been so good at fighting Indians, then marrying them and raising a family with them and building one of the largest spreads in this neck of the Sawatch, he could have become a stage actor.

He leaned forward. "Come on—tell me, Joe. Who killed Iris an' the others. Good men, all. I aim to exact revenge—Waycross revenge!"

"Oh, hush, Norman," Mannion growled. "You're making my head hurt worse, an' that's saying something." He glanced at the window to his left. It appeared dawn. Or was it dusk? He slid his glance to Waycross. "How long have I been out, anyway?"

"Levi an' several hands found you last evenin'...after they come across the horses packin' Walt, Coyote, Pike Payne, an' the kid, Willie."

He turned to his wife and said, "He can't ride—can he Momma?"

Mannion had never known the name of the rancher's wife. Waycross...nor anyone else Joe knew of...had ever called her anything except "Momma."

She hissed and shook her head, scrunching up her eyes. "I should say not." She tapped her own left temple with a wizened brown finger. "Blood' Joe—you stay bed!"

"Can't do that."

Mannion rose with a grunt and headed over to where his corduroy shirt and his buckskin mackinaw hung with his pistol belt and hat beside a mirrored dresser abutting the chinked log wall. Waycross's sprawling, two-story lodge was one of the more rustic Mannion had been in—decked out with a strange mountain hybrid of white and Ute furnishings, hides and game trophies all over the place, as well as headdresses, medicine shields, the stone-age weapons of the traditional Utes and the rifles and pistols of the Western white man. Norman had raised a passel of half-breed children here and was obviously raising—or at least was helping raise—a passel of at least quarter-breed grandchildren.

Most of Waycross's four sons had married women with at least some Indian blood. It was a taste that appeared to run in the family. Many of the people in and around this neck of the Sawatch jokingly referred to the Waycross spread as "Papoose Acres."

How ironic that thirty years ago Norman Waycross had been one of the fiercest Indian fighters in southern Colorado Territory.

"Lost too much time already, sawing logs when I should have been riding after Lodge." Mannion hadn't been able to catch the name in time before it had slipped out of his mouth.

Waycross stared up at him, near-jade eyes wide, lower jaw hanging. "*Ulysses* Lodge?"

"Forget you heard that," Mannion said, tucking his shirt into his pants.

"You hold on, now, Joe. If Lodge is the one who shot my men, I'm—"

The rancher fell silent when Mannion crouched over him, both hands on the arms of the man's chair. "Lodge shot Jane Ford in the San Juan. I know you know Jane and I have a history. Not a great one. But a history, just the same."

"It's no secret you love the woman, Joe."

So, the story had made it as far as the Sawatch. Mannion didn't doubt it. He'd always been a prime topic of conversation in this small pocket of Colorado. When he'd become attached to Jane Ford, even more so.

"She might die, Norman. Yeah, Lodge shot her in a fit of rage over a soiled dove he supposedly had tumbled for."

Waycross made a face. "Ach! Sick, ugly human being! Been hunting men in the Sawatch for years. No one's ever liked him. Now he's killed four of mine, and—"

"Keep them here, Norman," Mannion warned. "If you don't, I'll arrest you for interfering with a lawman in the pursuit of his duties. Look it up. It's a real law. And I will arrest you. I don't care if you have both feet in the grave!"

He straightened and turned to the girl standing by the door, looking none too bored suddenly. "Honey," Mannion said, "have one of your grandfather's men saddle my bay and bring him to the house for me."

The girl looked down at her grandfather.

Waycross stared up at Mannion, pensively puffing the stogie.

Mannion stared back at him as he stomped into each boot in turn.

Waycross glanced at the girl and waved the hand holding the stogie. "Do as the man says, Cecile. There's no reasoning with Bloody Joe."

"Hold your men back, Norman," Mannion said, wrapping his Schofields, bowie, and cartridge belt around his waist and cinching the buckle. "Keep them back. I'll bring Lodge back alive or dead. Likely dead, though I wouldn't mind seeing him hang. I know you have a dog in the hunt, but hold 'em back, Norman. I want him. For Jane."

"Awful selfish, Joe."

"It's my way, Norman. You know that." Mannion shrugged into his coat and very tenderly set his bullet-torn Stetson on his head. He knew how he must look—bandage around his head, the long line of a former bullet burn across his cheek, haggard as Moses. Again, he crouched down over Waycross, placing each hand on each of the pushchair's arms. "I'll run him down for both of us. Besides, it doesn't really matter who kills him, does it? As long as he's dead?"

"It does to you, Joe." The rancher's dark eyes were grave. "It does to me."

Mannion straightened, gave a savage grin and a hard smile. He brushed his thumb across his badge. "Hold them back, Norman. I'll shoot any man who comes within range of this here Yellowboy." He opened and closed his right hand around the neck of the rifle resting on his right shoulder.

Thank God the rancher's men had found his prized repeater.

He knew very well he was making one very sorry effort of showing his appreciation to the Quarter Circle Six for having saved his life and retrieved his gear. But Lodge was his. When the man had shot Jane, he'd become Joe's quarry. Joe's alone.

He had no right, of course. But there it was.

His rage, his need for revenge, could not be reasoned with.

CAW! CAW! CAW!

He heard that demon who'd taken his soul far back in his brain as he turned to kiss Momma and give her arm a squeeze in gratitude for the old woman's having tended his wound. Hell, maybe the smudging had even helped. Even the crow had in its bleak, dark, raucous way.

CAW! CAW! CAW!

Mannion squeezed Waycross's arm affectionately and then made his way to the door and downstairs.

Just before he was going to open the front door and step out onto the large, front, halve-logged stoop, a spidery hand wrapped around his left arm. He turned to see Momma standing before him.

How in hell had the little bird-like woman made it down the stairs as fast as he had? He'd made good time despite his still seeing double and the almost unbearable beating of the giant, tender heart in his temple.

Momma smiled up at him, slitting her eyes, which glinted in the lantern light issuing from the large kitchen to Mannion's left and from which also issued the succulent aromas of frybread, pancakes, maple syrup, and bacon. A dozen half-breed children sat at the long pine table in there, dark eyes turned toward the marshal and their grandmother in the broad, high-ceilinged foyer whose walls were trimmed with Ute talismans in the forms of bones, stones, and feathers.

The head of an albino bull elk peered down from its perch over the large, oak front door.

Mannion crouched over the little woman. She pecked his cheek, her lips feeling coarse and cool as sandpaper. "There not'ing wrong with your soul, Joe," she said, giving a wink and then grimacing before pressing her right index finger against his forehead. "Just your *head*!"

Mannion almost stumbled back against the door in astonishment.

She threw her head back and cackled a witch-like laugh toward the ceiling beams.

Outside, Mannion paused on the front steps. A cowboy was leading Red from the big barn around which the rest of the dozen or so Quarter Circle Six riders milled. The drover's chaps flapped against his denim-clad legs. The morning breeze nibbled at the broad brim of his soiled, cream Stetson. Five minutes later, Mannion was mounted up and trotting Red across the yard to the open front gate.

He glanced over his shoulder as the big lodge house was just then painted lemon yellow by the sun rising above the eastern peaks. Momma Waycross stood out there at the top of the steps, one hand raised to shade her eyes as she watched Joe ride out into the fresh mountain morning.

Mannion turned his head forward as Red trotted through the gate and out into the beautiful, savage mountain country beyond.

CAW! CAW! CAW!

How had she known?

CHAPTER 17

Deputy Henry McCallister opened the front door of Dr. Bohannon's office and stepped out onto the front stoop to find himself confronted by a good dozen or so of Del Norte's concerned citizens. It was as though the entire town's diverse population was represented—short, tall; motley, neat; poor, rich; Black, white, Chinese, Mexican, and even two Ute half-breed brothers who owned a pig farm and who were also regular Red Dog players over at the San Juan.

Two brightly attired whores stood side by side in the crowd, twirling parasols over their heads as they regarded the deputy expectantly, concernedly.

"How is she, Henry?" said the barber, John Dunham, owner and proprietor of Dunham's Tonsorial Parlor, which sat right across the main street from Hotel de Mannion. "Has she stirred at all yet? Said a *word*?"

A low, inquiring roar lifted among the crowd milling on the stoop and on the street before it where several horses were tied to Bohannon's hitchrack and where also sat two leather-seated carriages and even one Pittsburgh freight wagon in the traces of which two dusty mules stood hanging their heads in the late-day sunshine angling over the false facades in the west. A small black-and-white dog sat atop the water barrel strapped to the side of the wagon, just below the driver's boot with its set brake around which the leather ribbons had been wrapped.

The little dog watched the crowd attentively, as though it, too, were awaiting news of Miss Jane's health with bated breath.

Henry was sorry to have to tell them, "No, no, I'm sorry, fellas...uh, ladies. Both doctors said they haven't heard a peep out of her yet."

Another low roar lifted in frustration at the unsatisfactory reply.

Henry raised his hands, palms out. "Come on, fellas... um, ladies...keep it down, will you? The doctors have some hospital beds behind the office, and there's two more folks back there now including a lady having trouble with a birth. Keep it down, will ya? I'll make sure and spread the word soon as I hear there's any change in Miss Jane's condition!"

The single Black man, Abe Washington, who had a diggings west of town with his wife and two boys and who came to Del Norte regularly for supplies and to sip a beer or two and to give Miss Jane's roulette wheel a spin, lowered the soapy beer mug he held in his right, gloved fist, and said, "Why in tawnation did that big galoot shoot Miss Jane, anyways? How could anyone have had it out for Miss Jane? What'd *she* ever do?"

Henry could see by the sheen in the man's mud-black eyes he'd had more than just the half a beer he currently held in his fist.

The short, rotund, apron-clad Chinese man standing beside him—Wu Lin, who ran an opium den behind his laundry—turned to Washington and said, "I heard it Bloody Joe fault. Bloody Joe fault!" Wu Lin stomped his foot angrily.

"I heard that, too," said the big mule skinner, Gunter Grierson, also clutching a beer in his fist. Raking his own glassy-eyed gaze across the small crowd around him, he said, "I heard he was riled about some stunt the marshal pulled and shot Jane to get even!"

"I don't doubt that a bit!" shouted a whiskey drummer standing behind Grierson and all but dwarfed by the bigger man. "I'm just so sorry Miss Jane had to get caught between those two bull buffalos!"

The crowd roared its collective, angry agreement.

"Pipe down, fellas! Time to go about your business!" Henry urged, waving his hands above his head. "And don't believe everything you hear, now. That's not what happened. The marshal had nothin' to do with it!"

"Oh, sure he did," said one man, reluctantly dispersing with the others. "He always does. If you ask me," he added, nudging one of the young whores striding beside him with his elbow, "it's time to give Bloody Joe his walking papers once and for all..."

Then they were all wandering away, heading toward their various destinations, most of which appeared to lie on the main drag a half a block away on Henry's left while a few of the others made for the less reputable watering holes and hurdy-gurdy houses on the other side of this secondary avenue. Grierson climbed up into his wagon and the little dog gave a bark and slapped his little tail against the top of the water barrel as the mules and wagon lurched forward, also heading toward Main Street.

As the dust sifted in the wake of the crowd's passing, Henry stepped down into the street and gave a weary sigh. For him as well as for the entire town, it had been a long few days, waiting to hear about any possible improvement in Miss Jane's condition.

Waiting in dread to hear that...

No, that was too awful to think about.

Henry had never realized it before, but Miss Jane Ford had been the glue that had held Del Norte together. Everyone who knew her felt like family. Thus, everyone else they knew who knew Miss Jane they felt a kinship with. All the yearlong—through the blazing, dusty summers; the crisp autumns with the aspen and cottonwood leaves blowing along the street; the brutally cold and snowy winters that socked the town in from the rest of the world; and the long, soggy, muddy springs with their perpetually gray skies—Miss Jane Ford and her sprawling San Juan Hotel & Saloon were the center of the wheel that held Del Norte together. That fine establishment was the town's single social as well as drinking and gambling center.

Everyone who visited felt automatically happier and less lonely and isolated as soon as they entered, as though visiting a large, sprawling family they'd never quite realized they'd had.

And Miss Jane Ford was like the captain standing proudly in the prow of that most popular ship.

Henry—nor anyone else in Del Norte, apparently—could not imagine that ship sailing without her. Surely, it would soon become a derelict and run itself up onto muddy shores...

Henry gave a little shudder at that.

He glanced behind at the doctor's neat, square brick office with its long extension behind it, housing the hospital beds. Then he shuttled his gaze to the north, above and beyond the false façade of the secondary business on that side of the street. He couldn't see the

Sawatch Range from this angle, but he wondered how the marshal was faring up there.

Had he caught up to the crazed bounty hunter, Ulysses Lodge?

Was he hauling the man back to town by now—likely tied belly down across the big steeldust he called Beast?

Or had Bloody Joe finally met his match?

After all, it was widely known that Lodge knew the Sawatch like the back of his hand. Like a fisherman who plumbed only the holes known to be home to the most and largest fish, Lodge had hunted the Sawatch for years. That remote, extensive range running for nearly a hundred miles at a long, relatively narrow angle from southeast to northwest, was the favorite hiding place of outlaws who'd pulled jobs down on the eastern plains, from Pueblo and Colorado Springs in the south to Denver in the north.

It was the nearest wilderness, and a wilderness it was.

In that range there were many places for an owlhoot to fort up until his trail cooled.

Even the bravest U.S. deputy marshals and Pinkertons as well as Wells Fargo agents hated riding into the Sawatch. It was like riding into the proverbial lion's den or into a canyon you suddenly discover is a giant nest of rattlesnakes, with a viper hissing at you from every crack and cranny in the stone walls around you. Danger at every turn. Especially for men wearing a badge.

Henry himself knew this to be true, for he'd ridden into the Sawatch more than a few times with Marshal Mannion and had thought himself lucky to have ridden out alive. Nearly every time he'd ridden into that forbidden range, he'd thought he'd never ride out again, but would end with his bones strewn along the bottom of some long-forgotten canyon.

Forgotten by all, that was, except for the men who'd put him there—kicked out, as the saying went, with a cold shovel.

No, the only men tough enough for the Sawatch were the ranchers who'd been tough enough to fight the land away from the savage Utes, the most stalwart of miners, the hardest of the hardest-bitten outlaws, and Ulysses Lodge and Bloody Joe Mannion...

With a weary sigh but knowing where he was heading now that his shift was through for the day before even pondering on it much, he untied his reins from Bohannon's hitchrack and swung up onto the back of his coyote dun, Banjo. He reined the horse out into the street and then booted him west to Main Street. He jogged the horse down Main Street, heading north, swinging his head from left to right and back again, looking for the outlaws he'd kicked out of town several days ago—the men who'd shown up so uninvitedly at Grace Hastings's cabin behind the school.

Vince Chaney.

Shane Nordstrom.

Lonnie Russell.

And Dutch Deering.

The night after leaving Grace's place—inwardly, he allowed himself a little smile, able now to call her Grace as well as to think of her by her given name, liking how the sound rippled off even his silent tongue—he'd tracked the men down to a squalid watering hole at the town's western end. With Rio backing him with his shotgun, he'd ordered them out of town by sunup the very next day.

To Henry's surprise, the four men hadn't balked all that much. Oh, they'd grumbled and cursed and sulked, saying they hadn't done nothing wrong, smirking knowingly at Henry. But they hadn't mentioned Grace.

Henry hadn't thought they would.

They hadn't wanted it to get around that they thought Grace knew where stolen loot might be. They hadn't wanted to sic other men after it.

Grudgingly, they'd agreed to go.

Henry had scoured the town for them all the next day while making his rounds, and he hadn't seen hide nor hair of the scalawags. He'd scoured the town every day between then and now. Still, he'd found neither hide nor hair.

Something told him they hadn't gone, however.

Kicking them out had been too easy.

Now he reined the dun off Main and onto a secondary side street, heading off on his usual, furtive route toward the schoolhouse and Grace's cabin. He'd worried about her constantly since that day Chaney and the others had ridden up, but of course he hadn't been able to keep a constant eye on her. He'd checked on her several times a day, however, as he would check on her now.

So far…at least at the time of his last visit…Grace had seen no sign of them. She'd seemed deeply relieved, as had Henry.

Still, he was wary.

Now he reined up at the edge of the autumn-gold aspens behind the cabin. As he regarded the cabin's back wall, the flour sack curtains drawn over both rear windows, to the right of the back door, a cool autumn breeze came sighing in from the west, carrying on it suddenly the high, slow, somnolent voice of a woman singing:

*"I dream of Jeanie with the light brown hair,
Born, like a vapor, on the summer air;
I see her tripping where the bright streams play,
Happy as the daisies that dance her way."*

Henry smiled. A strange feeling came over him. He'd never known one so peaceful, so magical. And here it was —a sudden gift, an unexpected surprise. It was nearing the end of the day, and the shadows were growing long, the sunlight with a soft, velvety cast to it, a mixture of orange and safflower. Leaves rained down from the aspens around him, glinting gold as newly minted coins in the sunshine. The breeze blew softly, a rising and falling sowing, a lazy swishing sound in the woods behind him.

And the woman's pretty, soulful voice just beneath it, carried this way and that as the leaves swirled:

*"Many were the wild notes her merry voice
 would pour.
Many were the blithe birds that warbled them
 o'er:
Oh, I dream of Jeanie with the light brown hair,
Floating, like a vapor, on the soft summer air..."*

Smiling dreamily, his heart feeling so light he'd have sworn it was about to grow wings and fly, Henry booted the dun forward. Slowly, the horse approached the rear of the cabin, the slow, soft, leaf-crunching thuds adding to the slow, soft, melodic, entirely harmonious ambience of these fleeting minutes at the end of this crisp, cool, bright, and suddenly magical autumn day.

As he drew closer to the cabin, he could hear the tinkle of water, as well, tinkling in time, it seemed, with the woman's low, lazy, dreamy tone as she continued with:

> *"Many were the wild notes her merry voice*
> *would pour.*
> *Many were the blithe birds that warbled them*
> *o'er:*
> *Oh! I dream of Jeanie with the light brown*
> *hair,*
> *Floating, like a vapor, on the soft summer air..."*

Henry slowly swung down from the dun's back, looped the reins over the hitchrack, and stepped up onto the small, splintery wooden stoop fronting the back door. He removed his hat and canted his head toward the door as the sound of gentle splashing and the woman's voice mixed with the outside sounds of the breeze and the blowing leaves:

> *"Many were the wild notes her merry voice*
> *would pour.*
> *Many were the blithe birds that warbled them*
> *o'er:*
> *Oh! I dream of Jeanie with the light brown*
> *hair,*
> *Floating, like a vapor, on the soft summer air..."*

A slight pause, more slow splashing and then:

> *"I long for Jeanie with the day-dawn smile,*
> *Radiant in gladness, warm with winning guile;*
> *I hear her melodies, like joys gone by.*
> *Sighing round my heart o'er the fond hopes that*
> *die."*

A knot of emotion had grown in Henry's throat. His eyes were moist. Still canting his head toward the door, his hat held over his chest, he raised his right hand and knocked very softly three times with the back of that hand.

He cleared his throat. "Um, Miss...um, Grace? It's Henry."

"Oh!" she said with a start. He could hear water splashing as though she'd moved quickly, likely covering herself. "Oh...Oh, Henry. I'm, um...I'm bathing."

"I figured as much," he said. "No hurry. I'll wait out here. Or..." He winced, drew a breath, braced himself for her reply. "I can ride on if you like, leave you to—"

"Henry," the woman's voice came firmly through the door.

"Yes, Grace?"

A long silence. The breeze whispered and brittle leaves scuttled along the ground and across the stoop at Henry's feet.

Then her voice came, soft and intimate...

"Henry, come in here, please."

CHAPTER 18

HENRY TWISTED THE KNOB.

The latch clicked. She must have forgotten to lock it.

He studied the door for a few seconds, reluctant to go inside. His heart thudded a few times but then he opened the door a crack and narrowed one eye as he peered inside.

He started to draw the door closed again quickly when he saw her sitting in the square, aluminum tub, her rich, strawberry blond hair pinned loosely atop her head. The only thing concealing her body were soap bubbles.

She sat with her knees up, arms resting over them, hands entwined between them. Her head was slightly turned toward him, and her brown eyes regarded him with a vaguely wistful air.

"Oh, I, uh…"

"Come in," she said with a vaguely foxy smile.

No, there wasn't anything vague about it at all.

Henry hesitated, his heart continuing to beat a tom-tom rhythm against his breastbone. "Are you, uh…are you…?"

"Henry!" she said as she rose up out of the tub to

stand before him, bathwater and suds streaming down off her body until every bit of her, from the top of her pinned-up hair to halfway down her shins, was revealed. "For Godsakes, how many times do I—"

She stopped abruptly when he shouldered the door open, stepped inside, and kicked it closed. He pegged his hat and strode over to her, making no more bones about it. He shrugged out of his denim jacket, let it drop to the floor then bent down and picked her up in his arms with a grunt.

She gasped with the thrill of it, encircling her arms around his neck. He drew her away from the tub and carried her, dripping wet, into the bedroom part of the cabin, behind the parlor area.

He lay her down on the bed and then stepped back away from her, gazing down at her, his heart picking up its beat, his breath raking audibly in and out of his lungs. He unbuttoned his shirt quickly, awkwardly, missing buttons in his haste. She stared up at him, brown eyes wide, lips slightly parted, sitting up a little, drawing her legs together and to one side.

Her pale skin was wet and sleek. A flush rose in her cheeks. Her eyes sparkled in the light slanting through the curtained windows around them.

"Hurry," she said softly, huskily, pushing up a little farther on her elbows.

Henry gave a nervous laugh as he almost fell after prying one boot off with the other foot.

"Hurry," she said again.

———

A SCRATCHING SOUNDED.

Henry woke with a gasp, turning onto a shoulder.

He'd been asleep with a cheek on Grace's bosom.

She woke now, too, groaned luxuriously and said sleepily, "What is it, darling?"

"Heard something," Henry said, looking around the cabin lit by the lamp hanging over the eating table in the kitchen. The smoking lantern shunted more shadows around the shack than light.

"Just the wind," Grace said.

"Are you sure?" Henry started to reach for the pistol he'd dropped to the floor with his shell belt.

She placed a waylaying hand on his shoulder.

"Look there. Just the window." She directed his gaze to the back window right of the back door, where the branch of a lilac scraped against the lower right corner of the pane.

"Whew!" Henry said, lying back in the bed, wrapping one arm around Grace's shoulders. "I thought maybe..."

"Vince?"

"Yeah."

"I think Vince is long gone." Grace chuckled as she ran her fingers through the sandy hair tufted on Henry's chest. "You must have really put the fear of God into those men!"

She laughed again.

"Jeepers," Henry said, "I didn't realize they were so easy to cow."

"Vince can talk a good game," Grace said, "but deep down he's a coward."

"Even that Shane fella? He looked like a tough nut to me."

"Even Shane." Grace rolled onto her side and placed her hand against his cheek. "Don't you worry, Henry. They're gone. After seven years in the state pen, they want to have nothing more to do with the law. You just reminded them, is all."

"Well, I'm glad. I was worried about you, Grace."

"Thank you, Henry." She lowered her hand and snuggled against him. "I do so like having someone to worry about me. It's been such a long time." She glanced up at him, concern in her eyes. "If you must know, Henry, I've been lonely. So very lonely for years! I don't think I quite realized it until I met you. Then I realized it after all of these years I've been teaching...having to be so chaste lest the parents think I'm unfit to teach their sons and daughters..."

"I'm sorry, Grace. A woman as purty...as *pretty*...as you shouldn't have to be so lonely."

"Well, I'm not lonely now," she said, snuggling against him once more. She glanced up at him again, pleading in her eyes. "Tell me I never will again, Henry."

Henry frowned down at her, not sure what she was asking him. "What do you mean, Grace?"

"Oh, I don't know." Her eyes glinted with tears reflected in the lantern light. "I don't know what I'm saying. I guess I'm just hoping this wasn't the first...and it won't be the last..."

"Oh, heck, no. Grace, I, uh...I, uh..."

"No, don't say it, Henry." Again, she placed her hand on his cheek. "Let's just enjoy it as long as we can. In a couple of weeks the children will be coming back to school, and...well, you know..."

"Unless we..." She let her voice trail off and stared down pensively at the sandy hair tufted on his chest.

Henry nudged her slightly with his arm. "Unless we did what?"

She stared at his chest, frowning, as though there were some obscure message written there and she was trying to figure out what it said. Finally, she smiled and brushed her hand through the hair on his chest and looked up at him, again tears glinting in her eyes.

"Oh, never mind. It's too crazy to think about. You're twenty-three. I'm thirty." She lay back, hooking her left arm over her forehead, chuckling. "Oh, Grace, darling you have been too lonely. You've let your loneliness go and make you soft in your thinker box."

She touched her index finger to her temple and glanced up at him, laughing. It was a strange hybrid between laughing and crying.

She turned her head back forward and gazed across the room. She gave a deep sigh. "Ho hum."

Frowning, Henry rolled onto his side and rested his cheek on the heel of his hand. "Grace, are you saying what I think you're saying?"

"I don't know—what do you think I'm saying?"

"That you think...that you think that we should..."

She rolled quickly to face him, placing her hand against his cheek once more. "Oh, Henry, if we did, we'd have to leave here. Oh, my gosh—the scandal it would cause!"

Henry stared at her in mute astonishment.

Was she really saying that the two of them should be...should be...well, *married?*

He had to admit he hadn't thought that far ahead.

He also had to admit with some chagrin that he hadn't thought too far ahead of where he was now. In Grace's bed. His cheeks warmed a little as he considered the prospect of marriage.

Marriage!

His heart thudded a little.

He did love her, though, didn't he?

He'd thought for sure he did. He certainly had

enjoyed their time together, and what had happened over the past two hours had been pure, unadulterated magic. In fact, he didn't think he'd ever felt as good as he felt right now. At least, as well as he had felt before she'd mentioned marriage. That was a serious thought that needed serious attention.

"No, forget it, dear Henry," Grace said quickly, kissing the hair tufted on his chest then rolling her face in it luxuriously, sniffing deeply of him. "That's moving far too fast for both of us. Let's just enjoy what we have now…for as long as we have it."

"But, Grace, maybe…"

"Oh, nothing maybe." She smiled, gazing into his eyes. "Let's just enjoy tonight…or what's left of it, eh?"

Her smile grew wider.

He wrapped his arms around her shoulders and rolled her onto her back and closed his mouth over hers.

Suddenly, he lifted his head, frowning.

Chicken flesh crawled across his backside.

"What is it?" Grace asked.

He had the strange sensation of being watched. He shuttled his gaze to the window in the wall above his head and to his right. His heart lurched violently when he saw the pale oval of a face set beneath a felt hat brim watching him.

The face jerked back suddenly, the mouth opening in shock. Just outside that window, a horse whinnied shrilly. The face appeared again in a blur of swift movement, and a grunt sounded just before there was a muffled thud against the cabin wall, to the right of the window.

Another grunt and then the face and hat appeared again, farther away this time, pulling away from the window. The horse whinnied again and then there was the sudden thunder of galloping hooves.

The thunder dwindled quickly into the distance.

"Oh, my God!" Grace said.

"Someone was out there!" Henry said, scurrying off the bed and quickly stepping into his longhandles.

"Did you get a look at him?" Grace said, pulling the sheets and single quilt up over her breasts.

"No, but I have a feeling it was Chaney!"

Henry was in his longhandles and jeans in no time. He stomped into each boot in turn, set his hat on his head, grabbed his Winchester, and ran out the cabin's front door. He ran around the south side of the cabin, breathing hard.

He stopped when a horse whinnied straight out beyond him maybe fifty, sixty yards. The rider appeared to be having some trouble with his mount. In the starlight and by the light of a rising, half-moon, Henry could see the silhouette of horse and rider against the star- and moonlight as the horse pitched fiercely.

"Hold it right there, you lowdown, yellow-livered demon!"

Henry took off running, pulling his hat down low on his forehead. The horse screamed and the rider screamed, too, though it didn't sound like a man's scream at all.

Henry bit out a mocking chuckle as he continued running, seeing ahead of him the horse wheel and run back toward him, quartering away in the darkness on his left, reins bouncing along the ground to either side. There was no rider on its back. The rider appeared to be running into some brush ahead of Henry, maybe forty yards away.

"Stop or I'll shoot!" Henry yelled.

He stopped. He could hear the thrashing of brush as the runner kept on running back in the direction of the heart of town. There, he'd get lost in Del Norte's all-hour tumult.

Henry triggered the Winchester three times quickly, staring through his own, pale, wafting powder smoke.

There was a distance-muffled grunt and the sound of a body striking the ground.

Henry lowered the Winchester and took off running once more. He pushed through the brush and came out the other side, stopping and looking around.

Ahead, a silhouetted figure was just then running around the left side of a livery barn paddock, the horses and mules sidling away, whickering anxiously. The man wasn't moving very fast and appeared to be favoring one foot.

"Hold it!" Henry lunged into another run.

He drew within twenty yards of the hombre he was chasing just as the man was heading down an alley between a grocery store and a harness shop, dark at this hour, nearly midnight.

"Going to tell you one more time, Mister!" Henry shouted, his voice echoing off the walls of the buildings to either side of him. "Stop or take a pill you won't digest!"

The man stopped suddenly. He had his back to Henry.

Henry strode forward quickly, aiming the Winchester straight out from his right hip.

Henry slowed as he came within ten feet of the man, who appeared shorter than himself. A good six, seven inches shorter. Shorter than Vince Chaney.

Did Henry have a common peeper on his hands? Some drunk who'd ridden over to the pretty teacher's place to see what he could see?

Scowling incredulously, angrily, Henry said, "Turn

around slow, bucko. And I mean *slow*, or I'll drill ya where ya stand!"

"All right—I'm turning. I'm turning!" said a girl's exasperated voice.

A girl's *familiar*, exasperated voice.

The scowl on Henry's face grew even more incredulous as the girl turned to face him, lifting her head so her hat brim came up to reveal her eyes.

You could have knocked Deputy Henry J. McCallister over with a feather duster.

"Molly!"

CHAPTER 19

BLOODY JOE MANNION PULLED HIS HAT DOWN AGAINST a stiff wind and a cold rain.

His head throbbed behind the bandage Momma Waycross had been kind enough to wrap around his thundering noggin.

"Good thing it's made o' wood," he joked to himself as the rain turned suddenly to snow—painful javelins stinging his cheeks and eyes and making Red shake his head in disapproval.

He'd followed Chalk Creek out of Romley six miles but a good hour's ride to the south, and he'd been fighting the mercurial, mid-autumn weather every step of the way. He'd holed up in a flophouse in Romley for the night, getting word that, indeed, Ulysses Lodge had passed that way the previous day, not saying much to anyone but merely holing up with his big steeldust and a big American packhorse in the livery barn.

He'd ridden into town late, had breakfast the next morning in the Sewanee Café—six eggs, half a fletch of bacon, and a whole hill of potatoes smothered in bacon and sausage gravy. Belching, he'd tossed coins onto his plate, left, mounted up, and headed north along Chalk Creek toward St. Elmo.

It had been raining.

It had rained on Joe off and on throughout the day. When it hadn't been raining it had been snowing. Once when it hadn't been raining, he'd had to hole up under the overhang of a stone outcropping to avoid marble-sized hail. When the hail had stopped and the sun had come out, melting the hail, Joe had continued his journey north, knowing that Lodge had been headed for St. Elmo because the small but raucous mining town was the only destination out here for a man headed generally north.

Lodge had likely stopped in St. Elmo to eat, sleep, and possibly pick up supplies, though he likely hadn't needed them since he'd stolen supplies from the Quarter Circle Six men he'd killed. By now, he was likely continuing over the divide to Tincup.

From Tincup he'd head north, upstream along the Taylor River. From there, he'd try to lose himself in the high country on his way to the Sawatch's northern extremes, following the Taylor along the base of the divide, possibly forting up in the wilderness surrounding the Mountain of the Holy Cross, where the Taylor swung to the northwest, toward its headwaters in the higher reaches.

In that unforgiving country, Lodge would be like the needle in the proverbial haystack.

There was a chance he'd slip over the divide and head east for Leadville or head down out of the mountains to the west, toward Aspen and the Roaring Fork River, but Mannion doubted it. Lodge would likely stay away from larger settlements until he was sure he was no longer being followed. As it was, he knew he'd injured Mannion, might have even killed him. But as wary and trail savvy as

Lodge was, he'd assume Joe was still alive, still hunting him.

Which meant he'd make another play on him sooner or later, try once more to scour him from his trail.

Mannion hoped he could run the man down before he got into that rugged high country near the headwaters of the Taylor River. This late in the year, it could snow up there any old time, making travel even more hellish than it already would be, likely facing dangerous thunderstorms and hail every afternoon. This late in the year, pushing toward October, snowstorms were always a threat up in that cloud-tickling country, as well.

Mannion rode into St. Elmo now, the motley mining camp's cabins and tent shacks spread out on his right, the river on his left. The early evening air was spiced with the smoke of supper fires. He rode with an uneasy feeling at the base of his spine. There was always a chance Lodge was forted up right here, waiting for his hunter to become the prey once more.

Fool Joe once, shame on him...

Fool him twice...

As the cold rain sliced down at a sharp angle from low, jagged-edged, steel-gray clouds, Mannion surveyed the town warily. The only folks out were those prospectors in sack coats and pants and high-topped, lace-up boots, beards, and battered hats standing on covered boardwalks, watching the main drag down which Mannion clomped now atop Red and which was quickly becoming a muddy stream. To the left lay the Chalk River and, beyond, pine forest and beaver meadows fanning out toward the tapering lumps of several low mountains.

Mannion shivered inside his buckskin and the oilskin poncho he wore over it, fending off the rain. Damn, it was cold. Occasionally amid the rain he saw snow. The hard flakes formed crystals in the mud around Red's hooves, melting as the hard-driving raindrops obliterated them.

The main street followed the curve of the river, twisting and turning several times. Halfway through town, Mannion swung down a side street, noting a big grizzly carcass hanging upside down outside what was likely an itinerant hunter's wood-frame tent. Hanging from two posts, the bear's limbs were spread wide. A wheelbarrow loaded with guts sat on the ground near the beast's giant head. The bruin had likely been shot up around Gladstone Ridge, above Ptarmigan Lake.

The big beast looked like a man hanging there, halfway skinned.

Looked like Ulysses Lodge himself.

Maybe that's what Mannion would do once he'd run the killer down. Hang him upside down and skin him slow. That's how hot his anger still burned.

Jane weighed heavy on his mind. More than a few times since leaving Del Norte he'd wondered if she was still alive. Had he been up here on his vengeance quest, wasting precious time he might have spent with her while she was still alive?

She might have awakened and asked for him...

He shook away the thought. He was up here now. He needed to stay focused on Lodge.

He swung off the growing quagmire of the street and up to the Mountain Mary Saloon—a long, two-story log structure slumped under a peaked, rusted corrugated tin roof. Its windows wanly lit against the storm, the Mountain Mary was one of the few businesses that remained open all year in these chilly climes. Most of the other folks would likely be pulling out soon, heading either down to Salida or even farther east and lower down, to Denver, Colorado Springs, and Pueblo.

Two men stood on the front stoop that ran the length of the building.

They'd been standing to the right of the batwings, conversing—two lean, bearded men in wool coats and baggy denims. They gazed blandly at Mannion now, one with a smoldering quirley in one corner of his mouth. One held a beer mug in his hand. The other one, the smoker, had a beer mug resting on the loafer's bench flanking him.

As Joe reined Red up to one of the three hitchracks fronting Mountain Mary's, the bearded men glanced at each other then turned and, the smoker scooping his beer up off the loafer's bench, pushed through the batwings and disappeared inside.

"What's the matter?" Mannion asked, grinning, as he wrapped his reins around the hitchrack. "Don't like the company?"

Most folks in his neck of the Sawatch knew who Bloody Joe was. They'd either heard enough about him to recognize him or they'd seen him before. He'd hunted enough men in this massive devils' den for his reputation to precede him. Few other men had *cajones* enough to trail thieves, rapists, and killers into this wilderness pocked here and there with even more thieves, rapists, and killers.

Not Joe.

Joe felt at home here.

He hooked a wolfish smile at the thought, gray eyes slitting beneath the dripping brim of his Stetson.

He loosened Red's latigo, shucked his Winchester from the saddle boot, and stepped up onto the stoop. He paused to cock the Winchester then ease the hammer down and set the rifle on his right shoulder as he pushed through the batwings and took one step to the left, not wanting the doors to outline him against that gray, churning mess behind him.

When he'd first ridden up to the place, he'd heard the hum of conversation from within. Now, after the two bearded men on the stoop had gone inside, likely bringing news of the notorious visitor to their fair little mountain mining town, the place had gone quiet enough that Mannion could hear the roar of rain on the roof.

Thunder rumbled occasionally, distantly.

Dull lightning flashed in the windows.

Over a dozen men sat around the place—mostly bearded miners, prospectors, and woodcutters in wool, canvas, sack cloth, or denim. A few had the look of drifters clad in trail gear—mustached, hard-eyed men with pistols on their hips, some with rifles on their tables, saddlebags draped over chair backs, over gray or yellow rain slickers.

These were the hunted.

Mannion let his cold, wolf-eyed stare trail among the tables, at the men and a few weary-eyed, scantily clad women among them. He smiled suddenly, coldly, turned to his left and began walking toward the long, polished, mahogany bar that Mountain Mary had had shipped up from Heraklion, a mountain mining town just over the divide and which had gone belly-up when its own gold and silver had played out seven years ago.

She'd had the bar shipped up and over the divide to St. Elmo in sections. The backbar mirror, a good fifteen feet long, she'd shipped up and over the divide in one long piece aboard a hay and burlap padded lumber dray. The mirror looked as flawless and as polished as the bar she was so proud of and over which she was leaning now, grinning at the big, broad-shouldered, lean-hipped lawman in the high-crowned, wet, tan Stetson striding toward her now, opening and closing his gloved right hand around the Yellowboy's neck.

As Joe approached the bar, he kept one eye skinned on the mirror, wary of a bullet to the back. One or two of the hunted here might think he was here for them. He didn't care to let them know otherwise. Let them make their play. The rat population in these mountains was always in need of thinning.

Mary Karr, owner and operator of Mountain Mary's, smiled beneath the low-crowned, flat-brimmed black hat she wore as she rolled a lucifer match from one corner of her mouth to the other. A green and blue feather poked up from behind the band of the hat.

Mary was a well set-up woman in her forties, with many strands of silver in her long, blond hair. More silver than Mannion remembered. More lines around her eyes and mouth, as well. But then, hell—who didn't age? Especially in these mountains? As was her custom, Mary was dressed in a man's wash-worn, wool shirt unbuttoned far enough to give a man a hard time keeping his eyes on her face. Mannion couldn't see her below the waist, but he knew she was wearing, as was also her custom, baggy canvas trousers and Indian-beaded moccasins, the oncebright beads having long since faded with time.

Speaking in her Gaelic brogue still thick as Scottish fog over Edinburgh even after her twenty years in these mountains, she said, "Jesus, Joseph, and Mother Mary, what brings the likes of you to these parts so soon after your last visit, Bloody Joe?"

She let her appreciative, distinctly female gaze—Mary didn't mind letting a man know how she felt about the figure he cut—wander from his gray eyes and the salt-

and-pepper mustache mantling his mouth down to the tips of his wet, black boots then up again, letting them take their time, lingering at the nice breadth of manly shoulders forming a nice V above the still-flat stomach. "You gettin' a bad case of the suicidals, are ya, Mister Marshal?"

It hadn't been long since Mannion had passed through St. Elmo, hunting outlaws, of course, though occasionally he came up here with Vangie in the autumn, hunting elk with which to fill their winter larder. When they did, they stayed with Mary. No elk had finer meat than the Sawatch elk, nourished by the pure waters of the Taylor Gunnison, Eagle, and Roaring Forks Rivers as well as the finest, lushest grass and berries.

"You know me, Mary. I've always been attracted to wolf dens."

"You have, Joe." Mary leaned sideways on an elbow, exposed by the rolled up left sleeve of her shirt. She blinked her frosty blue eyes very slowly and curled her upper lip. "Though at one time, you came to visit the momma wolf. Just the momma wolf." She raised her eyes to indicate the second story, where her girls worked the line and she kept a couple of rooms of her own. "Remember?"

"How could I forget?" Mannion chuckled lustily and set his rifle on the bar. He removed his hat, waved the rain from the crown, and set it atop the bar, as well. He ran his left hand, leaving the right one free for the rifle, through his long, salt-and-pepper hair and said, "Those were the days."

"Not here for that now, are ya? Not for me." She leaned toward him, her eyes filled with knowing.

"No, not for you."

Though back in his younger days, when he'd first

moved to Del Norte and was shadowing bad men into these mountains, he'd often stopped for Mary. He hadn't patronized the whores down below in Del Norte. Even for an unmarried lawman, that had seemed wrong, somehow. Unseemly. Not to mention dangerous. He'd always wanted to be seen as above most men's weaknesses of the flesh.

Of course, he wasn't, but there you had it.

He'd preferred to appease his own primal urges up here in these rugged, dangerous mountains—all the more exciting for the ruggedness and the dangerousness—in the bed of Mountain Mary Karr, with a fireplace crackling in a corner of her small, intimately comfortable room with its soft, brass-framed feather bed, the rug of silver-tipped grizzly on the floor beside it.

He'd always been partial to the hot-blooded warrior women of Scotland and Ireland.

He thought of Jane again now and fought back a pang of guilt for coming here.

On the other hand, he'd had good reason. He saw validation of that assumption around Mary's right, discolored eye. Who else would have the gall to sucker punch Mountain Mary?

He reached out and ran his finger around that yellow and blue discoloration very gently, and said, "How you'd get the black eye, Mary?"

She took his hand in both of hers and said, "I got me a feelin' you've already guessed, Bloody Joe."

"You wouldn't have gotten it compliments of a big brute named Ulysses Xavier Lodge, would you?"

"Why, how did you know?" Mary said, pulling her head back, feigning surprise.

"Figured he'd come here, to St. Elmo. If he came to St. Elmo, he'd go to where everyone goes when they come to St. Elmo—Mountain Mary's. He often leaves a calling card, does Lodge. That's why Jane kicked him out of the San Juan."

Mary pursed her lips, slitted her eyes, and nodded slowly. "Came here lookin' for a woman. I told him there weren't any women here for him. He can bring a fist up fast for a man his size, Joe. No matter."

Mary stepped back away from the bar and pulled two double-barreled, sawed-off, twelve-gauge shotguns out from under the bar. She set them on the bar, dipped her chin, and smiled dangerously. Her frosty eyes gazed up at Mannion from beneath slender brows. "I just set these two pretty babies up here and drew the hammers back and told him one more time—and that *that* would be the *last* time I ever told him—there weren't any women here for him."

Mary smiled and lifted her firm, proud, Gaelic chin, adding, "He suddenly seemed to get the notion I was tellin' the truth, don't ya know? He backed away from the bar...real slow-like...then turned and fairly ran through those batwings."

She threw her head back, laughing. Sobering, she hardened her jaws as well as her eyes and said, "I'd have killed any other man who laid a hand on me. I'm savin' Lodge for when it really feels *good*!"

Mannion smiled. "Know where he went?"

Mary returned the gut shredders to their homes beneath the bar and hiked a shoulder. "Likely over to the Witch's place on Storm Creek. She'd take him when no one else in town would."

"Think he might still be over there?"

"In this weather?" Mary turned to glance out the sashed window in the front wall, to her right. "I wouldn't doubt it a bit. Holed up with one of the Witch's poor, long-suffering doves, no doubt. Mescin, Injun, half-breed, or darkie. I hear the Witch even has a humpback workin' for her. Men have strange desires. I hope he pays her well, at least, before he goes." She crossed her arms. "I don't shudder often, as you well know, Joe. But that big bastard—he makes me shudder."

Mary shuddered as if to demonstrate the truth of her statement.

"Yeah, well," Mannion said, "he'll be done making anyone shudder real damned soon. Give me one drink—will you, Mary?"

"Tarantula juice?"

Mannion smiled. "You know me too well."

Mary walked down the bar and returned with an unlabeled bottle and one shot glass. She set the glass down on the bar in front of Mannion and glanced at the bandage wrapped around his head. "That needs changing," she said.

Mannion knew blood had seeped through it from over the tattoo.

"In due time."

"I could change it for you."

Mannion smiled as he picked up the shot glass. "You could do more than that."

"Anytime, Joe. You know me."

"He shot Jane."

"Ah." Mary nodded slowly. "That's why you're here." She glanced at the bandage again. "He did that, too."

"I got careless, stupid."

"Most folks do when it comes to him. That's why he's still haunting the Sawatch after all these years." She ran her finger across the long, scabbed burn on his left cheek. "He do that, too?"

"Nah. That came before." He remembered his and

Rio's dustup in Leo Tollefson's roadhouse with Bronco Lewis's bunch. So long ago now…

She hooked another dry smile. "You have quite the life, Joe."

"It's about to get more interesting. I'm gonna kill the son of a bitch, Mary. Once and for all. Send him back to the demon that spawned his rancid hide." Mannion threw back the shot and reached for his hat.

Again, Mary grabbed his hand and leaned toward him, both elbows on the bar. "Don't get cocky, Joe. Don't get over-confident. I know how you feel about Jane Ford. Hell, every woman in these mountains knows how you feel about Jane." She drew her mouth corners down as though in fateful sadness. "He does, too. He'll know you're coming, and he'll be ready. He's always *been* ready for someone like you."

"Hell, Mary—didn't you get the telegram?" Again, Mannion grinned as he set his hat on his head. "There's only one of me."

He winked, picked up his rifle, set it on his shoulder, and swung around, noting the cunning, shifty eyes sliding his way as he strode toward the batwings.

Outside, thunder rumbled louder than before. The storm was growing closer.

Hell would pop this night. One way or the other. From one quarter or another.

This was the Sawatch.

CHAPTER 20

Dark now, twenty minutes later.

The storm had settled over St. Elmo, hammering the muddy little settlement with crashing thunder and witches' fingers of lightning stitching a quilt of bad weather across the murky, dark sky.

Squeezing the Yellowboy in his gloved hands, Mannion shouldered up to one of the livery barn's doors, from inside the barn, nudged it open a crack, and jacked a live cartridge into the Winchester's action. He'd heard running footsteps a few minutes ago when, after renting a stall for Red, wanting to get the weary horse out of the weather, he'd been rubbing him down with dry burlap.

There'd been several sets of footsteps, all owning the air of deadly furtiveness.

Now, with the horse secure, fed, and watered, Mannion shouldered the door wider, stepped out into the rain-hammered night, and kicked the door closed behind him.

He looked to each side of him, cringing when lightning flashed, revealing him out here, hunkered down inside his coat and poncho, and dropped to a knee in case shots came. When none did, he turned to his right and began walking along the front of the barn to the right front corner.

He held the cocked Yellowboy up high across his chest, right index finger curled through the trigger guard.

When he reached the corner, he pressed his right shoulder against the barn's log wall, switched the rifle to his left hand and snaked it around the corner, aiming down the barrel toward the rear.

Nothing but dark murk. As far as he could tell, nothing moved.

He lowered the rifle slightly and stepped out from the barn's front wall, moving toward the dilapidated corral just beyond it. As he did, he kept his eyes on the murk between the corral and the barn. Good thing he did. A shadow moved roughly halfway down from the front of the barn.

Mannion ran forward as a gun flashed and the bullet sizzled through the air behind him. He dropped to a knee behind the corral's near corner post, raised the Yellowboy to his right shoulder, and triggered two quick shots, the Winchester roaring beneath the storm's ceaseless rush and howl. He picked up movement in the corner of his right eye and turned to see another shadow stealing toward him from the front of the barn, the man slowing his jog to a walk and quickly raising the rifle in his hands.

Mannion swung the Winchester toward him, jacking another round into the action, and fired.

The second attacker howled and lurched back, firing his rifle straight up at the stormy sky before falling in a heap in a deep puddle fronting the barn's right door. At the same time, a bullet caromed over Mannion's left shoulder to plunk into the face of the post. He could feel the curl of air off his left cheek.

He wheeled, putting his back to the post and ejecting the Winchester's last spent round, seating fresh, and firing at the figure poking its head and shoulders above a water barrel off the corner of a feedstore.

The man's pale hat blew off his head.

The man gave a yelp and wheeled to run down the alley between the feedstore and a cabin boarded up against the coming winter. Mannion jacked another round into the Winchester's chamber, fired...jacked and fired again...and once more. He didn't see the fleeing attacker fall but he heard him give a strangled screech, indicating at least one of his bullets had hit its target.

Mannion lowered the smoking Yellowboy, smelling the peppery odor of the powder smoke mixing with the rain and brimstone smell of the storm and wet sage. Quickly, he thumbed cartridges from his shell belt into the Yellowboy's loading gate, taking a cautious look around. He was on a narrow side street. Only a few cabins and shops hunched beneath towering, storm-tossed pines.

When he had the Winchester fully loaded, with one cartridge seated in the chamber, the hammer lowered to half cock, he rose, pushing off the post, and continued his slow walk to the east along the murky, muddy side street. As he rounded a bend in the street, he saw a large house ahead, built in the Victorian style with towers, turrets, a sharply angled roof, and gingerbread trim. It was surrounded by a white picket fence. Tall pines looming over the house and yard bent back and forth in the wind, shy dancers at a party they'd been forced to attend.

The house had been built by an eastern railroad magnate who'd intended to open a gold mine just outside of St. Elmo. As the story went, he'd put the cart before the horse in building the house; the house had no sooner been completed than he'd been indicted on federal fraud and embezzlement charges and his mine investors had pulled out.

Heading off to the federal rock quarries, he'd sold the house to the widow of another mine owner who'd gone belly-up near Salida. Miss Caledonia Dane, known locally as "the Witch," had turned the snazzy digs into a house of ill repute, which had become even more disreputable over the past several years, after Miss Dane—suffering from alcoholism as well as from Apollo's Curse, or syphilis—introduced opium and refused service to no one. She hired any girl who wanted to work on her back for a fifty-fifty split of profits and turned no customers away.

Even, most likely, though Mannion couldn't imagine it, Ulysses Lodge.

It was a seedy, dangerous place even by Sawatch standards in general and St. Elmo standards in particular.

Looking around warily for more scoundrel vermin from Mountain Mary's, buoyed by coffin varnish to go a-huntin' the infamous Bloody Joe Mannion, Joe pushed through the gate in the picket fence, both fence and gate in badly need of fresh paint. The gate was barely clinging to its post, so that Mannion had to slide it with the toe of his right boot along the brick paving stones to open it.

Thunder crashed like cymbals, making the soggy ground beneath Joe's feet reverberate with its violence.

Ahead, lamplight guttered weakly in the two rain-streaked parlor windows to the right of the house's front door while the windows to the left of the door were dark. Most of the second and third-story windows were lit at varying degrees of brightness. Mannion thought he saw two silhouettes moving together, dancing slowly, in the window just beneath the roof's sharp peak.

His skin crawled at the Sodom-like air of the place despite the melodic tinkling of a piano sounding from within and which was drowned frequently by near and distant thunder.

His skin crawled further when, gaining entrance and stepping through the parlor, the walls on each side of which were adorned with sour-smelling wet coats of wool and animal hide hanging from brass pegs, he saw a half-naked man and a totally naked girl sprawled across a fainting couch abutting the wall to his right. Above them was a large oil painting of a beautiful, black-haired lady attired in a fine, metallic-green gown with white lace and a plunging bodice riding through green woods atop a coal-black, fiery-eyed stallion. The painting had two holes in it—one near the rider's left elbow, the other in the gilt frame.

There were four other people in the parlor beyond Mannion—three were comatose and slumped atop brocade- or velvet-upholstered chairs or sofas. Bottles, glasses, and brass-bowled opium pipes littered small tables here and there about the room whose pent-up air was laced with the cloying odor of the midnight oil. The fourth person in the room was playing a grand piano at the room's rear flanked by an enormous window over which red velvet drapes with gold tassels had been drawn, a small gap between them revealing the rain-splattered window down which the lamp-reflecting beads of moisture ran and beyond which lightning flashed.

The piano player lifted her beringed hands from the piano's keys. She lifted a beringed hand to her garishly painted mouth, coughed raucously for several seconds—a cough so deep and grating that it made Mannion's own lungs cry out in agony—then fixed her dark, long-lashed eyes set deep in dark hollows in the waxy, emaciated flesh of her face, on her most recent visitor.

"Name your poison, Jake! All the girls is busy—them that aren't three sheets to the wind, that is," she added, glancing at the naked girl passed out with the half-naked, bearded man on the fainting couch. "Entrance is five dollars. For that you get your fill of both liquor and..."

She let her voice trail off and the narrow swatch of her waxy forehead suddenly corrugated as her gaze held on the tall newcomer holding the Yellowboy up high across his chest, right index finger curled through the trigger guard.

"Wait," she said suspiciously, her deep, gravelly voice sounding like the loud purr of a sick cat, "you're not here..."

"Not here for that," Mannion said, glancing quickly around the room in which the once-tony but now shabby, expensive furniture was arranged willy-nilly, which meant it wasn't arranged at all except to give a man and a prostitute a modicum of privacy to discuss what might later happen upstairs, when they were alone. "I'm here for *him*."

Rain dripping off his oilskin poncho and the brim of his hat, Mannion opened and closed his hands around the rifle, eager to get to work. He glanced up the stairs running up behind the wall to the right of the two sleepers and the bullet-torn, oil-painted beauty riding through romantic woods.

From his vantage, he could see only a four-foot stretch of banister and four or five steps, the wall abutting the stairs concealing the rest. The parlor continued to the right of the stairs in which there was more haphazardly arranged furniture as well as two men asleep face down at a large, round table strewn with coins, playing cards, several shot glasses, and whiskey bottles.

The sleepers were—or *had been*—the sole survivors of a long night of poker, it appeared. The other players had likely retreated, pockets lighter than when they'd come, to the upstairs lairs of the Witch's girls or to home and likely a good tongue-lashing from indignant wives.

Mannion returned his gaze to the Witch herself, who studied him with a pensive air while puffing a cigarette protruding from a long, jade holder. She blinked once, twice, three times, long lashes curling at their ends, and said, "Law?"

Mannion just stared at her.

"Is he still here?"

"Who?"

Mannion just stared at her.

The Witch hiked a shoulder then rose from the piano bench, turning toward him, striding toward him, weaving around chairs, sofas, tables, and the occasional bottle or shot glass. She wore flowing silk robes that blew back in the wind of her walk and which gave her an angelic air. Albeit an angel spawned in hell.

Coal black, obviously dyed hair was piled high atop her head. Her waxy, deeply lined face had an unearthly quality, bespeaking someone neither alive nor dead, but hovering in some netherworld between.

Black eyes were as depthless as marbles.

When she stopped before him, close enough that he could smell the tobacco, alcohol, and opium stench oozing from her pores, her broad lips quirked up at the corners in a knowing smile. "You're Mannion."

"I didn't think we'd met." He'd never met her, but he'd heard the stories. She was almost as famous as he was in this stretch of the Sawatch.

"You're the only lawman either courageous enough or stupid enough to visit this end of St. Elmo. I heard the shooting out yonder." She gave her head a toss to indicate the way in which Mannion had come. "You made it through. Only Bloody Joe Mannion could make it through." She glanced around the room behind her and beyond the stairs and then lifted her gaze to the ceiling above her head. "Best hope none of these sleeping vipers wakes up or you might not make it out again."

"I'll take my chances."

"Who were you looking for again?"

"Lodge."

"Ah." She gave a tight smile.

"He here?"

"I don't know." The Witch hiked her shoulder again, drew deeply on the cigarette holder then gave another loud, grating cough as she blew the smoke out her nostrils. "He was. That's all I can tell you."

"Which room?"

"He went upstairs with Mi Lay." She laughed deep in her rotting lungs; it sounded like a horse's whicker. "Get it? Mi *Lay*?"

"Which room?"

She gave a half-hearted wave of a dismissive, beringed, claw-like hand. "Oh, I don't know. Second-floor hall, right of the stairs, third or fourth door on the left, I think." She stepped toward Mannion, placed a hand on his holding the Yellowboy by its neck. "Go easy, eh, big fella? My clients come here for the *peace* and *quiet*. They *work* hard. They *play* hard. They like to *rest* hard without threat of the *law*."

"No promises."

Mannion turned to the stairs, climbed them two steps

at a time, quietly, wincing when a riser groaned against his weight.

He turned right at the second-floor landing, strode past the first two doors, stopped at the third one. He canted his head toward the wood panel. Inside, nothing but silence. In fact, save for muffled snores up here and the storm's continuing thunder, the silence around him was almost total. All the vile vipers had slithered into their holes, slaked their lust, and descended into slumber.

Mannion twisted the doorknob slowly. When the latch clicked, he shoved the door open a foot, poked his head inside, then pulled it back out again. He winced and shook his head against the image of what he'd seen. He hadn't seen Lodge, but what he had seen in there wouldn't soon leave his memory.

He closed and latched the door and, clucking his distaste at the breed of man these poor girls were forced to "entertain," continued to the next door on the hall to his left.

He extended the Yellowboy out from his left hip, placed his thumb on the hammer, and squeezed the doorknob, stretching his lips back from his teeth just before the latching bolt clicked open. He paused, canting his head to the door, listening intently, drawing his index finger back taut against the Winchester's trigger. A longtime bounty hunter, Lodge was probably a light sleeper. Like lawmen, sound-sleeping bounty hunters didn't live to ripe old ages.

Mannion eased the tension in that finger just a little when no sounds came from within. Just a little. He shouldered the door open and filled the opening quickly with his large frame, extending the Yellowboy straight out from his right hip and drawing the hammer back to full cock.

He grimaced, grunted, again stretching his lips back from his teeth.

This time in horror.

Lodge wasn't here.

Only the girl was here—a frail, pale-skinned Chinese girl lying spread-eagled on the rumpled bed ahead and to Mannion's left. She was entirely naked.

And dead despite the dark eyes staring right at Joe in mute accusing while her mouth formed a large, round, dark 'O' of silent terror and disbelief at having had her neck laid open so wide and so deep that the slash, likely from a big bowie knife, had nearly taken her head off.

A mirrored dresser lay to the right of the bed, just beyond the curtained window between them.

On the mirror had been scribbled in thick, red lipstick and in a large, childlike hand:

YUR NEKST BLUDDY JO

Beneath that, two red dots above a broadly curved 'U'.

A mocking smile.

A door latch clicked. Mannion turned to see a big man with a gray beard looking out a partially open door on the hall's left side, as he turned to face the stairs. The man was entirely naked. He held a silver-chased Remington revolver down low against his right thigh.

He wrinkled his nostrils distastefully and said, "Ain't you Bloody Joe Mannion?"

Mannion pressed the Yellowboy's stock against his right hip, and grinned.

The man's eyes widened as he brought the Remington up quickly, "It's Bloody Joe Mannion!"

The second half of "Mannion" had been drowned out

by the Yellowboy's roar as it carved a round .44-caliber hole through the man's upper left chest, just beneath his collarbone, punching him back into the room as he lowered the Remington again and fired a round through his left, bare foot.

Mannion cocked the Winchester and began striding toward the stairs, hearing shouts and scuffling and fumbling behind the doors ahead and behind him—hell, all around him!

A door opened ahead of Joe. A man clad only in long-handles and wielding a sawed-off, double-barreled shotgun ran into the hall. Mannion shot him before he could get both barrels leveled.

Doors opened behind Joe and men ran out into the hall.

Joe wheeled and promptly shot three men like shooting ducks off a millpond.

He shot one more running up the stairs.

As he himself descended the stairs, the man who'd been sleeping with the doxie on the fainting couch poked his head around the corner, aiming an old Springfield rifle up toward Mannion. Joe fired from his right hip, drilling the man through his right shoulder. The man fell back, howling, against the front wall.

As he tried raising the Springfield again, Mannion shot him through his right eye, painting the wall behind him with thick, liver-colored blood and white flecks of bone and brain matter.

Mannion stopped at the bottom of the stairs and cocked his head to listen.

No more shouting or fumbling, no more drumming of running feet.

Again, the Witch's lair was silent.

The Witch stood ten feet away on Mannion's left, one

claw-like hand on a hip. She drew deeply on the cigarette holder, blew the smoke at the ceiling. "Well, well," she said angrily, coughing. "Bloody Joe does clean up well, doesn't he?"

More coughing until she was doubled over with it.

"He tries." Mannion pinched his hat brim to her, turned to the door. "Be seein' you."

"Not if I see you first!" the Witch shrieked as he drew the door closed behind him.

He could still hear her coughing as he descended the porch's wet steps.

CHAPTER 21

"Molly!" Henry exclaimed once more, staring in shock at the girl standing before him clad in a dark skirt and cape and a dark-green felt hat. "What in holy blazes are you doing out here?"

He remembered the face in the window.

Her face.

Molly's face.

Anger and humiliation burned in him once more. "What in hell were you doing peeping through Grace's...I mean, *Miss Hastings's* window?"

Molly steepled her fingers against the sides of her head, beneath her hat. "Oh, God—I didn't mean to... I didn't mean to...well...how could I know what you two would be doing in there? Besides, I didn't come to peep. I just came to satisfy my curiosity."

"About what?"

"About you...and why you skulk off from time to time. I figured there was another girl, and I couldn't help being jealous. I followed you from a distance the other day, saw you heading in the direction of the schoolhouse. There could be only one place you were heading on this side of town." Molly pursed her lips and shook her head, her eyes in the starlight bright with worry. "Oh, Henry—you don't know what you're getting yourself involved in!"

"*What?*" Henry exclaimed. "What're you talking about? Grace is a very nice lady." He stepped forward and closed his hand around Molly's right arm, just above the elbow. "Now, you listen, Molly—don't you dare blab a peep about this to anyone, you hear?"

She gazed up at him, her large, round, gray eyes incredulous. "No, no. Certainly not," she said, angrily flaring a nostril. "I'll let you dig your own grave." She jerked her arm free of his grip. "Now, if you'll excuse me, I have to fetch my horse!"

She wheeled and walked away in the darkness, back in the direction from which they'd both come.

"Stay here," Henry said, starting after her. "I'll fetch him for you!"

"Leave me alone, Henry!" Suddenly, Molly stopped and turned back to him. Bent slightly forward at the waist, she said with grave sincerity, slowly shaking her head. "Stay away from her, Henry. Stay away from her or you'll be sorry. You may have come back from Arizona with a gunman's confidence and a lawman's proud stride, holding your chin higher and loving how everyone's suddenly calling you by your given name—like I always *had!*—but you're still a simpleton when it comes to women. That Grace of yours is playing you like a finely tuned fiddle!"

She swung around and started to walk away but stopped suddenly with a startled gasp. Henry had heard it, too—a soft thud as though of a log being knocked off a wood pile. There was a high-pitched "meow" and then a cat appeared, leaping off wood stacked against the rear of the building to Henry's left, striking the ground with a thud, then dashing across the opening and disappearing behind the building on Henry's right.

Molly heaved a relieved sigh then strode angrily away, auburn hair bouncing on her shoulders.

"*Playing* me?" Henry ran up behind her and grabbed her arm again, turning her around to face him. "Playing me how?"

Molly looked around cautiously, biting her upper lip. Turning back to Henry, she said, "Not here. Meet me tomorrow after work by that big tree on Burial Rock Creek. You know the one—by that pool we used to swim in." She said this last with a touch of sadness for times gone by and turned and strode away in the darkness.

That made Henry a little sad, as well, though she'd been the one who'd ended their relationship. She'd given him the cold shoulder for accepting the job of escorting La Stiletta down to Tucson for Marshal Mannion. It didn't make him sad for long, however. Mostly, he just felt shocked and confused by what she'd told him, or what she'd warned him about Grace.

"Stay away from her or you'll be sorry!"

Henry stared after her, thinking about it.

"Ah, heck," he said, kicking a bottle strewn with other trash in this alley between two buildings on the east side of Main Street in Del Norte. "She's just a jealous girl. They get notional, girls do," he added, starting back in the direction of Grace's place. "Jealous girls most of all!"

He gave a dry laugh, but it sounded hollow even to himself.

Somehow, he'd let her get under his gallblamed skin!

Molly's warning echoing inside his head, he walked around the schoolhouse, its bell tower shouldering back against the starlit sky, and saw Grace standing in the open doorway of her cabin, between the rows of split wood Henry had stacked for her. She held a striped quilt around her buxom body, her pale shoulders showing above it, her shins and bare feet showing below it.

Her hair hung messily about her shoulders.

A pair of moccasins she wore around the house and yard were on the floor behind her. In the starlight he could see the faint sheen of perspiration on her forehead—likely leftover from their admittedly delightfully wild frolic.

Henry had never been with such a woman. In fact, he hadn't been with many women at all before Molly. He'd liked being with Grace very much. She'd introduced him to pleasures of the flesh he'd never known about much less experienced. Now Molly had gone and ruined the mood—dang her, anyway.

"Henry, who was it?" Grace lifted the toes of one foot and then the toes of the other foot, looking up at him worriedly as he approached.

Yes, who was it?

For a few seconds, Henry considered telling her the truth. That the face in the window had belonged to his ex-girlfriend, Molly Hurdstrom. Curiosity and jealousy had compelled her to ride her horse over to Grace's place and ogle them through a window.

He nixed the idea, though he wasn't sure why. He didn't believe a word of what Molly had told him about Grace. That he needed to stay away from her, that she was somehow dangerous.

That had just been Molly's jealousy talking.

"Don't know," Henry said. "Probably just some jake from town. He rode away too fast for me to get a good look at him."

"It wasn't Vince?"

"I don't think so, no."

"Oh, dear," Grace said, turning to stare off around the school in the direction of town. She turned her gaze to Henry, frowning. "Should I be worried?"

"Nah, I think it'll be all right."

"That man might spread the word about us, Henry."

"I think it'll be all right, Grace," Henry said. "Don't worry about it. If I hear any rumors, I'll stop them dead in their tracks. We'd best get inside."

"All...all right..."

Grace turned and walked into the cabin. Henry followed her inside, closed the door, walked into the bedroom portion of the shack and removed his shirt from its peg.

"What're you doing?" Grace said, standing off the end of the kitchen table. "Where are you going?"

"I'd best get back to my rooming house." Henry shrugged into the shirt. He gave a half-hearted smile. "My landlady might start getting suspicious."

"Oh, I'm sure she's dead asleep." Grace quirked an alluring smile. "The night is young..."

Henry chuckled, again noting the hollowness of his mirth.

"...playing you like a finely tuned fiddle."

What for the love of Pete had she meant by that?

Oh well. He'd find out tomorrow. Just crazy notions of a jealous, notional girl.

"Good night, Grace," Henry said, his saddlebags draped over one shoulder, his Winchester in his right hand. "I'll see you again soon."

He set his free hand on her bare shoulder, kissed her cheek, and walked to the door.

Grace turned her head to follow him with her gaze. "How soon?"

Henry smiled. "Soon."

He went out and closed the door behind him and strode around the cabin toward the stable.

"...playing you like a finely tuned fiddle!"

THE NEXT AFTERNOON, ON THE TRAIL HEADING northwest of Del Norte, Molly hipped around in her saddle and gazed back along the trail's east side, to her right. She'd thought she'd seen something back there, in the corner of her right eye.

"Whoa girl," she said now, drawing back on her chestnut's reins. "Whoa, Queenie...that's it, that's a girl." Molly reached down and patted the mare's right wither.

The horse had been a birthday gift from her parents a couple of years ago. Molly had taken the horse with her when she'd moved out of her family's house, stabling her in a livery barn near the house she roomed in. Molly's father and mother were trying to convince her to move back into their house, to live with them again, to forget about the old trouble involving the McClarksvilles—her having *shot* Adam McClarksville because he'd been about to kill Henry.

The situation had been an awful mess, not to mention a huge scandal. And while Molly doubted she could forget it, forget that her parents had tried so desperately to force her into marriage with a young man she hadn't loved—who'd been a common thug, no less, albeit a thug who'd haled from a rich family—she'd agreed to at least consider their urging. Now, with Henry out of her life, she had to admit she felt an almost irresistible pull to return to the comfort of her parents' home, the house she'd grown up in. She'd been awfully lonely in recent weeks though she knew that her and Henry's breakup had been entirely her fault.

What a fool she'd been.

She'd been jealous of the prisoner, the comely La Stiletta, he'd been assigned to escort to Tucson to testify in a trial against her Mexican bandito boyfriend. Molly should have known that Henry would stay true to her. She'd let her jealousy get away from her.

Now she'd likely lost Henry forever.

She just hoped she had lost him to *her*...that woman.

She absently rubbed Queenie's right wither as she gazed behind her at the rocks and cedars stippling the trail's right side. She was sure she'd seen something move. Queenie swished her tail and turned her head to gaze in the same direction Molly was, ears pricked as though listening.

Molly glanced at the horse, patted her wither once more, frowning curiously, and returned her puzzled gaze to the brush. "Did you see it, too, girl? Do you hear something, Queenie?"

Fear touched Molly. She stared along her back trail, hoping she'd see Henry following her out from town. No sign of him, however, between her and Del Norte, which was a long, jagged, tan line along the southeastern horizon, tucked into a broad, fawn-colored fold between the Sangre de Cristos in the east and the San Juans in the west.

Molly became aware of the large, open space she was in.

And that she was all alone in it.

Apprehension staying with her like a burr clinging to her skirt, she booted the mare on ahead but kept taking cautious looks around her. Finally, when she'd ridden roughly a mile beyond where she'd stopped, she decided she was just feinting at phantoms again. Her fear was the result of her own paranoia.

It had started in earnest when she'd left home and no longer had the protection of her parents. All sorts of bad things could happen to a girl alone, and of course lying awake in her own dark room at night, she'd imagined all of them.

Before their breakup, Henry had purchased a small gun for her to carry in her reticule, in case any of the drunk miners or cowboys in the customarily raucous Del Norte got overly "handsy" or downright objectionable. She'd placed the gun in her saddlebags before leaving her room, so she had it with her now. Thinking of the gun gave her comfort.

Henry had taught her how to shoot it, and she'd become fairly good with it. To her it was just a gun though to Henry, who liked guns, it was "a Henry Deringer .41-caliber pocket pistol with black walnut stock and a checkered bird's head grip, foliate engraved German silver mountings, a petite back-action lock with a generous hammer spur, etc., etc...."

To Molly it was just a gun. She was glad she'd brought it with her today.

She rode over a low pass and then through a dry arroyo and there ahead, in a sheath of autumn-yellow cottonwoods and aspens with a sprinkling of Ponderosa pines lay Burial Rock Creek. The stream meandered down from a large, stony badlands area the centerpiece of which was Burial Rock itself, which legend had it was where the Ute Indians from this area once buried their dead to keep them away from carrion eaters—aside from carrion-eating birds, Molly thought.

As she approached the creek, she swung onto a secondary path that led upstream to the east. She came to the large cottonwood that stood back from an open, horseshoe bend in the creek, and from a deep, dark-blue pool where she and Henry used to swim together, far from the prying eyes of Del Norte.

She regarded the water longingly as she stopped Queenie and swung down from the saddle.

A cool wind blew, lifting little, white ripples from the pool, making her auburn sausage curls dance along her jaws.

She tied Queenie to a sapling then turned to the big cottonwood fairly glowing lemon yellow in the autumn sun. She smiled, remembering days gone by. Then she walked over to the big tree and sat down at its base, leaning back against the bole.

She removed her dark green felt hat and fiddled with it pensively, waiting for Henry.

She wished he'd come. It was after five thirty. The apprehension of earlier had never totally left her. It returned in earnest now as the mare, who'd been cropping grass along the stream, lifted her head abruptly to stare into the brush and stunt cedars to Molly's right. She thought she'd heard something, too—a soft snapping sound, as though someone had stepped on a twig.

The mare whickered, shook her head as she continued staring in the direction from which the sound had come.

"What is it, girl?" Molly said, softly.

Molly cast her own fearful gaze into the brush.

"Is anyone there?" she called, hearing a tremor in her voice.

When only the wind and the murmur of the creek replied, she gained her feet slowly and walked over to the mare. She opened the flap of the saddlebag hanging down the sorrel's right hip, reached in, and pulled out the

Henry Deringer .41-caliber pocket pistol, which she'd tucked neatly into a small, burlap pouch.

She removed the pretty little piece from the pouch, turned, and holding the gun halfway out in front of her, began walking slowly, fearfully toward the brush from which the snapping sound had issued.

Again, the sorrel whickered.

"Who's there?" Molly said. "I know someone's there. Show yourself!"

She approached a white-stemmed aspen, the ground around it carpeted in bright yellow leaves, which crunched beneath her feet. She started to swerve around the tree when Grace Hastings, clad in a heavy cream wool sweater and low-crowned black hat, stepped out from behind it. The woman closed her left hand around Molly's derringer and ripped it out of her hand.

"I'll take that!" she said and tossed the gun away.

Molly was about to cry out but then the woman bunched her lips and shook her head with deep frustration. "Oh, why did you have to go and make me do this?"

Then she smashed the barrel of her own revolver against Molly's right temple with a grunt.

Molly felt the stinging in her head just before her knees struck the ground, and she was out.

CHAPTER 22

Mannion reined Red to a halt and frowned down at the old Indian trail he'd been following since the day before around noon, after the rain had stopped and he'd been able to continue his pursuit of Lodge without being swept away by flooded washes and ravines, plenty of which stitched this part of the Sawatch.

The Taylor River had swung away from him, swerving to his left to lose itself up in the high, cold reaches where the river was born. Mannion had continued north before swinging east across Pine Creek and then into the fir- and boulder-studded canyons off the north slopes of the Collegiate Peaks. He'd seen little of Lodge's spoor within the past few hours, but he knew where the man was headed now. He'd learned to think the way Lodge thought. The savage man-beast was leading Mannion up here into this godforsaken, at times nearly impossibly rugged terrain, to try once again to scour him from his trail.

He'd lead him up around Treasure Vault Lake and into the even more remote and rugged wilderness flanking the Mountain of the Holy Cross.

If he didn't kill him sooner, that was.

Sooner or later, between here and there, Mannion knew, Lodge would make another play on him. Maybe not this afternoon—it was nearing evening, the sun losing its intensity and the shadows spilling out from the western crags—but maybe tomorrow. Maybe the next day or the next.

Lodge would make another play.

He'd wait awhile.

Tracking a man was an odd thing. The decisions he made and which you observed and came to understand drew you close to him. In an almost spiritual, mystical sense. Mannion had come to know Lodge in that sense. He'd come to know his mind, how he thought. What he'd come most to know about him was how much fun the man was having, leading Mannion up here to kill him.

Lodge loved to kill. Some men did. It gave them an almost spiritual, mystical sense of power. It gave them a godlike feeling. It was almost a sexual experience or maybe it went beyond sex. To such men, killing was an excitement they could not find in any other way.

Standing in that room at the Witch's place in St. Elmo, staring at that poor, dead girl, Mannion had come to understand the thrill that killing the girl had given Lodge. The thrill of killing her to taunt Mannion. Joe wished he hadn't come to understand it, because by coming to understand it, he'd felt it himself.

It made him feel dirty. It made him feel as though his soul, if he still had one, had been corrupted.

Now as he stared down at the deep, white, semicircular scratch a shod hoof had recently made—probably only a few hours earlier—in the side of a large rock beside the trail, Joe felt as though he were once again peering into the bleak murk and filth of the bounty hunter's brain. It was a devil's lair chock full of green-horned demons, not unlike the Witch's place where he'd demonstrated his gruesome killing skills.

Lodge had been born without a soul. Joe knew that without a doubt. He had a brain. He was not a stupid man. He was trail savvy and sharp, as smart as any rogue grizzly staying ahead of men hunting him after one beef-eating spree after another. Mannion had known such grizzlies. He'd hunted a few himself. Like Lodge, they'd come to enjoy the pursuit as much as the killing itself.

It excited them.

Lodge was excited now.

He'd killed the girl for the thrill of killing her. But even more than that, he'd killed her because he knew it would incense Mannion even more than before and solidify his desire to catch up to and kill Lodge as soon as he could. It would make him even more eager and determined, cause him to track even faster and possibly even carelessly.

Mannion looked around.

Tall crags stood on the other side of a lake ahead and to his right. The lake was a large, dark-blue jewel set in a solid granite bowl, with mostly rocks and boulders but a few tufts of tough, wiry grass and evergreen shrubs around it. Joe thought Lodge was holed up in those crags somewhere, likely watching him, smiling as he studied his pursuer through field glasses.

"Come on, Joe," he could almost hear the man calling to him. "Keep comin', Joe. Keep comin'. You're close. *Real clossse...*"

Rage and exasperation burned in Mannion.

He hated being toyed with. He hated being played like this.

Lodge could have waited for him at the Witch's place.

He could have killed Mannion then and there. At least, they could have had it out. But, no. The bounty hunter, thrilled to an almost sexual degree to be hunted, wanted the chase to continue. So, he'd killed the girl to egg Joe on, to taunt him, and he'd continued running, leaving just enough of a trail that Joe, given his keen tracking skills, could follow.

Follow Mannion did, continuing up and over a high, windy divide and dropping into a forested valley on the other side. He camped that night in a notch cave, knowing that while the sky was clear when he'd stopped for the day, a storm would likely blow in after dark.

It did.

Again, rain turned to snow and then back to rain.

It was a chill, soggy dawn that saw Mannion rise and build a low fire for coffee, with dry wood he'd gathered before the storm. He continued along the narrow, winding horse trail Lodge had been following and would likely continue to follow up into the wilderness surrounding the Mountain of the Holy Cross.

By noon, the ragged clouds had scattered and a clear, cerulean blue sky—an autumn sky, for sure—opened, and Joe put the Collegiate Peaks behind him. The Holy Cross was a vast formation ahead of him, appearing from this distance of a good fifty miles a giant anvil suspended above the earth, the gauzy space below it appearing a flat pedestal of white clouds.

Mannion rode up and over another rocky divide and into another, narrower valley angling northeast. As he rode, he saw a large, granite outcropping ahead and to his right. Several thumbs of solid rock jutted out over the valley, obscured by the crowns of larches, spruces, and tamaracks.

Mannion drew back on Red's reins and surveyed the

formation carefully, squinting against the sun beating nearly straight down from that faultless vault of sky. The cold air, seemingly unheated by the sun, was winey with spruce resin and the heady smell of balsam.

In the distance, crows cawed.

Finally, Joe reined Red off the left side of the trail and into deep forest. He came to the ruins of an old trapper's cabin, nothing much remaining but a caved in sod roof, rotting frame timbers, and an all-but-hidden sheet-iron monkey stove. It never ceased to amaze him how far some men would trek to toil alone. At the same time, he could feel the same urge deep inside himself.

He stopped Red, dismounted, and shucked his Winchester from the saddle boot. He dropped the reins in the shade of a balsam, near a freshet trickling out from a rocky spring ringed with firs. He loosened the saddle cinch, withdrew a coil of rope from a saddlebag pouch, shoved it into a large, inside pocket of his mackinaw, then patted the horse's left wither.

"You stay, boy. I got me a suspicion. I might still be addled by that braining the big son of Satan gave me, but it's a suspicion, just the same."

He gave the horse one more reassuring pat then tramped off through the trees.

He climbed partway up the next ridge and followed the curve of the slope to the east, around the backside of the granite formation that was now about a hundred feet below him on his right. When he was nearly directly north of where he'd first stopped Red at the valley bottom, and maybe three hundred yards away from that spot, he followed a boulder field down toward the formation spread out below him.

The formation appeared ancient lava likely spewed from the earth's bowels beneath the higher, blown-out, cone-shaped ridge farther to the north, behind Mannion now as he clambered his way through the rocks and boulders to a relatively flat shelf.

He moved at a crouch around the semi-circular area, holding the Winchester down low in one hand, carefully, cautiously scrutinizing the terrain around him. The short hairs were standing up beneath his collar.

His quarry was here.

Somewhere.

Mannion had no evidence of that. Still, he believed it to be true.

He'd come to know how Lodge thought. The man would try to effect an ambush from somewhere on the granite formation. It was perfectly positioned above the trail to allow for a clear shot at a man passing below.

Mannion came to the rocks and boulders at the shelf's southern edge. He stepped through them, angling downward to yet another semi-circular shelf below. He was stepping from right to left between two tall, tooth-like rocks when he stopped suddenly.

He lifted his chin and worked his nostrils, sniffing.

What his keen sniffer detected were ashes and something sour. Cold ashes and death.

He turned back to his right and stepped through a natural corridor of solid rock, a cabin-sized boulder slanting over him on his right, smaller, vertical rocks on his left. He followed a bend in the corridor and came to a small, sandy-floored clearing.

He stopped, heart thudding.

Dead ahead lay a large pile of gray ash.

To the right of the ash, trail gear was piled and draped over rocks—canvas sacks, warbags, two pairs of saddlebags, and two saddles. A bedroll, neatly rolled and tied, leaned against the rock over which one saddle was draped. A food sack hung from the saddle's apple. A speckled blue coffeepot sat on a flat, pale rock to the right of the mounded ash.

To the left of the camp, flies buzzed loudly over what remained of a smoky-gray mountain lion carcass. As Mannion approached the carcass, his eyes watered against the sickly-sweet stench of death and blood. He stopped over the carcass and gazed down at it—a big male. It had been gutted, the innards tossed into the rocks beyond to gather more flies that formed a wavering, black cloud.

Two haunches were missing, leaving only the tail hanging off the bloody end of the spine, partly exposed ribs, the head, and the two front legs. The cat's square head with large, round ears lay at an odd angle. One large, glassy, light-brown eye stared dubiously up at Mannion. Several of the cat's bones, chewed clean, some broken and the marrow likely having been sucked out, lay charred amid the gray ashes of the now-dead fire.

Mannion dropped to a knee and looked around, heart thudding slowly, evenly against his breastbone.

Where are you, you big son of Satan?

He rose to a crouch and, crouching, stepped away from the dead cat, heading roughly south along the sloping, rock- and boulder-stippled formation. When he heard a deep, quiet whicker, he froze in his tracks, heart picking up its beat.

A horse.

He followed the sound to his right and, dropping to one knee, peered through a gap in the rocks and down into a small clearing in which two horses were hobbled—Lodge's big steeldust and the big, American sorrel he'd taken from the Quarter Circle Six men. The clearing was carpeted in hock-high grass where the horses had not yet cropped it. Along the base of the stone wall curving around one end, to Mannion's right, a little freshet trickled, fed by a spring flowing out from a mossy crack in the rocks. A chipmunk was just then sitting on a rock beside the trickle, nibbling a nut and eyeing the human intruder.

The steeldust lifted its head. It was working its leathery nostrils, sniffing the breeze, eyes narrowed almost dreamily.

Suddenly, it turned its head to stare right at Joe through the rocks.

Mannion tensed and said very quietly, "Easy, now, big fella. Just...take it...easy..."

All he needed was for the horse to give a warning whinny.

Slowly, he scuttled back away from the gap in the rocks. On one knee, he looked around.

Where in hell was Lodge?

He looked around the area he was standing in. It was carpeted in fine, white gravel. Moving forward, he spied what appeared a faint shoe print in the gravel. A man's large moccasin print. He looked around, found one more. Near the print was a large gob of expectorated chewing tobacco.

Joe followed the big man's trail down through more rocks.

When he descended the formation at a steep angle for maybe fifty feet, he stopped suddenly. He's spied something in the rocks below him, at the edge of yet another semi-circular shelf.

A man's moccasin-clad foot!

It protruded from a narrow gap in the pale rocks. The heel was lifted, putting most of the weight of that foot on the toes, which Mannion could not see from his vantage. Lodge was holed up in those rocks, kneeling, likely drawing a bead with his rifle on the trail below, believing that Mannion was about to ride through there aboard Red.

Joe drew a deep breath to calm his fast-beating heart.
Calm. Nice and calm. Nice and slow.
You've done this before. Ain't your first rodeo, Joe, my boy...

However, he'd rarely hunted a man as savvy as Ulysses Xavier Lodge.

Very slowly and quietly, he seated a live round in the Winchester's action and curled his right index finger through the trigger guard.

He took one more, deep, calming breath then stepped slowly, quietly between two rocks, dropping several more feet to the level of the formation on which Lodge was kneeling, ready to effect his ambush. Ahead of Joe now were ten feet of open, sandy ground between him and his quarry.

He took one more step...one more...

Now, quartering slightly right, he could see both of the man's moccasin-clad feet and then the backs of his canvas-clad legs and then his broad back and the heavy, buffalo hide coat stretched over it and the heavy, sloping shoulders.

The back of the man's head was topped with Lodge's customary, bullet-crowned, floppy-brimmed hat.

The bounty hunter leaned forward and to his right, aiming down the barrel of the Winchester, which he had snugged up taut against his right shoulder, the barrel propped on a flat rock in front of him.

Joe stepped closer, closing the distance between him and his quarry, breathing very slowly, very shallowly, aiming his own Winchester straight out from his right hip.

He was five feet away from the man, resisting the

urge to shoot him in the back of the head and be done with it. No, he'd take him alive if he could. No point in doing Jane's shooter any favors. He'd love to watch Lodge die slow out here, but he'd rather the man wait out his grisly end in the bowels of Hotel de Mannion, pondering his fate, then take that long, seemingly endless walk to the gallows, and hang.

Four feet...

He stopped suddenly when Lodge lifted his head, brushed his right arm across his forehead and said through a guttural snarl, "Goddamn, your wretched hide, Bloody Joe! Show yourself, gallblast ya!"

Mannion continued forward and snugged the barrel of his Winchester up taut against the back of the bruin-man's stout neck. He smiled. "Right here, Ulysses. What's the matter—you miss me?"

CHAPTER 23

"You're doing very well, Doctor!" Vangie called as she watched Dr. Ben Ellison riding her blue roan, Cochise, around the circular breaking corral late in the afternoon. "Very well, indeed. Just remember to keep your knees together and don't bounce in the saddle. Put some weight on your stirrups and try to move *with* Cochise, not against him."

"Easier said than done!" the doctor laughed as, clad in his three-piece suit albeit without the coat just now, and his crisp brown bowler hat, he made one more turn in front of Vangie, who was striding around in the corral's center, watching horse and rider trot around her.

"No, you're doing fine. Keep in mind, there's no sin in holding onto the saddle horn. That's what it's for!"

"Now you tell me." Chuckling the doctor drew back on Cochise's reins, stopping the horse near Vangie. "I didn't want to look too much like a tinhorn in front of you, Miss Mannion."

"Vangie," Vangie said, suddenly feeling a little bold with this handsome, learned man despite her naturally retiring nature.

This was the second time he'd been over here to the Mannion stable and corrals, riding and watching Vangie ride, taking pointers, and she had to admit she did feel as though she were coming out of her shell a bit. She wasn't sure why. She and Ben—yes, she'd come to not only address him as Ben, as he'd insisted, but to see him as Ben, as well. They couldn't have been more different or come from such different backgrounds.

She was a frontier gal, born to the breaking corral and sired by none other than the infamous and notorious town tamer, Bloody Joe Mannion himself. Ben had been raised by a wealthy Eastern family who'd made their money for the past several generations in the shipping trade.

Like Ben, his brothers and nephews had been educated in the finest eastern colleges. They were all doctors, bankers, or lawyers. Vangie had no idea what the young doctor saw in her, but she was pleased that he must see something beyond the dirt under her fingernails and the horse shit riming the soles of her stockman's boots.

"Please, forgive me," Ben said now, smiling down at her from Cochise's back. "Vangie it is, of course. I'm sorry that I sometimes slide back into my own innate formality."

"Well, I'm sorry," Vangie said, "if I sometimes slide back into my own—*oh, no, hold on!*" she cried, clapping both hands to her mouth when she saw Cochise lean forward and flatten his ears against his head.

"Oh, Lordy!" Ben wailed just before Cochise dipped his head still lower and raised his hindquarters sharply, kicking straight out and up with his rear hooves.

Vangie screamed as Ben was catapulted straight up and over Cochise's bowed head to hit the dirt six feet in front of the stallion before rolling in a cloud of dust and finely ground horse apples.

"*Ben!*"

Vangie ran to the dusty, rumpled medico as Cochise went running around the corral, tail and head arched, whinnying merrily, thoroughly satisfied with himself. Vangie dropped to a knee beside the medico. He'd been lying belly down in the dirt but now he pushed up onto his hands and knees, groaning and shaking his head as if to clear it.

"Ben, are you all right? Oh, God—please tell me you're—"

"I don't know," Ben groaned, rolling onto his right side and holding that arm up close against his body. "Landed on my arm and..."

"Do you think it's broken? Should I fetch Doc Bohannon?"

Ben shook his head. "I think I'll be all right." He moved the arm a little. "Just a little sore, is all."

"Are you sure?"

"I should get up and move around a little."

"I'll help."

When the doctor rolled onto his hands and knees again, Vangie grabbed his left arm and helped heave him to his feet. She reached down for his dusty bowler, which had come off in the tumult.

"Water," he said.

Favoring his right arm, he let Vangie help him over to the fence. They crouched through it together and then Vangie removed the canteen she always kept hanging from a nail in the post by the gate. She uncapped the flask and held it out to Ben as he leaned back against the corral, shaken and dusty, still favoring his arm.

"Does he do that often?" he asked, accepting the canteen with his left hand.

"Not to me." Vangie cast the stallion, standing in the middle of the corral now, reins dangling, snorting and shaking his head defiantly, a hard glare. "He learned he can't get by with that nonsense with me, though he did get by with it a few times early on. Just like you, I was caught entirely by surprise."

She looked at Cochise again, jutted her chin angrily over the corral, and said, "Incorrigible beast!"

The stallion pawed the dirt and shook his head.

Ben laughed as he turned to cast his own gaze at the fine blue roan. "Testing me, eh? Just showing me that while I was able to ride him and he obeyed my commands—a few of them," he added wryly, "I still need to be wary. He's the bigger one. He's in command."

"I may not be the bigger one." Glowering at Cochise, Vangie thumbed herself in the chest. "But I'm the one in command!"

The roan blew again, kicked up more dirt, and went galloping around the corral, his fine, blue-black mane blowing and glistening in the sunshine.

"Now he's showing off." Vangie turned to the doctor. "How's the arm? Do you think it's broken?"

"Nah." Ben raised the limb of topic above his head, flexing it several times. "The joint's just a little bruised is all. It'll heal in no time."

"I'm so sorry, Ben."

"Don't be." Ben looked at the galloping horse again and threw his head back and laughed. "Quite the relationship you two have."

Vangie laughed then, too. As she kept her eyes on her horse, her expression softened. "Strange as it may be, he's my closest friend. My only friend, I reckon." She looked at the doctor. "I tell him everything."

"I don't doubt that a bit, Vangie Mannion." He gazed at her wistfully, admiringly. "You two are a lot alike. I can see that. Defiant, independent souls. I can see how close you are."

Vangie just stared at the handsome stallion, her own wistful smile quirking her mouth corners.

"I hope you have room for one more friend in your life, Vangie."

She turned to Ben, frowning. He gazed back at her, his gaze sincere.

"Well," he said, finally breaking the awkward silence. "I guess, now that Cochise has taught me who's boss, I'd better pack up my aching pride and get back to the office, do my nightly checks on Miss Jane and the two other patients."

He pushed away from the corral fence and donned his hat.

"Do you mind if I ride to Doc Bohannon's office with you?" Vangie asked. "I saw Jane earlier, but I'd like to see her again. You never know when..." She shrugged. "Well, you know..."

"Yes, I know," the doctor said fatefully.

There'd been no change in Jane Ford's condition in the week since she'd been shot. The town and Vangie and even the two doctors, Vangie thought, were losing hope.

"Of course." Ben glanced at the surrey he'd rented from one of the livery barns in town and gave an incredulous frown. "In my...*carriage?*"

"Do you mind? I can walk back. Let me just strip the tack off of Cochise and I'll be ready to go!"

"Oh, no, no—of course I don't mind." Ben smiled suddenly as he watched her crawl back through the fence and strip Cochise's saddle off his back. "Just never took you for a carriage-ridin' gal."

"Well, you just never know about folks," Vangie said, removing Cochise's bridle. As she set the saddle on the corral fence and tossed the bridle over it, she crawled back through the fence and smiled up at the young medico. "I have even been known, at least a time or two, to wear a dress and even brush my hair out long."

"That I would love to see."

"Well, maybe sometime...," Vangie said, blushing with self-consciousness, knowing what a shameless coquette she was being and not caring one iota.

"Sometime," Ben said. "Perhaps a steak dinner at the San Juan...?" He arched a hopeful brow.

"With French wine?"

"With French wine, milady!"

"All right, then," Vangie said.

She turned to the carriage. Ben did the same. Somehow, they ran into each other.

"Whoa!" Vangie said.

"Yes, whoa!" the doctor said, grabbing her arms and laughing.

He sobered quickly.

Vangie found herself staring up at him, her right foot on his left one. She did not move. Ben stared down at her, tightening his grip on her arms.

Slowly, he lowered his head to hers, very gently closed his mouth over her slightly parted and eagerly waiting lips.

Henry McCallister closed the jail wagon's rear door and glanced at Bronco Lewis and four other prisoners staring belligerently back at him through the strap-iron bars. He closed the padlock through the hasp, locking the door, and turned to one of the two deputy U.S. marshals tasked with hauling Lewis and the four other prisoners, which the circuit court judge had just that day ordered be sent off to the territorial pen, and said, "Well, have a nice ride, fellas. Hope you don't run into any bad weather on the way down the mountains to Denver."

"We fought rain on the way up, we'll likely fight it on the way down," said big Deputy Cisco Walsh as he lit a long, black cheroot, waving out the match and blowing smoke through his broad nostrils. "That's what happens when you draw the short straws—ain't it, Gav?"

The other federal, Deputy Gavin Crews, was just then setting his sheathed Winchester and warbag under the driver's seat at the front of the wagon. He pulled his mouth corners down, beneath his dark, waxed and curled mustache, and said, "That's what happens."

Apparently, the chief U.S. marshal in Denver had his deputies draw straws to see who would be assigned the unenviable task of driving the jail wagon up into the Rockies to fetch prisoners down to the pen.

Crews pinched his hat brim to Henry as he climbed aboard the wagon's right side. "Take 'er easy, Henry. We'll pick up that game of Red Dog where we left off last night...when I draw the short straw again. I likely will soon. Always seem to!"

Walsh climbed into the driver's side of the wagon, took up the reins of the two stout mules in the traces, released the brake, and shook the ribbons over the mules' backs. The jail wagon squawked forward, the sour-looking prisoners jostling with the pitch and sway.

"Hey, Deputy!" Bronco Lewis called through the rear

door's bars. His wrapped and swollen ankle kicked out before him; he gave a lewd gesture.

"My sentiments exactly!" Henry called after the man.

That was one prisoner he was not going to miss at all.

Rio Waite chuckled on the porch of Hotel de Mannion, where he stood beside the hulking Cletus Booker, Marshal Mannion's latest edition to his deputy staff. Booker stood there atop the porch steps beside Rio, dwarfing the older man, looking around and tapping the hide-wrapped club in his right hand against the open palm of his left hand. He was peering around the dusty main street as though looking for more heads to bust.

And he probably was.

That was why the marshal had hired Booker, who'd been fired from a previous deputy town marshal's job up high in the San Juan range when he'd gotten crossways with the town council. Booker liked to bust heads. To Marshal Mannion's way of thinking, more than a few heads in and around Del Norte needed busting. That's what Booker was for.

Booker didn't say much but usually only grunted responses to questions. But he was good at busting heads, all right. And that's what Del Norte, with its steadily rising crime rate, needed.

At least, two railroads hadn't come to town, as they'd planned to. Both had been thwarted only a few miles outside of Del Norte due to corruption in both companies and right here in town.

None other than the town's former mayor, Charlie McQueen, had gone to federal prison when he'd been found guilty of conspiring with both railroads to cheat their investors. The railroads hadn't really been in competition, after all. They'd been in league with one another to cheat both companies' investors.

And Charlie McQueen was doing hard time now, turning large rocks into little rocks, because he'd conspired with both companies to not only cheat investors but to kidnap Vangie Mannion and lure Bloody Joe, who'd gotten savvy to the mayor's and the railroads' devilish scheme, into a deadly whipsaw.

Thus, Del Norte was railroad-free and, unlike most businessmen in the area, Bloody Joe was happy about that. He'd been a town tamer in enough towns to know that the coming of a railroad turned even the most formerly peaceful towns into Sodoms and Gomorrahs.

Henry glanced up at the angle of the sun now and turned to Rio, still gazing after the jail wagon, and said, "Hey, Rio—what time you got?"

The older deputy plucked his old, dented turnip out of a vest pocket, opened it, and said, "Five minutes after five o'clock." He narrowed a cagey eye. "Why—you got somewhere you gotta be, lover boy?"

"*Five after five?*" He'd been so distracted by the jail wagon and the two deputy U.S. marshals that Henry had plum forgotten he'd been supposed to meet Molly out at Burial Rock Creek over a half hour ago. "Ah, heck!" he said, and ripped Banjo's reins from the hitchrack fronting the jailhouse.

He turned the coyote dun out into the street and fairly leaped into the saddle. "Be seein' you fellas! I'll be back in two shakes of a whore's bell!"

Or somewhere thereabouts, he thought as he booted the dun into a hard gallop, leaning forward over the horse's poll and pulling his hat brim down low over his eyes.

When the outlying shacks and stock pens of Del Norte slid back behind them, he and Banjo fairly tore up the trail. A quarter mile from town, he eased the dun into a lope. Fifteen minutes later, Henry swung the horse onto a secondary trail angling off the main trail's right side. Five minutes after that, he reined up near the old, sprawling cottonwood that stood back from the deep, dark pool in which Henry and Molly used to swim together, frolicking like forest sprites here in the cottonwoods, aspens, and scattered pines.

"Molly?" Henry called, looking around.

Oh, no, he thought. *She probably got tired of waiting for me and rode back to town.*

But, no. If she'd done that, he'd have met her on his way out here.

Henry rode Banjo around the clearing between the pool and the cottonwood, leaning out from his saddle, gazing at the ground. He picked up the tracks of a horse that had ridden into the clearing the same way Henry had, from the direction of the main trail. He picked up the tracks of another horse that had ridden into the clearing from the opposite direction of the main trail, from upstream.

Both horses had left the clearing together, staying close to the stream, following it downstream to the main trail, where the trail crossed the stream via a rickety wooden bridge.

He followed these tracks and, gaining the main trail, paused and stared northward, frowning curiously, worry building inside him.

"Now, who in holy blazes had Molly met out here?" the deputy asked himself aloud as the dun's hooves drummed across the bridge. "And why had they headed north together?"

Henry gazed down at the tracks on the north side of the bridge.

The two sets of tracks were so close together that it appeared one horse had been led by the other.

Which meant Molly had likely been taken against her will.

"That tears it," Henry said, casting his gaze northward once more. He booted Banjo into another hard run. "Let's go, Banjo. *Hy-ahhh, boy*!"

CHAPTER 24

ULYSSES LODGE GRUNTED HIS SHOCK AT FEELING THE maw of Mannion's Yellowboy pressed up taut against the back of his neck, just above the collar of his stinky buffalo hide coat. The man's shoulders tightened.

"Hold still or I'll drill a pill through your neck."

Mannion reached down and pulled the man's Colt from under the right flap of the man's coat and tossed it away. He felt around for the man's knife, found it on the other side of his shell belt from his pistol, slid it from its sheath, and tossed that away, too.

"Now, pull your hands away from the rifle. Leave it right where it is. Just pull your hands away."

Lodge opened both his paw-like, gloved hands.

The rear stock of the rifle dropped to the ground, the barrel coming up to smash against the man's mouth. Lodge jerked his head back, gave another grunt.

"Raise your hands," Mannion said, shuffling back away from his quarry. "One move for the rifle, and I'll shoot you through the back. Break your spine. Leave you right here, paralyzed, waiting for the wolves to clean your bones after dark."

"Go to hell," Lodge said in his deep, gravelly voice.

But he raised his hands a little higher than his shoulders, palms out.

"Now, stand up...real sloww," Joe said, aiming the Yellowboy straight out from his right shoulder, training the barrel at the back of the big man's head. Tight curls of shaggy, gray-flecked, cinnamon hair tufted out from beneath the man's hat. The curls were greasy and speckled with dust and weed seeds. The man himself smelled like how Joe imagined a bear would smell fresh out of hibernation in the spring.

Lodge drew up his right knee. He planted his right elbow on that knee and slowly rose, grunting and grumbling, pulling up the left knee, then, as well.

When he stood facing away from Joe, looking out over the trail from which he'd intended to scour his hunter, Mannion said, "Turn around slow. The key here is *slow*, Lodge. I have my finger drawn back so tight against this trigger that for the life of me I can't figure out why you're not down and howling yet."

It was a true statement.

He wasn't sure why he hadn't shot the man yet.

He kept seeing Jane lying there in the doctor's bed, her face as pale as the sheets around her, and did not know how he'd kept himself from drilling a bullet through Lodge's thick hide by now. He'd wanted to take him alive, but he'd honestly not believed he'd be able to do so.

Part of him hoped Lodge made a move on him so he could drill the man in the guts, leave him here, writhing and howling. Leave him here for the wolves and bears and other carrion eaters to finish him.

Lodge shifted his high-topped moccasin-clad feet until he stood facing Mannion, hands still raised a little higher than his broad shoulders, fingers halfway curled inwards toward his palms.

God he was big. Big and ugly.

Joe at six foot four didn't have to look up at many men, but he had to look up at Lodge. He felt small as he stood in this man's shadow angling across him. Half-man, half-bear. He looked like the offspring of one of those wild creatures the old mountain men claimed to have seen—half-man, half-beast, walking upright, faces with generally human features, but with long hair and hair all over their bodies.

The wild man, the old salts had called the inexplicable beast.

Lodge could be the offspring of one of those.

Only, Lodge was human enough to be truly foul.

As if to validate Mannion's estimation of the half-man, half-beast before him, Lodge smiled, showing his crooked, rotten teeth. A jeering grin, for sure. Blood oozed from the cut on his lower lip from when the barrel of his rifle came up to smash him in the mouth.

"Hi, Bloody Joe. Figgered we'd meet up again sooner or later. How's your head?" His smile broadened. "How'd you like what I did to that girl?"

That mocking twinkle in the beast's eyes fanned the flames of rage burning inside Mannion. He wanted to smash the butt of his Winchester against the man's face, to break his jaws. He wanted to ram it into Lodge's belly, knock the wind out of him. He wanted to drill a .44-round into each of the man's knees.

Sheer will kept him from doing so.

He knew if he started, he wouldn't be able to stop.

He wanted the man to die slow. He wanted, ideally, to haul him back to Del Norte, to lock him up in the basement cellblock to wait out the days or weeks it would take for the circuit court judge to ride up from Salida, to doom the man to the gallows, and for Lodge to await and ponder that grisly end.

Second by second, minute by minute, hour by hour...

Could Mannion do that?

He wasn't sure. He'd try. For Jane's sake. She deserved the finest edged revenge. Of course, he was taking a chance that Lodge, as savvy a character as Mannion had ever known, might get away from him. But sore head and all, he was up for the challenge.

Mannion took another step back and to one side, keeping the Yellowboy aimed at Lodge's face. "Over there...to your gear. Nice and slow."

The big man shrugged then spat a wad of chaw onto a rock to his left. "All right, Joe. Whatever you say," he said with forced agreeableness.

Mannion kept a good seven feet behind the man as they walked Indian file back through the rocks toward Lodge's gear. Joe kept out of range of the man's long, thick arms, knowing from experience that while Lodge was as large a man as Mannion had ever known, he could move as quickly and with the agility of a mountain lion.

Yeah, he was taking a chance, taking him alive. But he wanted the man to pay top dollar for what he'd done to Jane.

He'd likely killed her though Mannion made a conscious effort not to think about that possibility now, as he'd been trying to do over the many long days he'd been ghosting her shooter's trail. Must be well over a week now. He'd been so intent on tracking his quarry he'd lost track of the days.

"Stop," Joe ordered when the dead painter, the mounded gray ashes, the coffeepot, and the rest of the man's gear shifted into place ahead of him. "On your knees, Lodge."

Lodge chuckled then got down on his knees. Mannion walked around in front of him, keeping the Yellowboy aimed at the man's broad, sun-darkened forehead. He reached around behind him for his handcuffs, dropped them into the sand and gravel between the big man's knees.

"Put those on nice and tight. Let me hear 'em click."

Lodge held the cuffs up in front of him. He closed the right one around his right wrist until it clicked. He was about to do the same to the left wrist, but Joe stopped him with, "Uh-uh. Behind your back."

Lodge looked up at him, one eye narrowed. He shrugged again, grinned, showing all those sickly-looking teeth, then slid his hands around behind his back. Mannion stepped to one side and watched the man close the second cuff around his left wrist until it clicked, locked.

Mannion smiled.

He walked around behind the man, fished the rope from the inside pocket of his coat, shoved Lodge belly down in the sand and gravel and went to work, tying his feet together and then tying both tied feet to his cuffed wrists, effectively hogtying him.

By the time he finished, Lodge was no longer grinning.

That made Joe smile.

Then he stepped up into the rocks until he had a good view of the valley below, stuck two fingers in his mouth, and whistled for his horse.

———

A HALF HOUR LATER, HE HAD LODGE'S BIG STEELDUST saddled and Lodge sitting in the leather, hands cuffed behind his back, ankles tied to each other beneath the horse's broad belly. He'd tied the bounty hunter's bedroll over the man's saddlebags behind him.

From Lodge's stolen stash, he'd taken what trail supplies he'd thought he'd need for the journey back to Del Norte. Those supplies he and Lodge would carry on their own horses. He didn't want to fool with a packhorse, so he left the Quarter Circle Six mount unsaddled. It would likely eventually find its way back to its home ranch.

As they climbed up out of the valley, Mannion retracing his steps, relieved to have the long hunt finally over, a long, shrill, snarling cry sounded from somewhere up the forested slope above him, on his left.

Painter, Mannion knew. Nothing else made a sound like that.

Joe halted Red to scan the forested ridge. The pines and aspens were too thick for him to see more than a couple of dozen yards up the slope.

Mannion glanced over his left shoulder at his prisoner. "The mate to that wildcat you killed?"

Lodge didn't say anything. He just gazed up the ridge, one eye narrowed to a slit. He had a look of deep consternation on his bear-like features.

Mannion chuffed a wry laugh and booted Red on ahead along the narrow, meandering trail. But that painter's angry, snarling whine echoed in his ears, touching him with a cold hand of apprehension.

It was midafternoon, but Joe wanted to travel as far as he could before it was too dark to travel further. He and Lodge rode for two and a half hours before gathering clouds had formed a steel-gray lid over the valley they were in, and the night's darkness was spilling down from the western ridges. Thunder rumbled distantly as Mannion cut his charge down from his saddle and got him situated in a rocky nest beneath the overhang of a steep, stone ridge.

He forced him to sit Indian style then bound his ankles and looped a rope from his ankles around his neck, and slipknotted it. Thus, bound and with his hands cuffed behind his back, Lodge was going nowhere.

Mannion unsaddled and tended both horses, graining and watering them and giving them each a good rubdown. He hobbled Red and Beast just down the slope from Mannion's and Lodge's camp, in a well-sheltered notch encircled by large boulders, with only narrow gaps between them. The mounts would be sheltered by the outward slanting ridge wall from the coming rain as well as from the brunt of the wind and possibly hail Mannion knew was coming, as well.

He gathered enough wood for the night and had a fire going, a pot of coffee steaming, before the rain came. He offered no coffee to his prisoner. Lodge would go without coffee, maybe only a little water to wash down a biscuit or two later. If Joe was feeling generous, that was. At the moment, he was not.

A thinner man than Lodge was now would hang for shooting Jane and killing the Witch's Chinese doxie.

Brooding, Mannion sipped his coffee and nibbled the last of his jerky from his own foodstuffs. He'd delve into Lodge's cache in the morning.

They sat there, Mannion on one side of the fire, facing out from the slanting ridge wall, Lodge on the other side of the fire, facing Joe. Neither man said a thing until they'd ridden out the storm, which was surprisingly brief, with neither snow nor hail, just a short-lived shower and some thunder and distant lightning.

Once the storm had rolled on and the low clouds had parted and drifted away on a cool, building wind that moaned in the crags towering over men and horses, a raking snarl sounded from a near ridge. Lodge lifted his chin from a short doze, opened his eyes, and gazed across the fire at his jailor.

He blinked once then fixed his animal eyes on his captor.

"Painter," he said. It was more of a grunt.

Inexplicably, he smiled.

Mannion was staring off into the thickening darkness relieved slightly by kindling stars, the apprehension of earlier building inside him.

The mate of the cat Lodge had killed had tracked them.

CHAPTER 25

THE NIGHT WORE ON.

Mannion wanted to sleep but every time his chin sank and slumber began to wash over him, he lifted his head abruptly as another snarling moan sounded from the forested mountain rising straight out from Mannion's position here at the base of the inward-slanting stone ridge.

Each time he was nudged out of a doze, he tossed a little more fuel on the fire, wanting to keep the flames built up. Like most wild animals, wildcats were repelled by fire.

To Joe's right, the two horses milled uneasily. Horses were afraid of painters more than any other creature save possibly grizzlies. Occasionally, Joe glanced down the slope on his right, into the nest of boulders to see the firelight glistening in the eyes of the mounts staring warily out in the direction from which the snarls had come.

Occasionally, Mannion glanced at his prisoner. Lodge didn't seem at all disturbed by the puma's presence on that ridge on the far side of the rock-strewn canyon.

Hard to tell what the big man was thinking. Wild animals were easy. But wild animal mixed with a man was a real challenge.

If Mannion fathomed to guess, the man was pleased at the fear he sensed in his captor. Joe Mannion wasn't afraid of many things, but he'd tangled with enough wildcats to know they were nothing to tangle with. Them and grizzlies. Yeah, he had a healthy fear of such beasts.

After another long silence issuing from that far ridge rising in the star-capped darkness, Mannion again felt his chin sagging. His hands started to go numb around the Winchester he held across his knees. Sleep, like a deep shadow, stole over him. He'd just heard himself snore when that long, tooth-gnashing, grating wail rose from the opposite ridge once again, louder than before.

Mannion jerked his chin up with a gasp, closing his gloved hands around the Winchester on his knees. Flushing with embarrassment at his unseemly reaction, he glanced to his left again, across the glowing coals of the near-dead fire. Enough shifting, umber light delineated his prisoner's bearded features with his animal-flat, deep-set eyes that he could see the man was smiling as before.

Joe wasn't sure why, but Lodge's odd reaction to the nearness of a beast that could pounce and kill so quickly aggravated his own unease. Then it occurred to him that the man wasn't smiling at his captor's unease. At least, that wasn't the only thing he was smiling about. No, Lodge was smiling because he welcomed the possible death at the razor-edged claws and fangs of a wildcat as opposed to the long, lingering death his human captor intended for him.

Yeah, that was it.

Trussed up as he was, Lodge was defenseless. The cat

would likely kill him quick. If Mannion got him back to Del Norte in one piece, Lodge would have several weeks to consider his forthcoming dance at the end of the hangman's rope. Several weeks to hear the pounding of the hammers knocking the scaffold together in the lot beside Hotel de Mannion.

Lodge would far prefer to have his life end here, tonight, by a beast he probably felt more of a kinship with than he did his fellow human campmate.

The horses had stirred frenetically at the cat's last snarl and shuffled their hobbled feet uneasily. Then they'd gradually quieted down. But now, as Mannion tossed a couple of more stout branches on the fire, they started their fearful commotion once more, whickering loudly, swishing their tails, turning to stare across the canyon toward the ridge rising on the other side of it.

"What's that all about?" Joe heard himself mutter aloud, staring in the same direction as the horses, feeling a chill witch's hand of fear splay its fingers across his back, between his shoulder blades.

He looked toward the horses. One set of eyes stared out toward him, reflecting the orange firelight. The horse was *staring* out beyond him, toward a clump of trees lining a creek on his far left, maybe fifty yards away. The horse—Red, Joe saw now—whickered deep in his chest and pawed at the ground with both hobbled front feet.

Mannion switched his gaze back toward the stunt cedars and aspens rising on the far side of the creek. Had the painter made its way along the horseshoe-shaped ridge and then down through the rocks to the creek? As if in response to his silent question, a rock went rolling down that distant ridge, making distance-muffled clattering sounds before thumping up against a tree on the far side of the creek.

Joe glanced at Lodge. The bounty hunter was staring toward those trees silhouetted in the darkness, some of the leaves reflecting the silver light of the stars twinkling over the canyon. Lodge was smiling. It wasn't a happy, delighted smile. It was a pleased smile.

His end was coming. The cat would cheat the hangman.

"Not if I have anything to say about it," Mannion said, grunting as he heaved himself to his feet and loudly racked a cartridge into his Yellowboy's breach.

Behind him, the horses continued to stir, now with even more excitement than before.

The cat was moving closer. Steadily closer to the fire, toward the scent of the man it knew—maybe had even watched—kill and butcher its mate.

"Sit tight, Lodge," Mannion said, holding the Winchester up high across his mackinaw-clad shoulders as he moved off into the darkness, following the curve of the ridge toward the trees fluttering their leaves on the far side of the creek. "We'll be getting some good shuteye in no time."

"Careful, Bloody Joe," Lodge called behind him in his strange, at once singsong and guttural voice, the voice of an animal that was only half man. "I piss-burned her good."

"Yeah, well, she's piss-burning me," Joe said, weaving his way around tufts of evergreen shrubs and rocks, making his way toward the creek.

The ground sloped down toward the cut in which the creek meandered.

Mannion stopped at the top of the cut and looked down at the water, lightly windswept and glittering like a snakeskin in the starlight. He could smell the sickly-sweet smell of something feral, not at all unlike the smell of Lodge himself. The smell was coming from the other side of the creek, maybe in the trees stippling the opposite bank and which at this altitude, were nearly all bare except for a few conifers scattered among the aspens.

Mannion looked up the slope behind him. He could see the fire's dull glow reflecting off the rock wall behind Lodge, to the right of where Joe had corralled the horses. In haste to go after the cat, he'd forgotten to add more wood to the fire, to keep the beast away from both his prisoner and the horses.

Damn.

Don't cheat the hangman, Joe.

He gave a dry chuckle and then looked around, looking for a way down into the twelve-foot-deep cut that wouldn't turn his ankle. He walked upstream to his right a few yards, to where the bank wasn't as steep as where he'd just come from, and started down, holding the Winchester in his right hand, his left arm out for balance.

He gained the bottom of the cut easily then forded the shallow stream via rocks, slipping off one rock and dampening his right boot and part of his trouser cuff. He cursed then stopped when he gained the stream's opposite side and then stared up at the opposite bank.

He shuttled his gaze to the trees on his left. They sloped down from higher up on the opposite ridge. A breeze swept down from the ridge, touching Mannion's nose again with the smell of a wild thing.

Mannion raised the Yellowboy to his shoulder aimed along the barrel, sliding the barrel among the trees, hoping to pick out a target among the branches silhouetted against the starlit slope behind them.

"Where are you, lady?" Joe muttered.

He moved to his right, keeping the rifle aimed up at the trees, looking for the large dark clump of the cat perched in one of the branches, awaiting its stalker. Cats were smart. It had likely spied Mannion moving down the slope in its direction; she knew he was coming for her.

The snarls had been meant to lure him in...

Cats could be that smart.

Mannion continued walking slowly along the shore of the murmuring creek, aiming up at the trees stippling the bank above him. He took another step...another...and another.

He stopped.

Two dull yellow lights shone in the darkness roughly halfway up a stout-trunked, lightning-topped cedar. The lights went out and came on again as the cat blinked. The eyes lifted and starlight glinted off the two large, savagely downcurved fangs as the great beast opened its jaws and sent an eardrum-rattling snarl echoing across the canyon.

Mannion froze as the shock waves of the cat's sudden appearance and then its spine-crackling roar rolled through him. He drew the Winchester's hammer back and fired.

Too late.

The black mass of the cat had leaped quickly from the branch it had been perched on and into a snag of willows and evergreen shrubs fifteen feet to the left of the cedar, lifting a great thrashing and an angry moaning sound. Ejecting the spent cartridge and pumping a fresh one into the Yellowboy's action, Mannion ran downstream, aiming the Yellowboy up toward the shrubs he'd seen the cat leap into.

Without a certain target, he fired once, twice, three times, quickly pumping the cocking lever.

A great cry vaulted out away from the left side of the shrubs and then Mannion saw the big, square head with the laid-back ears and the two yellow eyes. He fired one eye blink before the cat leaped from its perch at the edge of the bank, his slug plowing into the ground where the cat had just been before it stretched its body out into a high arc ahead and above Mannion.

Joe watched in terror as the body with its arching tail and widening jaws and two glowing eyes plunged toward him, the cat's head and shoulders smashing into his own head and shoulders just as he got another round racked into the Yellowboy's action. The cat slammed him onto his back in the stream behind him, the back of his head glancing off a half-submerged stone. He lay dazed and grinding his teeth against a new orchestra of pain kicking up off-key music between his ears.

Instinctively, he reached for the Yellowboy that had fallen into the creek beside him, just before the cat had leaped off of him with a continuous, angry groan issuing up from deep in its chest.

As the great cat splashed across the creek, Mannion sat up and turned, swinging the Yellowboy around. The cat was a long, leaping silhouette bounding up the embankment. Joe aimed quickly and fired, evoking a shrill snarl from the beast just before the cat cleared the lip of the bank and lunged away, gone.

Mannion cursed then planted the butt of the Winchester in the stream, using the long gun to hoist himself up out of the water. He ran stumbling across the stream then, using the Yellowboy again, scrambled and hoisted his way to the top.

He stared up the slope toward the camp. Only a very dull glow there now. The fire was all but out.

As Mannion stumbled into a shambling run, Lodge's burly voice called out, "She's comin' for me, Joe! She's a comin'!"

Mannion couldn't see the cat in the darkness, but he could hear the thumps of its padded feet, the air raking in and out of its great lungs, the enraged snarling issuing continuously from its throat.

A guttural laugh vaulted out from the base of the ridge wall ahead and above Mannion. "She's almost here, Joe, an'—boy, oh, boy—does she have a mad-on!"

CHAPTER 26

Henry checked Banjo down suddenly.

The dun's heels kicked up dust as they skidded along the trail horse and rider had been following for the past half hour out from Burial Rock Creek.

The autumn sun had tumbled beyond the western ridges, there was only a little orange light left over there, and night was closing fast. He had to lean out far from his saddle and squint his eyes to see where the two horses he'd been following, one trailed by the other, slanted off the trail's west side. Henry straightened in his saddle and stared off in that direction, noting some broken country that way—dikes, haystacks, buttes, and mesas across whose slanting tables shadows were stretching long and fast.

Somewhere out in those buttes—the Heathcliff Buttes, they were called, after a pair of brother prospectors named Heathcliff—a lone coyote yammered.

Behind Henry rose the mournful calls of a dove.

Molly's captor was leading her into that broken country. At least, whoever had taken Molly wasn't heading straight on into the Sawatch. At least not yet. It appeared they must be intending on stopping for the night, maybe intending to make camp in that busted up terrain dead ahead, where the Heathcliff brothers had made a go of it once, long ago, and had failed.

Henry had pushed Banjo as hard as he could and, doing so, he'd closed the gap between Molly and her captor just enough that a few times, from the tops of high hills, he'd been able to make out their distant silhouettes on the trail ahead of him. Molly's captor was pushing his own and Molly's horses hard.

Why?

Where were they heading?

Who was that person on the horse ahead of Molly?

And just what in holy blazes was this all about?

Part of him knew, of course. He wasn't an idiot. The part that knew, however, was being suppressed by the part of him that refused to believe that Grace Hastings had anything to do with abducting Molly.

If he really thought it through, though, he knew that logic would indicate otherwise. Molly had intended to meet Henry to explain her warnings about Grace.

"...she's playing you like a finely tuned fiddle!"

Had Grace ridden out to Burial Rock Creek to keep Molly from explaining those warnings?

But how would Grace even know they'd planned to meet?

When Henry's mind perused such quiet, half-conscious mutterings, it flashed on those moccasins that had been on the floor of Grace's cabin when she'd been waiting for him in the open doorway, after he'd discovered that Molly had been the one peeping through the window at them. His mind's eye also flashed on the perspiration he'd seen glistening on Grace's forehead and above her rich upper lip.

Had she followed Henry following Molly then hurried back to the cabin ahead of Henry?

Gazing in frustration now across the sage-carpeted open ground between himself and those first buttes, dikes, and mesas all peppered with pines, cedars, and autumn-changing aspens, he muttered, "Time to find out."

He whipped the rein ends against Banjo's right hip.

Horse and rider went galloping off across that darkening plain, though Henry had to slow the mount down to make it easier for him to follow the two pairs of horse tracks, as with each minute that passed, the light grew weaker and weaker, and he had trouble picking them out of the sage and the hard ground pushing up small tufts of wiry, brown needlegrass. There was only a little green light left in the sky when, another half hour after he'd left the main trail, he hunkered low atop a rock-strewn dike, holding a spyglass to his right eye.

His hat was on the ground beside him.

In the night's near total silence save an occasional, vagrant breeze and the screech of a hunting nighthawk, he could hear Banjo cropping the autumn-cured grass down the slope behind him.

Sixty yards ahead of him and maybe a hundred feet below, a fire glowed in the gap between two forested mountain ridges. He could make out the silhouettes of several people milling about the fire, some gesticulating wildly, as though angry. He thought at least one of those silhouettes formed the shape of a woman.

Grace?

He thought he could make out the movement of horses picketed in the trees on the other side of the fire, beyond the human figures.

He couldn't see Molly.

She had to be down there, though.

And Henry had to spring her from whatever devil's nest she'd landed in.

And he needed to know why Grace had taken her in the first place.

He reduced the spyglass, slipped it into its doeskin sheath, and let it hang from its thong around his neck. He donned his hat, crabbed back away from the lip of the dike, then rose and hurried back to Banjo. He took up the dun's reins, swung into the leather, and booted the mount halfway down the dike before turning him hard right and following a little, rocky cut down to a crease and then up the forested ridge beyond, angling north, in the general direction of the camp and the fire lying in the gap at the ridge's base.

He rode high on the ridge so the crackling of Banjo's hooves in the forest duff wouldn't be heard from below. He was glad the wind was out of the southwest, so the horses of those around the fire wouldn't wind him and Banjo and alert their riders.

If the female form was Grace down there, the riders would have to be the men led by Vince Chaney—Shane Nordstrom, Lonnie Russell, and Dutch Deering. Henry couldn't believe he was actually considering that possibility, but who else could it be? They were the only men he'd ever seen in Grace's company, not that she'd seemed all that happy about it.

When he figured he was roughly straight above the campfire, he stopped Banjo and tied him to some shrubs before unsheathing his Winchester carbine.

"Stay, boy," Henry said quietly, knowing the command wasn't needed since he'd tied the mount, but his nerves were on edge and the words had slipped out of him unconsidered.

He couldn't wrap his mind around any of this...

Holding the Winchester low, he descended the slope which was so steep in places he had to slow his pace and descend it sideways, grabbing tree branches to break his descent. When he'd dropped down the slope maybe fifty yards, he started to see the fire's glow below him and to his right.

He angled toward it, moving slowly down the steep slope, his feet sometimes sliding in the sand and gravel so that he reached out for low branches to break his fall.

When he was close enough to the camp that he could start to hear voices pitched in angry tones and frustration and see cinders from the fire rising before turning black and disappearing against the velvet darkness of the sky, he moved up behind a pine and dropped to one knee.

The camp was nearly directly below him now, maybe twenty feet out from the base of the slope he was on.

Men's voices grew clearer until he could hear one man—he thought it was the hard-eyed, temperamental rascal, Shane Nordstrom, grate out the end of an angry sentence with, "...your own damn fault, Grace. Why in the hell did you to have to romance the damn deputy, anyway? If you hadn't—"

"Oh, shut up, Shane!" Grace said, though it didn't really sound like her voice at all. It sounded like the hard, angry voice of a cold, cunning, and very frustrated woman. "I told you why I did it. I did it because I thought it would be better to have the law on my side rather than against me, in case anyone found out who I was. Who I was related to. You men didn't help any—showing up when you did and all but telling him about the loot!"

Grace, standing to the right of the fire, clad in a skirt and blouse and a heavy, black shawl with the hood up, swung around to gaze down at the person sitting back against the base of a leafless aspen, her hands tied behind her back, her ankles—*Molly's* ankles—tied before her.

"We have bigger fish to fry," Grace added.

"Oh, God," Molly moaned, slowly wagging her green-hatted head. "Oh, jeepers, jeepers, jeepers." She looked up at Grace with beseeching eyes. "Whatever you do to me, just please don't hurt Henry!"

Standing on the other side of the fire from Grace and Molly, Vince Chaney mocked the girl. "Whatever you do to me, just please don't hurt Henry!"

The hardcase leaped in the air, giving a bizarre, mock pirouette, then turned and raised his hands to his downcast face and gave a poor imitation of a girl crying. "Boo-hoo-hooooo!"

Shane Nordstrom stood beside him. The other two men, the wiry blonde, Lonnie Russell, and the short, stocky redhead, Dutch Deering, sat on a log to their left, Deering holding a bottle between his spread knees.

"I say we kill her right now and get it over with," Shane said, showing his teeth as he glared across the fire at Molly. "We're gonna have to sooner or later. What in hell are we waiting for?"

Grace turned to him sharply. "No killing!" She switched her gaze to Chaney and added, "I will not be involved in murder!"

"Well, what the hell we gonna do with her?" Lonnie Russell said from his perch on the log. "If we let her go, she's gonna go back to town and blab about us an' the loot!"

"So far, there's only us," Grace said. "There isn't any loot. At least, not yet. There may never be any loot. I'm only going on a hunch that that map Casey drew will ever lead us to it!"

"What if it does?" Shane said.

Grace shrugged a shoulder and stared into the fire. "We'll cross that bridge when we come to it."

Dutch Deering took a long pull from his bottle then lowered it, sighed, belched, and said, "Don't matter if there is or is not any loot. You, dear Grace, took the girl. That's kidnapping. Now, bringing her out here where we've been toiling nigh on two weeks now, looking for the loot, you've involved us in that kidnapping."

He thumbed himself in the chest with the hand holding the bottle. "I for one don't intend on spending another seven years in that federal hot house. If we don't kill the girl, she's gonna go back to town and tell that *Marshal Bloody Joe Mannion*, no less, what happened, and Bloody Joe's gonna come gunnin' fer us!"

"I won't!" Molly yelled. She looked from Grace to Chaney to Nordstrom and then to the other two men. "I promise I won't mention a word! Oh, please, believe me!"

"Oh, please believe me!" Chaney mocked her.

"You go to *hell*!" Molly bellowed at him, jutting her head and chin out and deepening her voice. "I've taken all the mockery from you I'm going to take, you...you... slimy old scalawag!"

Henry had to chuckle inwardly at that but then he tensed when Chaney glared at her then moved slowly around the fire toward her, cat-like, unholstering one of the two six-shooters holstered on his hips.

Henry heard the ratcheting click as he cocked the piece, holding it straight down at his side but keeping his cold, hard gaze on Molly. "I do believe I'm gonna claim the honors of silencing this little, starch-drawered ringtail."

Grace stepped in front of him, placing her hands on the man's chest. "No, Shane, please. You promised me...

when I told you about the map I found in the Bible...you promised me that there would be no killing involved. No matter what happened."

Chaney looked at her. "I lied, Grace."

He brusquely swept her aside with one arm. Grace gasped as she stumbled back away from him. Chaney took another step toward Molly and raised the pistol at Molly.

"No, no, no!" Henry said, snapping his Winchester to his shoulder and drawing the hammer back to full cock. "Hold it right there, dammit. I got you all dead to ri... ri...*riiiightttss*!"

As he rose from his knee, the boot he planted against the slope slid out from beneath him. The ground came up to smash without mercy against his back and the back of his head.

The air left his lungs with a single *WHUFF!*

The Winchester went flying out of his hands as though plucked from his fingers by God's own will.

And then he was rolling...rolling...rolling down the belly of the slope, the fire and the four men and one woman and Molly gawking up at him, eyes wide, lower jaws hanging slack, becoming clearer and clearer as they grew closer...and closer...and closer.

He glimpsed his Winchester sliding down the slope beside him, vibrating, firelight glinting off the bluing, kicking up sand and gravel in its wake. He tried to reach for it in vain.

He slammed against the bottom of the slope, belly down, and lay still, the wind knocked out of him.

He groaned and rolled onto his back.

Four rifle maws stared down at him, black and round.

So did the four faces of the hardcases—Chaney, Nordstrom, Russell, and Deering.

Crunching footsteps grew louder.

Then Grace stared down at him. She shook her head once, fatefully, and said, "Henry, you damn fool!"

Raking air in and out of his battered lungs, Henry smiled. "Nice seein' you, too, Grace. Just thought maybe you'd read me a chapter of *Ivanhoe's* all."

CHAPTER 27

Up the dark hill beyond Mannion a great snarl fairly exploded out of the mountain wall a hundred yards away and hidden by the nearly complete darkness now that the fire had died. The snarl came roaring back at the lawman, a veritable freight train of sound as it echoed off that velvet-black bastion blotting out the stars.

A man's bellowing wail joined that of the cat, filling Mannion's head with the din. He set his jaws hard against it as he ran stumbling over rocks and brush tufts until his right boot hooked a rock. He grunted loudly as that foot was kicked out from beneath him and he struck the ground hard on his head and chest.

"Oh, *hell!*"

His temple had still grieved him but now that grief rose to another crescendo, knocking him half unconscious and causing him to grind his teeth against the agony. That railroad spike of misery he'd felt when he'd first been brained had gotten just a little duller and rustier as it once again probed his tender brain plate.

He couldn't hear the cat's snarl and the man's wail from above and ahead of him for the tolling of cracked bells in his own head. The night was alive with the tolling of those bells and the searing misery in his head as well as his urgent need to continue up the slope to the camp.

He writhed on his back and then, summoning strength and doing his best to suppress the misery, he gave a great bellowing wail of his own as he heaved himself onto his belly. He gave another wail and bellowed a curse as he pushed up onto his hands and feet. As he did, he felt reverberations through the ground beneath him and thought he heard the clatter of horse hooves on rock.

He looked around for his rifle, saw the glint of starshine off steel, then picked up the Yellowboy and brushed the sand and dirt from its frame. He drew a deep breath and continued up the slope, moving more slowly now, frowning curiously.

Aside from the continued ringing in his ears, the night had fallen silent.

Eerily silent.

The silence of a crypt.

He knew what happened. At least, he thought he knew.

The big cat had killed its supper and was likely feeding up there to the right of the dead fire—wherever it was. It was so dark now he couldn't make out a thing up there against the velvet-black backdrop of sheer, stone ridge.

He slowed his pace and levered a cartridge into the Yellowboy's action. He aimed the gun straight out from his right hip, thumb caressing the cocked hammer, index finger drawn taut against the trigger.

If the cat was feeding, it would be even more dangerous than before.

Mannion kept walking, one slowly, cautious step after

another, gazing into that darkness, looking for the two round, yellow lamps of the cat's eyes.

Nothing.

He couldn't hear anything, either. No snorting or snarling or the tearing sounds of fang and claw rending clothes and human flesh.

As he came within fifty yards of the mountain wall, he smelled the sickly-sweet odor of cat. Mannion couldn't hear or see the beast's moving shadow ahead of him, but he could smell it, all right.

Funny the horses weren't stirring in their makeshift, stone corral.

Mannion stopped, staring straight up the slope, close enough to the wall now that he could just make it out in the starlight. He swept the gravelly ground along the base of the wall, getting his bearings. He was several feet right of the camp. Between him and the ashes mounded in the fire ring, something large and irregularly shaped lay on the ground.

Lodge? What was left of him, anyway?

The smell of cat was still strong.

Mannion moved slowly over to the object in question, keeping his finger taut against the Yellowboy's trigger. The smell of cat grew stronger. Joe reached into a shirt pocket and fired a lucifer to life on his thumbnail, holding the match out in the night as deathly still and quiet as the inside of that crypt.

He saw what had caused the smell of cat grow stronger.

So strong that the stench was threatening to bring tears to his eyes.

The cat lay before him—a large, rumpled, fawn-colored rug.

The eyes shone in the light of the flickering match.

Blood glistened on its belly, which Joe could see part of, as the cat lay twisted on its left side. Two or three inches of pink tongue curled down over the side of the beast's half-open mouth.

"Good Lord," Mannion whispered, then dropped the match when the flame burned down to his fingers.

He looked around suddenly, fear causing those short hairs to stand up on the back of his neck.

Somehow, his prisoner had freed himself from the ropes and killed the cat. One of Mannion's bullets must have struck the puma, weakening it just enough that the big man-beast himself, Ulysses Lodge, had been able to get his cuffed hands around the cat's neck and either broke the neck or strangled the beast. Doing so, he'd likely broken the chain on the cuffs, freeing his hands.

Mannion swung around, tracking the shadows with the cocked Yellowboy, his heart drumming. He expected an attack from any quarter at any second. But then he remembered the reverberations he'd felt through the ground and the clacking of hooves on the stony ground.

He hurried over to where his and Lodge's gear was piled between the fire ring and the rock wall. *Had been* piled. Lodge's saddle and saddlebags were gone.

Heart beating still faster, Mannion lowered the Winchester and strode over to peer through a gap in the large rocks forming the makeshift corral. Both horses were gone. Lodge had quickly saddled his and ridden off but only after hazing Red away from the camp, prolonging the time it would take Mannion to get after him again.

Rage boiling over inside him, Mannion swung around and stomped an angry foot, threw his head back, and bellowed a curse at the stars.

The curse rocketed around the canyon, echoing.

After the last echo had dwindled to silence, a man's deep-throated, distant, self-satisfied laugh sounded from a high northwestern ridge.

Then silence reigned once more.

———

Something touched Mannion's cheek as he slept.

It was at once leathery and bristly.

"Go 'way," he heard himself mutter. "Go 'way...let a man sleep..."

A loud snort.

Joe grunted and half a blink later his Russian was in his hand and cocked. Red pulled his head back with a start, and whickered.

The horse regarded its rider dubiously from five feet away.

"Oh," Joe said, raising the Russian's barrel and depressing the hammer. "You, Red."

Mannion looked around. The sky was low and gray and a fine, granular snow was falling, the small flakes nudged this way and that by a cold breeze. It was well after dawn. The sun was up but remaining far behind the sky's low, gray lid.

Mannion shoved his pistol into the empty holster of the coiled shell belt beside him, on which both Russians and his bowie knife were sheathed and cursed again. He'd overslept. The braining he'd received last night after the one he'd received a few nights ago from Lodge had damn near done him in.

He'd needed that sleep.

Lodge had likely gotten good and far ahead of him, but Joe had needed that rest.

After last night's violence. After the last *several* nights of almost no sleep. He'd been pushing both himself and Red hard.

He felt like a damn fool.

"I shoulda shot that son of a bitch through the back of his neck when I had him dead to rights." He turned to Red, still regarding him dubiously, the horse's fine head lowered, the end of its snout three feet from Mannion's nose.

"Why didn't I? Huh, Red? Will you tell me that?"

He tossed his snow-dusted blankets back and heaved himself to his feet. Red backed away from him and shook his head.

"Yeah, I know, I know. I wanted the son of Satan to hang." Mannion started rolling his soogan. "Should've just shot him and headed back to Del Norte. Headed back to Jane." He pulled the leather thongs from his pants pocket and tied each to an end of his hot roll. "I can't ever do the easiest thing. Gotta make it double hard for myself."

He gritted his teeth and pressed the heel of his left, gloved hand to his left temple. "It's the brainings. I'm not thinking right." He chuckled dryly. "Who'm I trying to kid? I'm just vengeance hungry. I just want the sumbitch to pay in the worst way for taking Jane away from me."

He turned to Red again. "Isn't that a laugh, though, Red? Shit, I'm the one who let Jane get away. Maybe it's just easier to blame Lodge."

When the pain abated, he gathered the rest of his gear, saddled Red, hung his food-stuffed war bag from his saddle horn and, nibbling a piece of jerky, swung up into the saddle. He put the big bay down the slope then back onto the trail through thick forest that he and Lodge had taken into the canyon.

As he doubled back toward the formation where he'd hunted Lodge down, it occurred to him that maybe it wasn't really Ulysses Lodge he was hunting at all. No, no. Maybe he was hunting himself—leastways, the part of him he couldn't control.

The beast in him.

Mannion chuckled and wagged his head.

"Oh, Jesus," he said. "Those brainings really have made me squishy in my thinker box!"

Crossing a pass where the wind turned the granular flakes to hard pellets stinging his cheeks, he drew his hat down low on his forehead and booted Red into a lope down the pass's other side. "Come on, Red. We got some ground to cover!"

He didn't run the horse far, however. The higher they climbed into the mountains, nearing the formation where Mannion had run Lodge down, the harder it snowed, and small drifts were being shaped by the wind to angle across the trail like long pillows tapering at each end. Those drifts could be slippery or hiding a sharp rock that might damage one of the bay's hooves.

Mannion didn't need a lame horse.

His own foggy brain was enough of a handicap out here in the perilous, high-and-rocky country.

He stopped Red where he'd stopped him before, well south of the formation on which Lodge had holed up, intending to effect an ambush. Believing there was a possibility the bounty hunter might try the same play again—he'd have to climb up to his old position to gather the guns Mannion had taken off him and thrown into the rocks—Joe turned Red off the trail's right side, instead of the left side, as he'd done the previous day, then left the horse in a snag of snow-dusted pines and boulders.

He scouted the formation on foot, taking his time, knowing a bullet could come from any quarter. When he scouted the area where he'd left the bounty hunter's weapons, kicking the snow away, he found the guns and the man's bowie knife gone.

But there were plenty of large moccasin prints slowly being obliterated by the building wind.

Lodge had been here, all right.

And, judging by the tracks, he'd come and gone. However, he'd left a good bit of blood in the snow in the area from which he'd retrieved his weapons. Large droplets speckled the snow around the man's moccasin prints.

As Mannion inspected a few such droplets, he saw something poking up out of the snow. He plucked the thing out of the snow with his bowie knife and held it up to inspect it.

A bloody, half-frozen longhandle sleeve.

It was badly torn.

Likely by the cat's teeth or claws. The bounty hunter had cut it off and likely bathed the torn arm in the snow. There were plenty of gobs of bloody snow lying around.

"Ah," Mannion said, dropping the half-frozen sleeve. "So you're wounded, eh, big man?" Joe nodded slowly, pondering the information. "I see, I see."

He wasn't sure whose advantage that was.

Under normal circumstances, he'd consider it his.

Now he wasn't so sure.

As per his own daughter's sage observation, a spooked dog was a dangerous one. A wounded dog was even more dangerous.

Mannion managed to follow the man's shambling footprints to where Lodge had left his horse when he'd climbed the formation to retrieve his guns. Joe stared off along the trail Beast had made weaving through the pines as horse and rider had continued their journey north and east—likely heading toward Treasure Vault Lake and the Mountain of the Holy Cross.

Up there in those high, rocky, snowy reaches, the trail would end.

For one of them, at least.

Mannion stuck two fingers in his mouth and whistled for Red.

CHAPTER 28

HENRY MCCALLISTER FOUND HIMSELF STARING UP AT the four grim faces of the hardcases aiming down their rifles at his head. Grace stood a little off to one side, also staring down at him, incredulous.

"That's very funny," she said now in response to his quip about his having ridden out here to have her read a chapter of *Ivanhoe* to him. "The situation you find yourself in isn't one bit amusing, however."

Anger boiled up in Henry as he returned her glare. "What did you expect me to do when I didn't find Molly where we were supposed to—"

"Yeah, what'd you expect him to do?" Vince Chaney said, glancing at the woman standing to his right.

He was to the left of the others as Henry stared up at them, the hard-eyed tough nut, Shane Nordstrom, standing right of Chaney, then Dutch Deering and Lonnie Russell, respectively.

Chaney kept his own glowering stare on Grace. "Did you think he was just going to ride back to town and not try to track 'er." He slid his jeering gaze to Molly. "I mean, I would have. She's one cantankerous little ringtail—I'll give her that!"

"Shut up, brigand!" Molly intoned, jutting her chin up at the tall, lean, angular-faced man.

Grace raised her hands to her face and stared down at Henry with a look of deep consternation and exasperation. "I guess I didn't think it through very clearly." She swung around and walked a few steps away and then came back, lowering her hands and looking at Chaney. "Now, what are we going to do?"

"We have to kill them both," Nordstrom said matter-of-factly, keeping his own hard, black-eyed gaze on Henry. "There's no other way. They both know enough to be dangerous."

"Know about what?" Henry said, still feeling mostly in the dark. "I take it you're all out here looking for the loot Grace's brother took out of your camp that night." He switched his gaze back to Grace. "You really had me fooled, though, Grace. I have to admit. Molly was right. You *were* playing me like a finely tuned fiddle!"

"Oh, Henry—why did you have to come out here?" this from where Molly was tied to the tree to the left of the slowly dying fire. Her voice was high and pinched with emotion. "Now they're gonna kill you, too, and"—she hardened her voice as she shuttled her angry gaze to Grace—"all you were doing was spending time with who you thought was just an innocent, lonely lady schoolteacher. Hah!"

Chaney gave a dry chuckle as he reached down and pulled Henry's old Remington from its holster and tossed it into the brush. He picked up the Winchester, which lay several feet to Henry's right, and tossed that away, as well.

"Innocent, lonely lady, eh?" Chaney said, smiling jeeringly at Grace as he set his rifle on his shoulder. "You *was* playin' him like a fiddle, weren't you?" He glanced at the youngest member of the group—the skinny blonde man, Lonnie Russell, who was maybe in his late twenties while the others were in their thirties. The stocky redhead, Dutch Deering, could be in his forties. "Get some rope and tie him with the girl so we can keep a close eye on both of 'em."

Shane Nordstrom kept his hard-eyed gaze as well as his Winchester leveled on Henry. "Why keep wastin' time? We're gonna have to kill them both—the deputy and Miss Starchy Bloomers over there. Let's get it over an' done with!"

"Go to hell!" Molly screeched.

That made the men laugh.

As Lonnie Russell jerked Henry to a sitting position by his shirt collar, pulled his arms behind his back, and started to loop a rope around his wrists, Chaney shoved Nordstrom's rifle down with his right hand. "Now, now, now. What's the damn hurry, Shane? There might be another way."

"There has to be another way," Grace said, steepling her fingers beneath her chin. "I cannot and will not abide cold-blooded murder!" She stepped up close to the belligerent Shane Nordstrom and said, "Look, I didn't have to tell you men about that map I found in my Bible. But I did. Now, we have to go about this my way. We look for the loot and leave these two alive. Once we've found the loot, we can clear out of this country, leave a note in town informing the marshal where he can find them. By the time he finds them—"

"Hell, he'll come after us!" Nordstrom said, laughing without mirth as both Dutch Deering and Lonnie Russell prodded Henry over to the tree at which Molly was tied.

Deering shoved Henry down and proceeded to wrap the rope around Henry and Molly and the tree between them. "He's Bloody Joe Mannion!" Nordstrom continued. "He won't let us get away with the loot, not to mention kidnapping his own deputy and the kid's sweetheart!"

"Former sweetheart," Molly corrected him, her tone pitched with accusing.

That had been meant for Henry, he knew.

"I'm sorry, Molly," he said now while Shane and Vince continued to argue about his and Molly's fates. "You were right." He looked up at Grace who had turned to stare down at him, an expression of what appeared genuine contrition on her face.

It *appeared* genuine, but he now knew it was likely a lie. Like everything else about her. At least, regarding their relationship. She'd wanted to marry him, eh? Now he thought he was getting an inkling about why.

"She was playin' me like a finely tuned fiddle," he added, flaring a nostril at the woman.

Grace moved slowly toward him while Russell and Deering retook their places by the fire, Deering picking up his bottle and popping the cork.

"I have to admit," Grace said now, stopping only a few feet from where Henry's feet were tied together, extended straight out before him, "I had intended to use you to help me. You seemed nice enough when we met in the post office that day. I thought I could trust you."

"To do what?" Henry asked. "Help you find the loot?" He couldn't imagine what else she would have needed him for.

Grace nodded. "I knew I needed help. I couldn't find it on my own, much less get it out of the country by myself. You see, I found my brother's map quite by chance. He must have slipped it into our family Bible that night in Buena Vista, when he came to me for help. I found it a year ago. When I was flipping the pages, it fell out onto the floor—a crudely drawn, blood-stained map of a pocket of this area."

"That why you applied for the teaching job when Mrs. Bjornson retired? So you could move here and look for the gold?"

"Yes." Grace crossed her arms on her chest, leaned on a hip, and kicked one foot out, scowling down at him. "Don't judge me too harshly. I've worked a lot of years at my profession. My *best* years. The last one was up in Forsythe. Forsythe!"

It was high in the mountains above St. Elmo.

"The children didn't want to learn. Their parents only sent them to school because they misbehaved too badly or were too useless to keep them at home! So...sure, when I found that map, yes...I...I decided why *shouldn't* I look for the gold, try to improve my lot in life? The loot wasn't doing anyone any good, hidden away where Casey had stashed it!"

"And where is that?" Henry wanted to know.

"I don't know." Grace glanced at the men around her.

Chaney and Nordstrom had stopped arguing. Vince was pouring himself a fresh cup of coffee while Shane stood off in the shadows, looking ominous as he held his rifle up high across his chest, staring toward Henry and his fellow captive, Molly.

"The map is very crude," Grace continued. "Casey knew this area. I do not. He drew the map only to remind himself, it seems, of where he'd stashed the gold. I can't make heads or tails out of it. All I know is the cache lies somewhere north of Del Norte, along the main trail out of town."

"How'd you throw in with this bunch?" was another thing Henry wanted to know.

"They rode back to my place...the day they'd visited my cabin and found you there, as well."

Henry shot an indignant look at Chaney, who sat on a log, grinning, elbows on his knees, steaming tin cup in his hands. "I told you four to haul your freight!"

They all laughed.

Henry felt the flush of embarrassment and self-righteous indignation rise in his cheeks.

"We don't listen to no small-town law," Nordstrom bit out, his face hidden by the fire's dancing shadows. Chaney had added more wood to the flames, building them up.

"What can we say?" Chaney said, shrugging. "She needed someone's help. She thought she'd get it from you. But then she decided we might be more help to her." He shuttled his gaze to the teacher. "Didn't you, Grace?"

"I decided not to involve you, Henry. You're a good man. You need a better woman than the one I seem to have become." Grace swung around and kicked a rock. "Damn that map, anyway!" She pressed the heels of her hands against her temples again, slowly walking away from the tree to which Henry and Molly were tied. "It's caused me nothing but trouble."

She fired a hot glare at Vince and then at Shane. "It's caused me in my greedy desperation to throw in with just the kind of men I've spent most of my life avoiding! Men like my brother!"

Shane threw his head back and laughed. Henry could see the white line of his teeth in the darkness around his head though his eyes flashed malevolently in the firelight. The tough nut sobered abruptly and said, "Stow it, Teacher, or we'll cut you out."

"You will *not*!" Grace intoned taking three steps toward Nordstrom, fists clenched at her sides. "I had your word." She looked at Chaney. "I had *both* your words that we'd split that loot evenly among the five of us!"

Again, Nordstrom threw his head back and laughed his mocking laugh, apparently thoroughly satisfied with the teacher's struggle with her own morality...over what she'd previously believed her relationship with right and wrong had been. With the kind of *person* she was.

Suddenly, she was feeling unmoored. By right she should be, Henry thought.

At the same time, he couldn't help feeling a tad sorry for her. He'd believed her to be good, and he still did. She'd just had one hell of a large temptation laid before her when her brother's map fell out of that Bible.

Henry looked at her. His thoughts were churning. He needed to find a way to keep himself and Molly alive for as long as he possible could. "Why don't you let me take a look at the map?"

Grace turned to him. She and her four male cohorts all said at the same time, "*What?*"

Henry shrugged a shoulder. "I know the country. I know this gulch you're in. Used to fish a creek upcountry a ways and gentled horses for a rancher just up the creek and east, under Indian Butte. That's north of here. Close to the trail leading into the Sawatch and Cottonwood Pass. Since Casey was wounded when he hid that money, and likely in a hurry to get away from you four"—he glanced at Chaney and Nordstrom—"and to reach his sister's place, he'd have stashed that loot close to the trail. Prob'ly somewhere he'd holed up for a night."

The men and Grace shared conferring looks.

"Well?" Grace asked, finally, addressing Chaney, who appeared the brains of the bunch though Nordstrom was most definitely the muscle. "What do you think? We could spend the rest of our lives looking for that cache, given how little we have to go on from Casey's map. We need someone who might recognize some of the landmarks he drew."

Molly said on the other side of the tree from Henry, "My god, Henry—are you actually *seriously* considering throwing in with these people?"

"Why not?" Again, Henry shrugged a shoulder. He looked at Grace and then at Nordstrom, who he'd deemed, given the man's natural truculence, held Henry's and Molly's fates in his hands. He was ready to shoot them both and throw them to the wolves. "If you promise to let us live..."

A long silence as the men thought it over. Even Shane seemed to be considering it as he stared flatly at Henry. He now held the rifle, which only a few minutes ago he'd seemed on the verge of using, down low across his thighs.

Finally, Chaney sipped his steaming coffee and looked across the fire at Henry. "You know this country pretty well, eh?"

"Pretty well, yes."

Chaney looked at Nordstrom. Nordstrom looked back at him. He didn't say anything, but his silence must have been answer enough for Chaney, who turned back to Henry and said, "All right."

He tapped both his gloved thumbs against the rim of his steaming, tin cup. "If you can lead us to the cache, using Grace's map"—he lifted a hand to tap his right thumb against his coat over his left breast—"which I got right here, we'll turn you an' the girl free."

He glanced at the other three. "What do you think, boys? Fifty thousand in gold coins would be worth lettin' these two live—don't you think?"

Russell and Deering were staring at Shane. Now they smiled, shrewdly, with cold cunning that Henry could see right through—he hadn't just dropped off the turnip wagon. Lonnie Russell turned to Henry and Molly and said, "Why, sure, sure. That'd be worth keepin' em' alive—don't you think, Dutch?"

"Heck, yeah," the big, double-jowled redhead said, slowly swirling the contents of the bottle he held between his knees. "Heck, yeah," he repeated before glancing at Shane and adding, "Why not?"

Again, Shane didn't respond. He just stood staring at Henry.

"All right, then." Grace walked over to the fire and extended her open hand to Chaney.

Keeping his cunning gaze on Henry, Chaney reached into his shirt pocket and withdrew a ragged leaf of paper and set it in Grace's outstretched hand. She brought the paper over to Henry, dropped to a knee beside him, and held the note out before him, tipping it so that the orange firelight danced across the lined, badly stained, and rumpled page.

Henry gazed down at it.

There were several crudely drawn lines likely indicating land formations and one circle with spokes drawn through it. A wagon wheel? A heavy-winged black bird of some kind hovered over what appeared a small cabin at the base of what appeared a ridge, though the possible cabin had been so hastily and carelessly sketched it could be a stable or a small stock pen, as well.

Heck, it could be anything.

A circle with a thick X drawn through it lay to the right of the cabin or stock pen or whatever it was, with squiggly lines surrounding it. That must mark the location of the cache.

"I think I know where this place is," Henry said, his heart thudding anxiously with the lie. "It's just north a ways, tucked into some buttes. Hard to find, though. Little, abandoned ranch up thataways. Tomorrow, I'll show you."

He gave Grace a direct look, hoping like holy blazes she swallowed the lie.

She stared back at him, probing him with her own direct gaze.

The others stared at him, as well.

No one spoke. The fire snapped and crackled. A cool breeze made a low rushing sound in the grass surrounding the camp. A pine cone dropped from a near limb, making a soft thump in the brush.

"You might've bought you an' the girl a few hours, Deputy," Shane said in his cold, flat voice. "But I'll believe it when I see it."

"All right," Henry said, nodding equanimously. "That's fair."

His throat was as dry as dust and his hands, tied tightly behind him, were sweating.

On the other side of the tree, Molly made a sound that was half fateful sigh and half sob.

CHAPTER 29

Henry didn't sleep much.

At least, not during the first part of the night. He was too nervous.

Also, he kept trying to work loose the ropes tying his wrists together behind his back. He tried to be as inconspicuous as he could, because Vince Chaney arranged for himself and the other three men to take turns keeping watch. They were worried that when Henry didn't show back in Del Norte, Bloody Joe Mannion himself or one of the other two deputies might get suspicious and ride out looking for Henry.

Grace's cohorts were so preoccupied with the loot, stolen seven years previously, that they hadn't heard about the shooting of Miss Jane by the bounty hunting scoundrel, Ulysses Lodge, nor about the marshal having gone after the man, likely tracking him into the Sawatch Range. Grace herself had probably forgotten. No word had been heard from the infamous, notorious Marshal Mannion since he'd ridden out on his vengeance quest, horns sharpened.

Henry wasn't surprised the marshal had not returned to Del Norte. Lodge would be a wily foe even for the likes of Bloody Joe. Henry knew the marshal would track Lodge to the ends of the earth if he had to.

Henry saw no need to set the outlaws straight about the marshal's hunt. Let them worry about being tracked. That would keep them on edge. Men on edge often made mistakes.

The only problem was that one of the four men was awake all night, keeping the fire built up enough to keep the coffee warm. They likely would have done that anyway, though. At least, they tried to stay awake. Cutting several glances across his shoulder at the fire, Henry had seen each of them nod off a time or two, waking with starts when, in one case, a cigarette had burned to scorch Lonnie Russell's fingers or, in another case, when a coyote had given its mournful wail from a near ridge and Dutch Deering had jerked his bearded chin up off his chest and caused his hot coffee to slosh down the sides of his tin cup.

All four remained awake enough, occasionally scrutinizing their two prisoners, that Henry had to work as quietly and with as few movements as possible. Which meant he didn't make much headway against the ropes. Russell and Deering had tied the knots so tight that Henry couldn't have moved his wrists much even if he hadn't been under the outlaws' scrutiny.

He wasn't sure if Molly slept or not, over there on the other side of the pine. He guessed not much, though the two didn't exchange words. Even if the outlaws and Grace had not been only a few feet away, what was there to say? Henry felt like a damn fool to let himself be played so utterly and thoroughly by the lovely schoolteacher. He felt lousy about getting Molly involved in this scrape though he supposed she'd gotten involved on her own.

But only because she cared for him.

Grace had awakened often to sit up and look around edgily. Occasionally, she and Henry shared a wordless look. Then she either got up and walked off into the woods to clear her head or to tend nature, or she just flopped back down with a frustrated grunt against her saddle. She was having trouble sleeping.

Good, Henry thought. Why should she get a good night's sleep when he couldn't?

Around two or three in the morning, judging by the position of the stars glittering seemingly just a few feet above the pine crowns, he finally gave up on trying to loosen his wrists and nodded off. A hard kick to the side of his right thigh woke him.

"*Ouch!*" he complained, opening his eyes to see the black-eyed, granite-faced Shane Nordstrom glaring down at him.

"Wake up, Treasure Man. Let's go find that loot!" The outlaw gave a cold grin, eyes flashing darkly in the gray dawn light sifting through the forest around the fire that Henry could hear snapping and crackling, making the coffeepot give a soft *whushing* sound as the water heated. "Let's see if you're alive to sleep another night at the end of this day...or find yourself and Miss Starchy Britches in a shallow grave!"

He gave a dry laugh then pulled his bowie knife from the sheath on his left hip. He sawed through the knot of the long rope Deering and Russell had wrapped around both him and Molly and the tree between them. He cut the rope binding Henry's feet together, freeing them. He gave Henry a dark look as he rose and walked around to Molly's side of the tree.

Presently, Molly gave a frightened cry.

"Oh...please, don't!" she said in a pinched, quivering, high-pitched voice.

"Hey!" Henry said. "What the hell are you doing?"

Fear and anger rose in him as he turned to see Nordstrom kneeling beside Molly and holding the sharp edge of the bowie against the delicate skin of her neck. The savage-looking knife looked so cruel against the girl's flawless, peaches-and-cream skin, which that ugly knife could cut so easily, with only a slight increase of pressure in the outlaw's gloved, right hand.

Nordstrom smiled up at him. "Giving you a little preview of what's gonna happen to little Miss Starchy Britches if you're lyin', Deputy! Don't look too purty, now, does it?"

"Get away from her, damn you!" Henry lunged toward the man to kick him.

Nordstrom dropped the knife and grabbed Henry's ankle just before Henry would have buried the toe of his right boot into the underside of the man's chin. Nordstrom heaved up off his knee, rising, lifting Henry's right foot as he did, giving a wail of anger as he threw the deputy over on his back.

Henry struck the ground hard, unable to break his fall in the least with both hands bound in front of him and both feet having been yanked out from beneath him.

Anger seething in him, enraged by the challenging grin on the savage outlaw's hard, ugly face, Henry scrambled to his feet, swung his bound hands back behind his right shoulder then swung them forward, wanting nothing so much as to club the man's head clean off his shoulders!

Grinning, the outlaw ducked.

Henry's bound hands made a *whooshing* sound as they slashed through the air where Nordstrom's head had just been. He spun almost entirely around with a surprised grunt before he got his boots set beneath him. Nordstrom straightened and delivered two straight jabs to Henry's mouth with his left fist, cutting his lips before burying his right, clenched fist deep into the deputy's solar plexus.

Henry gave a deep-throated grunt as the air went gushing out of his lungs. He dropped to his knees and hung his head, tasting the copper of fresh blood on his mouth, groaning as he tried desperately and, at the moment, futilely to suck air back into his lungs.

"Stop it!" Molly screamed again, as she'd been screaming for the past twelve seconds of the skirmish—if you call it that. "Stop it! Stop it! *Stop it!*" came her ear-rattling command, glaring up at Nordstrom who stood over Henry now, hooking another cold grin at him. He pulled the big .45 Colt from the holster on his right hip and clicked the hammer back. "I should kill you for that right here and now."

"Nordstrom!" Grace said, running from where she must have been off in the woods, tending her morning ablutions. "Stop it this instant." She ran up between the savage brigand and Henry and gave Nordstrom a violent shove backward with the heels of her hands, causing her hair to tumble out of the loose bun it was in. "Are you *crazy*? Have you no sense *at all*?"

She glanced at Henry and then returned her castigating glare at the black-eyed outlaw who appeared unfazed by the remonstration. "I for one believe Henry does really know the area Casey sketched on the map! What would you do—kill him and destroy our chances at finding that cache just to suit your own savage *whim*?"

"I don't believe a word out of his mouth!" Nordstrom returned, glaring down at the woman before him, who was considerably shorter.

"Now, now, now," Vince Chaney said, smiling good-naturedly as he stepped between Nordstrom and Grace.

He and the other three men had been saddling their horses and seemingly enjoying the show. Good ol' Shane! There he goes again—a keg of dynamite with a short, lit fuse!

"The woman *does* have a point—you know, Shane?" Chaney said, placing a forestalling hand on Nordstrom's chest. "No point in killin' the kid until we're sure he's lyin'. And then, well, if turns out he is lyin'"—he winked at his big, thick-set, broad-shouldered partner dressed almost entirely in black—"you'll get first shot at him."

"What about the girl?" Dutch Deering was just then picking up the hat he'd set down in front of his horse, to let the mount drink from it. Now he tossed out what little water was left in the hat and set the ratty topper down on his red-haired head. He smiled lustily down at where Molly was still tied to the pine, hanging her head, sobbing. "Can I have first shot at the girl?"

Chaney and Nordstrom turned to the big, redheaded, red-bearded man, chuckling.

"Me—I get seconds!" Lonnie Russell intoned raucously where he was just filling a tin cup at the fire.

"There will be none of that!" Grace said, looking up at Chaney. "Vince, there will be none of that! All we're here for is the money. That's all. No...nothing..." She glared, her fair cheeks mottled red with exasperation, at Deering and Russell. "Nothing like that at all. I won't stand for it!"

Russell and Deering looked away, seemingly sheepish. But Henry, who was finally able to drag a few, shallow breaths into his battered lungs, had more than a feeling that Grace carried little weight here among these savages.

The idea of what these men might do to Molly after they killed him—which they'd surely do when they realized he had, indeed, been lying about his knowledge of the terrain sketched on the map—caused his spine to stiffen, his guts to churn, with dread.

Somehow, he had to get him and Molly away from these four. Five, counting Grace, who'd been blinded by her own lust for wealth though he could now read in her eyes that she was realizing the error of her ways.

Of the depraved nature of the men she'd entered with into an unholy alliance.

———

"Henry, do you have any kind of a plan at all?"

This from Molly, spoken quietly into his left ear from where she rode behind him on Banjo's back. The outlaws had Henry and the girl riding double. The easier to keep their eyes on them. Chaney was leading the zebra dun by a lead rope, taking Henry's directions, though for the life of him Henry had no idea where he was directing them.

His right hand was tied to the saddle horn, his boots tied to the stirrups. The outlaws had left his left hand free so he could study Casey's minimal map. Molly rode behind, unbound. Even if she suddenly leaped off the horse's back, she'd be easily run down or—horror of horrors!—shot. She knew it and Henry knew it and the outlaws knew it.

They were about an hour's ride north of where they

and the outlaws had camped. Grace rode behind Henry and Molly. Nordstrom rode behind her. He was followed by Russell and Deering, respectively—all of them riding Indian file on this narrow horse trail that led north and slightly west of Del Norte and into some buttes and mesas that may or may not look like any of the formations Casey had hastily scribbled on the map in Henry's hand.

"The only one I can think of is pray, Molly," Henry said, turning his head slightly to his left and keeping his voice down.

"Well, I've been doing that much!" Molly said in frustration and overly loud into his left ear.

Nordstrom had heard her.

"You two keep quiet up there," he called in his customarily belligerent tone. "You know the rules!"

"Oh, go to hell!" Molly shot back at the brigand from over her left shoulder.

The others laughed. At least, the men laughed. Grace rode as stoically in her saddle as she'd ridden since they'd broken camp after Henry and Molly had had a small bowl of beans and bacon and a little coffee to wash it down with before they'd been ordered into the saddle.

"Molly, dangit," Henry remonstrated the girl under his breath, grinding his teeth, waiting for a gunshot that would knock the girl off the saddle behind him.

When none came, he silently gave thanks to whatever guardian angel—if there was such a thing—looked over headstrong brunettes.

When the wind came up, muffling conversation, and Chaney and Henry and Molly were separated by a good thirty yards from the others riding behind them, as they climbed a twisting bluff shoulder into stunt pines, cedars, and boulders, Henry turned his head slightly left and said, "How in blazes did you find out about that loot, anyways?"

Keeping her own voice blessedly quiet, Molly said, "I was riding back from berry picking, and I saw the teacher and those obvious outlaws having a serious conversation behind the school. That got my suspicions up about her. It was almost dark. I rode around behind them and listened in on them talking about the loot—Miss Hastings telling them she had a map but would need help locating the gold."

Henry sighed and shook his head. "You were taking a big chance, Molly."

"Yeah, well, I'm curious. Besides, I wanted to know what you were getting into."

Again, Henry sighed. When there was another wind gust to cover his words, he said, "You should've come to me right away."

"I would have but I felt so foolish...eavesdropping like that. Besides, I was still miffed at you."

"You were miffed at *me*? Hah!"

He'd said it too loudly.

From behind Grace, Nordstrom yelled, "Don't make me ride up there!"

Just after noon, when the autumn sun was blazing straight down but the wind still had a cool bite to it, Vince Chaney stopped his horse and hipped around to cast an all-business look at Henry. "All right, kid. Where we goin'? I don't see anything resembling any of the formations on that map."

Henry's heart thudded.

The moment of truth.

"Uh, well..." He looked down at the map then studied the terrain around him.

His gaze held on a low, bench-shaped ridge. He

looked down at the map and then again at the formation. Hope rose in him.

Could it be...?

Nah. But, maybe...

"See that ridge over yonder, to the left of the trail?"

"I see it," Chaney called back to him.

"That's where we're headed!"

CHAPTER 30

Mannion was gaining on his quarry.

He could tell by the freshness of the tracks he was following through the downy pillow of recently fallen snow that sparkled like blue diamonds in the high-country sunshine.

He rode now up through a narrow canyon, boulders tilting toward him from among tall spruces, firs, and tamaracks carpeting steep slopes on both side of the wash. He kept his eyes glued on the terrain ahead and around him, watching for another possible bushwhack. Every so often, he dropped his eyes to the hoof tracks before him. They were following the angling canyon this way and that into the high, rocky, breathtakingly rugged and remote country up around Treasure Vault Lake in a bowl-like valley off the southern flank of the Mountain of the Holy Cross.

The tracks were only an hour or so old.

They were leading toward a high pass that was a massive gray crag looming straight north of Joe and Red.

Beyond the crag jutted an even higher one—a

massive, anvil-shaped formation known as Mountain of the Holy Cross.

Lodge was moving slowly. He was in misery from the teeth and fangs of the cat that had sought him out to avenge the death of its mate.

Mannion knew how the cat had felt.

Jane...

Occasionally the hoofprints told Mannion where Lodge had stopped his big steeldust. The bounty hunter had clambered down out of the saddle and made shuffling prints in the downy snow as he'd walked back several yards to peer around a bend and down the trail dropping behind him. Likely looking for his pursuer. Often, Lodge had dropped to his knees in the snow and placed his right, gloved hand down beside his right knee, leaning heavily on that hand. Mannion had seen where the gloved fingers had dug deeply into the snow.

Yeah, the cat had torn Lodge up good.

But he was still on the run. He'd keep moving until he could move no more.

Mannion held Red to a fast walk. The snow and the possible rocks it hid made for slow going. He could not risk Red throwing a shoe or injuring a hoof or fetlock. Hell, the snow might hide a deep cut of erosion that Red could plunder unwittingly and break a leg.

Without his horse up here, this far from civilization, Joe would be a dead man. Especially with the dark purple clouds he saw sliding toward him from the northwest, ahead and on his left. A storm was moving in. Those clouds were a giant shade slowly being drawn over the lamp of the vast, arching, cobalt, Colorado sky.

A wind was building, beginning to swirl the fallen snow around. It was humming and chuffing, occasionally thrashing the high crowns of the trees looming over him, on both sides of the trail.

As he followed another round bend in the trail, around a large belly of pitted granite on his left, a *thump* rose on Mannion's right. He stopped Red instantly with a slight tug on the reins, which he held in his left hand. The Winchester was already cocked, a live round in the chamber.

Now he swung the barrel out from his saddle pommel and thumbed the hammer back as he aimed up the steep, seven-foot slope on his right, aiming into the heavily shadowed but sun-dappled forest beyond.

He eased the tension in his trigger finger.

A large, red fox sat atop a large rock roughly twenty feet back in the trees. It stood shifting its feet edgily and arching its tail, growling softly, inquiringly. Mannion saw snow feathering the sun-dappled air above and behind the animal, and the long scuff marks in the snow mantling the larger rock behind it.

The animal had made the thumping sound when it had dropped down from the higher rock to the lower one, investigating the man and the horse on the trail below it. The little fox, likely dropped that spring, lifted its black snout and laid its red ears back against its head, and made a yodeling sound.

It dropped down over the edge of its perch, made another *thump* as it struck the snowy forest floor then ran off across the belly of the slope through the trees to Mannion's right. It descended the slope at an angle then crossed the trail ten feet behind the lawman and Red then bounded up the opposite slope to disappear into the forest on the trail's west side.

The light thuds of its small feet and the quiet panting

sounds dwindled beneath the building rush of the wind in the trees.

Red whickered and sidestepped, unnerved.

"Easy, Red," Mannion said, drawing back firmly on the reins as he lowered the Yellowboy's hammer into its cradle. "Just a fox is all. Likely knows a storm's on the brew and is heading home to is hidey-hole."

Mannion rested the Yellowboy's barrel on the pommel of his saddle again and nudged the bay ahead. He considered looking for his own hidey-hole to wait out the storm. On the other hand, why not push on? He was so close to his prey that he might very well run Lodge down...or find him dead along the trail...before the full force of that squall delivered its wrath.

Mannion smelled blood. He was as eager as the cat had been to sink his own proverbial teeth into his prey.

Lodge feared him. Mannion could smell that, too. He knew Mannion was behind him, closing the gap between them. Intending to do him in, once and for all. He was desperate. Maybe even panicking. He was badly injured. Maybe even still losing blood though Joe had spied none along the trail. Lodge had likely taken time to wrap the wounds with bandages from his saddlebags.

Still, he was injured, likely soaking those bandages with fresh blood. He had a fierce predator dogging his heels and an angry-looking sky closing over him fast.

Yeah, he was scared, all right.

He might make another move soon, Mannion silently opined, keeping his eyes roaming even more slowly and sharply on the terrain ahead and around him.

The clouds settled over him within the next hour, the snow coming down at a forty five degree angle. Horse and rider rode up out of the canyon and headed across the rocky pass between two boulder-strewn ridges. The sky was deep purple, threatening as hell. The wind was howling, the snow blowing thickly around Red's legs, sculpting deep drifts at angles across the ancient horse trail that followed the narrow gap between steep ridges that was the pass.

The whip-crack of a rifle touched Mannion's ears.

Red picked it up, too, and stopped of his own accord, giving an edgy whicker.

The whip-crack came again.

Mannion lifted the Yellowboy's barrel and thumbed back the hammer. He looked around at the rocky ridges towering around him, obscured behind the gauzy white curtain of thickening snow and showing a murky gray of stone bastion against the deep purple of the angry sky. His spine stiffened as another crackling report of a rifle again caromed around him, echoing.

The shots did not seem to be fired at him, however.

They were too far away.

Still, he turned Red off the trail's left side and into some rocks and pines. Partly concealed, he reached back into a saddlebag pouch for his field glasses. He pulled the glasses out of their case, raised them to his eyes, and adjusted the focus.

Another whip-crack echoed.

He followed the echoes to their source, which seemed to be a tall thumb of rock resting up against an even taller formation to the shorter thumb's right. The shorter formation appeared in the shape of a leaping stone flame, complete with ragged crest. At this crest, Mannion picked out movement through the glasses.

Again, the thunder of the rifle sounded.

This time, Mannion spied the orange stab of flames and the puff of smoke quickly torn by the wind.

He tightened the focus until the head and shoulders

of a man wielding a rifle near the top of the leaping stone flame swam into clearer view. He saw the big, bearded head topped with a bullet-crowned, black hat, and wide shoulders ensconced in a buffalo hide coat. The brim of the hat was being nibbled at by the wind and tufts of the man's thick, curly hair blew out behind his ears. Joe watched as Ulysses Lodge again cocked his Winchester then aimed to his left and ahead of him. He was apparently focusing his attention on something far off to Joe's right, above both his position and the position of Lodge himself.

"What in the hell you shooting at, ya old scudder?" Mannion muttered as Lodge aimed carefully over the frame of his Winchester, propping the barrel on the stone shelf in front of him.

Smoke and flames stabbed from the barrel.

The rocketing report reached Joe's ears three seconds later, the echoes chasing each other skyward quickly muffled by the wind.

Mannion slid the binoculars' single field of magnified vision to his right, to the steep, rock- and boulder-strewn slope east of his position. Again, he asked himself what the big bear of a man was shooting at. At first, he thought maybe an animal of some kind.

A mountain goat?

Bighorn sheep?

Possibly an elk or a bear?

What the hell—was he going to take time to dress out game and cook it knowing full well that Mannion was hot on his heels?

Well, maybe not hot on his heels but lukewarm, anyway...

Joe swept that steep slope with the glasses, finding nothing but rock and trees that, appearing like strewn matchsticks from this distance, formed large fields of slash created by previous rockslides.

His shoulders tightened.

Ice water pooled in his belly.

Rockslides...

Quickly, he slid the magnified circle of vision back toward Lodge, finding the man again just as more smoke and flames lapped from his Winchester's barrel. The echoing crackle of the long gun reached his ears and sent a cold rod of dread sliding up along the stiffness of his spine.

Feeling his heart pumping, his breath coming fast, he quickly slid the glasses back right and up near the crest of the massive, rock-strewn stone ridge...just in time to see several rocks shudder and leap out of the positions they'd likely held for eons and to tumble down the slope, freeing more rock from their own age-old positions as they tumbled against others...those other rocks loosing *more* rocks as they tumbled against even more.

The son of a fang-toothed, green-horned demon was starting a rockslide, and those rocks had nowhere to go but straight down toward where Mannion sat astride his big bay, partly concealed by trees and boulders at the very top of the pass, between two rock walls, one of which was coming right down at him!

Rocks rolled and leaped and rolled and leaped again until more and more were rolling and leaping, and the thunder of the mountain's collapse was a veritable roar inside Bloody Joe's head, accompanying the bells tolling a warning of certain annihilation!

Mannion didn't bother casing his field glasses. He thrust both the glasses and the case back into the pouch from which he'd produced them. Then he looked around quickly, wanting to ride ahead and off the top of the pass in the direction of where Ulysses Lodge was shooting from.

He quickly surmised he and Red wouldn't make it. That end of the pass was a good hundred and fifty yards away!

As the slide built and built and the stony ground beneath Red's own shifting and dancing feet pitched and lurched with the force of the million tons of rock coming down that mountain, Joe swung Red around and gave the bay its head, galloping hell-for-leather in the direction from which they'd come.

When Joe glanced to his left, his eyes widened, his heart turning a somersault in spine-splintering shock. The first rocks and boulders of the building slide were growing larger and larger as they hurled toward him, the closest ones sixty yards away but leaping a good twenty, thirty yards with each bounce.

He could see the cracks, pits, and fissures in them as they, all shapes and sizes, approached...

Joe put his head down and pulled his hat brim low, whipping his rein ends against Red's hindquarters. *"Run like hell, boy, or we're gonna be nothin' but smashed bone an' cherry jam under a whole damn mountain of rock—hidden even from God!"*

Red turned his head to the left. When he saw the same rocks that had Mannion's close attention, the horse's left eye widened until Joe could see a good inch of white around the iris. Red swung his head back forward, gave a screeching cry of bald-assed terror, and lunged into an even faster stride—more speed than the big stallion himself even thought he'd had in him.

As a wagon-sized boulder leaped right toward horse and rider, doubling in size with each sixteenth of a second, Joe cursed and silently told himself, "Ah, hell... we're not gonna make it..."

He closed his eyes and lowered his head to Red's neck as though that would somehow ease the blow that was less than a second away.

CHAPTER 31

Henry couldn't believe it.

Maybe he and Molly wouldn't die, after all.

If the outlaws kept their promise, that was. Which was doubtful. But at least they'd each had a few hours left to breathe and smell the crisp autumn air and hear the birds and take in the pretty, rolling, sage-carpeted countryside around them.

Maybe they even had a few hours more.

Henry was pretty sure he'd found—more like *stumbled upon*—the little gap between buttes that Casey had hurriedly sketched on his map. But they hadn't found the treasure yet.

Ahead of him and Molly riding astride Banjo, Vince Chaney checked down his claybank, stopping both his own horse and Henry's dun. The others rode up around Henry and Molly and stared down into the hollow in the buttes below, frowning incredulously.

Shane Nordstrom turned his perpetually angry gaze to Henry. "This don't look like nothin' I see on that map, Sonny Boy."

"Henry, are you just fooling around?" Molly wanted to

know where she sat Banjo's back behind the deputy. She'd spoken just above a whisper so not to incur more of Nordstrom's wrath.

They'd both incurred enough of that.

"Pull us up there, and I'll show you," Henry told Chaney.

Chaney turned and clucked to Henry's dun, jerking the horse up by its lead rope. Nordstrom sidled his own mount away from Chaney, making room for Banjo.

Henry held the note up in his left hand where both Chaney and Nordstrom could look at it. "See that curved line there? I'm pretty sure that's a bluff," he said, able only to point with his chin since his right hand was tied to his saddle horn.

Then he jerked his chin toward the bluff before them, on the other side of the hollow. "It's that bluff there, I'm pretty sure." Again, he looked at the ragged map the breeze was fluttering in his hand. "See that black bird flying over it. I'm pretty sure that bird was Casey's shorthand for Crow Ridge. That bluff there is Crow Ridge. See the little cabin and stable at the foot of it?"

"Yeah, yeah, we see it," Nordstrom said in his customary dry, impatient, belligerent tone.

"That's indicated by that little box there on the map, under the curve that makes the bluff. Now, just by lookin' at the map, no one would know that bird indicated Crow Ridge. Not if you don't know the country. It was Casey's way of being secretive about where he stashed the loot. Casey must've known the country."

Grace cut in with, "He once told me he'd worked up around Del Norte. He was probably a ranch hand...when he wasn't rustling or robbing stagecoaches." She crossed her arms on her chest, over her cape, and shook her head as she stared soberly into the hollow.

Henry said, "Marshal Mannion and I were out here a coupla years back, trailing rustlers. They were holed up in what's left of that shack down yonder."

He paused to study the shack hunched near the base of the bluff, flanked by a thick fringe of brush running in a semicircle along the bluff's base. There was some open ground between the cabin and a small stable and two interconnected corrals. Like the shack, the stable's roof was halfway caved in. The corrals had seen better days, as well. Pig's ear and buckbrush and sage had grown high around it, and several of the slats were down, the gate lying flat on the ground, also nearly hidden with brush and wild shrubs.

"Marshal Mannion thought the place had probably been knocked together during the War Between the States, when lawmen had been even rarer out here than they are now, by a small pack of rustlers long-roping stock raised by Honyockers from Nebraska and Kansas, who'd moved west to escape getting tangled up in that bloody war."

"Enough with the history lesson, Sonny Boy," Nordstrom cut in.

Henry's heart beat anxiously. His nervousness caused him to blabber. He could hardly believe he might very well have just lucked into finding Casey's cache. At least, he was pretty blame sure he'd at least located the shack and the bluff indicated on the map.

He once again cautioned himself, though, that even if he had stumbled onto the cache, he and Molly were far from out of the woods. He might have bought them some time by riding out here, but they were still likely crowbait...just as soon as Chaney and Nordstrom got their hands on that gold.

Yeah, Henry had bought him and Molly some time.

But now he needed to get them away from these four tough nuts before they turned them both toe down and buried them in shallow graves, never to be seen in Del Norte ever again.

He happened to glance across Chaney at Grace. She was looking across Chaney back at Henry. The deputy could tell that she was thinking the same thing he was. Her eyes were grave beneath the brim of the black felt hat she wore.

He jerked his glance away from hers, having no time for her sympathy, if that's what he'd seen in her eyes. Sympathy and contrition, maybe? Even if those emotions were real, little good they'd do Henry and Molly when the outlaws found that gold.

"Well, well—what do you think, Shane?" Chaney said, looking across Henry at Nordstrom sitting his gray to Henry's right. "Maybe the kid wasn't so full of beans, after all."

Staring into the hollow between bluffs, at the moldering shack and equally moldering stable and corral all but buried in brush, Nordstrom offered a noncommittal hike of his left shoulder. "Maybe, maybe not. I reckon proof'll be in the pudding, won't it?"

He grabbed the map out of Henry's hand, placed his gloved right finger on the circle sort of obscured by squiggly lines behind the shack marked on the map, to the left of the tumbledown stable.

"If this marks the spot of the cache, it shouldn't be long till we get our hands on it." Nordstrom cut one of his trademark threatening looks at Henry. "Should it, kid?"

Henry didn't like that look at all.

He hadn't liked any of Nordstrom's looks, but he liked this one least of all. It told Henry that his suspicions that he and Molly were nearing the end of their ropes had been right. The outlaws were not going to keep their promise to let them live if Henry led them to the loot.

"Hy-ahh!" Nordstrom howled, grinding spurs into his horse's flanks.

"Hy-yahh!" both Russell and Deering yelled to their own mounts, booting them into mounts and into Nordstrom's rising dust.

Chaney chuckled eagerly and put spurs to his own mount, starting down the bluff toward the hollow. Banjo started after him, jerked along by the lead line.

"Vince!" Grace said.

Chaney checked his mount down abruptly and curveted him. Banjo stopped abruptly, as well, just before he would have rammed Chaney's claybank. The dun turned, whickering uneasily and twitching his ears. In the dust rising around him, Chaney regarded the teacher with an expression of curiosity mixed with impatience.

"It's agreed, right?" Grace cut her eyes to Henry and Molly sitting Banjo between her and Chaney. "We've agreed to let them live." She gave her head a slow wag, her eyes dark with foreboding. "There is no way I can condone cold-blooded murder."

Chaney glanced at Henry and the girl. For a few moments, he seemed to be thinking about it. Returning his gaze to the teacher, he smiled and said, "Oh, sure, sure, Grace. Don't worry about it. I know how to take the venom out of Shane's sting. I can reason with him. Not many can, but I can." He turned his head forward and booted his horse on down the rise, jerking Banjo, Henry, and Molly along behind him on the lead line.

When they reached the trough in which the cabin sat, Chaney had just gotten his mount and Henry's mount stopped when Molly said in her impatient, angry, frightened way, "I have to tend nature!"

Chaney scowled at her as he swung down from his saddle. Nordstrom and the other two men had already dismounted and were striding quickly, eagerly into the brush to the left of the tumbledown stable. Henry smelled mold and wood rot.

"Oh, go to hell," Chaney said. "You done just tended nature not twenty minutes ago!"

"That was almost an hour ago," Molly protested. "And I have to go again!"

Henry glanced at her. She'd been right. It had been at least an hour since they'd last stopped for Molly to take a short nature hike out into the brush, Grace flanking the girl with a pistol and Nordstrom's orders to shoot the girl if she tried to run. Henry had a feeling it was nerves making her need to go so often.

"I'll watch her, Vince," Grace said, swinging down from her own horse's back. She rode a sorrel gelding rented from one of the livery stables in town. "Let's cut Henry down, too. He hasn't had any water or a chance to tend nature since we left camp this morning."

Chaney swung toward her, his usually amiable features set with dire warning. "Listen, Grace—don't go gettin' any ideas about those two. Like helpin' 'em get away? Forget about it. You were plannin' on diggin' up that loot and keepin' it for yourself. Or you and lover boy here," he added, cutting his eyes at Henry.

Henry felt his cheeks warm with embarrassment. They turned even warmer when he saw Molly casting a cold, accusing look at him.

Grace's cheeks also flushed, and she glanced down at the ground in front of the hem of her dark wool skirt.

"All I'm sayin' is," Chaney said, dipping his chin at her

and looking up at her from beneath his sandy brows, "you're cut in. It's up to you whether you get cut *out*!"

He punctuated the warning with a dark nod.

He pulled his bowie knife and walked over and freed Henry's hands from the deputy's saddle horn, Henry's feet from the stirrups. When the deputy had swung down from the saddle, Chaney ordered him to hold his wrists together. Then Chaney stepped back, drew his pistol, cocked it, and aimed it at Henry's belly.

He glanced at Grace.

"Tie him. Tight," he ordered, showing his teeth.

CHAPTER 32

GRACE PICKED UP ONE OF THE CUT ROPES LYING IN THE dust and sage beside Banjo, then stepped up in front of Henry. Molly stood a good distance behind Grace, staring at Henry with that dark, frightened, angry expression she'd had since Henry had first found her trussed up at the outlaws' camp the night before.

Grace did not look at Henry until she'd tied the ropes tightly around his wrists. Then she looked up at him, gazed into his eyes with a hard-to-read expression—more sympathy? contrition?—before she stepped straight back then pulled pistol out of one of the saddlebag pouches draped across her horse's back. It was a snub-nosed, .38-caliber New Line Colt revolver.

"I've got them covered," Grace said, quietly but firmly, clicking the pocket pistol's hammer back. "Don't worry. They won't be going anywhere."

Chaney glanced toward where the other three men were stomping around in the brush, arguing, obviously desperate to retrieve the loot at long last. After seven long years of prison time. Chaney looked at Grace, Henry, and Molly. He wanted to stay with them to make sure they pulled no tricks, but he also wanted to get after that loot. In the devious mind of the outlaw, he might have suspected his pards might try to squirrel away some of that gold for themselves before he even saw it.

"You see to it, Grace!" he said, pointing at her warningly with his left arm and outstretched finger while holstering his Smith & Wesson with his right.

He turned and stomped into the brush to the left of the stable.

Grace had backed up to stand beside Molly, both women facing him. Keeping her eyes on Henry, Grace said to Molly, "Go ahead. Tend your business. If you try to run off, I'll shoot him."

She clicked the snub-nosed Colt's hammer back.

Henry stared into her eyes. They were hard to read. But he didn't believe she meant it. Or maybe he just didn't want to believe it.

"Some *lady* you took up with, Henry," Molly said, sneering, glancing at Grace then turning and walking off into the brush west of the stable, a little south of where the four outlaws were stomping around, looking for the loot.

Henry looked at Grace. He looked at the cocked Colt in her hand.

"They'll kill us," he told her. "You know that, don't you?"

Grace didn't say anything. Henry thought he could see her chest rise and fall a little more quickly and heavily than before, behind the black cape she wore over a cream sweater.

"If you cut me loose—"

"Stow it!" Grace said tightly, cutting him off.

"It'll be just like you shot us yourself," Henry persisted.

"I said shut up!" Lowering her voice and softening her tone a little, Grace added, "Please, be quiet, Henry. This is hard enough on me. I'm a wreck—can't you see that?"

"Well, I'm so awfully sorry."

"Please!" she said, louder than she intended. She looked quickly toward where the men were stomping around, unseen in the brush. They could only be heard, not seen.

Henry thought he'd found a chink in the teacher's armor. Encouraged, he continued to probe that soft spot. "Cut me loose," he said. "We'll all three ride out of here. It'll be like you weren't even a part of this. I won't tell the marshal. I won't tell no one. Heck, I'll even say you helped retrieve the loot, when you found your brother's map in your Bible."

"Oh, God, Henry—you won't tell *anyone*!" Grace made a strangling sound—a half sob, half laugh.

Henry frowned. "What?"

Grace wiped a tear from her cheek with the back of her free hand. "You won't tell *anyone*, Henry! Haven't I taught you *anything*?"

Again, she made that strangling sound. She began to slowly lower the pistol, as though, despite its small size, it was too heavy for her to keep aimed at his belly. Her shoulders jerked as she sobbed.

"Grace," Henry said, moving slowly toward her, raising his tied hands to her, "please..."

He'd moved to within four feet of her and was lowering his hands to the pistol she now held straight down in her right hand, when the crunching of brush grew louder behind her. So did the volume of the men's frustrated voices.

"Dammit, he's been lyin' to us!" Shane Nordstrom

yelled. "There is no damn loot in that brush. He led us on a wild-goose chase!"

Henry glanced over his shoulder to see the four men emerging from the brush, Deering and Russell plucking nettles from their coats. Chaney and Nordstrom were walking a little to the left of the other two, as Henry looked toward them. Chaney angrily shoved the branch of a lilac shrub out of his way. As Nordstrom stepped out from behind the lilac, to Chaney's right, he glared at Henry, red-faced with both fury and frustration, and began to slide his big Colt from its holster.

A crackling sound and a girl's clipped cry sounded from the brush on Henry's left, farther south and west of the stable than the outlaws had been.

Henry turned his head that way and yelled, "*Molly?*"

He started to run toward the source of the girl's cry when both Chaney and Nordstrom palmed their revolvers and aimed at him, crouching, Nordstrom yelling, "*Hold it, Sonny Boy, or I'll drop you right there!*" He gave a shrewd grin. "It's a trick. Hah! Miss Starchy Britches is tryin' to pull the wool over our heads!"

Chaney turned to the teacher. "Grace, you were supposed to keep an eye on her."

Grace turned from where she'd been gazing into the brush to her left, to slide her tear-filled gaze to Chaney. "I...I..." She lowered her chin and sobbed.

"Oh, Christ!" Nordstrom barked, raising his Colt, aiming at Henry's head. "This ends right here!"

Crackling sounded in the shrubs to Henry's right. Molly stepped out from the breeze-tossed branches. She held her right hand behind her back. She held her left hand straight down at her side. It was clenched into a fist. She looked to Henry and said just loudly enough to be heard above the wind, "I found the loot."

"*What?*" all four outlaws said at the same time, eyes widening in surprise.

They all four had their pistols out but now their heads swiveled toward the girl.

Molly turned to them, suddenly fashioning a cold, shrewd gaze of her own, gray eyes reflecting the crisp autumn sunshine. She raised her left hand, opening it. Several small objects glittered in the air before tumbling into the wiry grass and sage, making the changing sounds of coins.

Gold coins!

"The saddlebags are stashed in a hole. Must've been the start of a well. It was covered with rotten wood planks. I broke through them." Molly's smile broadened. "The saddlebags are there, stuffed full of coins just like those there."

She pulled her right hand out from behind her back. In it was a .44-caliber Colt revolver with tarnished bluing and worn walnut grips. "This was there, too," she added, holding the revolver in both her small, pale hands, clicking the hammer back with a ratcheting click.

All four outlaws raised their greed-glittering eyes from the gold coins winking in the sage between them and Molly and Henry and Grace. She aimed the pistol at Nordstrom and said as the wind blew her long, auburn hair about her fair, sunburned cheeks, "You let us go like you promised, and it's all yours. *I* promise. My word is good...unlike the word of some others!"

She'd spoken this last with her own brand of arrogant sauciness.

Henry would have laughed if his heart wasn't racing so fast and beating so hard. His palms were sweating as he shuttled his anxious gaze between Molly and the four desperados.

They'd all stiffened, eyes wide with sudden caution, guns half lowered before them.

Oh, no, Henry thought, reading the expressions in the desperados' eyes. They hadn't ridden all this way to be hornswoggled by a teenaged girl wielding a gun in all likeliness she couldn't hit the broadside of a barn with—from inside the barn!

No, no, no, no! Henry silently willed the men.

To no avail.

Nordstrom's nostrils flared and his eyes hardened in sudden rage as he jerked his Colt up and over at Molly. Henry saw the .45's large, round maw blossom smoke and flames as it and Molly's own Colt roared at the same time. Molly screamed as Henry turned to Grace, ripped her New Line Colt out of her hand and, turning toward the outlaws, slammed his left shoulder into her, throwing her to the ground.

As Grace gave a scream of her own, Henry flung himself straight forward. The outlaws were kicking up a fusillade now as their revolvers thundered, some of the bullets directed at Molly, some at him, the bullets whistling through the air where he'd been standing a moment before. He brought the New Line up in both his tied hands and, quickly picking out targets, three of the outlaws crouched over their own roiling weapons before him, clicked the hammer back and fired.

He cocked and fired, hearing the grunts and curses of his dancing victims, until the New Line's hammer clicked on an empty chamber.

Smoke wafted in the sunlight and breeze before him.

All four were down. Nordstrom had gone down first. He was the only one moving, writhing, holding his left hand to his right shoulder and cursing up a bitter storm. The others lay still in the sage where they'd fallen.

Henry whipped his head toward Molly. She lay on her belly eight feet away from him, both hands flung to both sides. Her smoking Colt was still in her right hand.

Between himself and Molly, Grace was just then sitting up, dirt and seeds in the hair hanging down past her shoulders. Her eyes were round and wide in shock, cheeks ashen.

"Molly!" Henry cried.

He awkwardly gained his feet, dropping the empty Colt, and hurried toward the unmoving girl. As he did, Grace picked herself up. She was staring toward the four dead or wounded outlaws. Suddenly, she raised her hands and screamed, "Shane, no! Hasn't there been enou—"

Her plea was cut short by a revolver's roar.

Grace screamed and flew back against Henry. He tried to catch her but she glanced off his right shoulder and fell to the ground. He whipped his head toward the outlaws. Grunting and cursing, Nordstrom was trying to gain his feet, holding his smoking .45 in his right hand.

As the outlaw swung the .45 toward Henry, Henry took one long, running stride forward.

The .45 roared.

The bullet whipped over Henry's right shoulder to spang off a rock beyond him.

Henry dove forward, ripped the Colt out of Molly's hand. Just as Nordstrom got his boots set beneath him and clicked his own revolver's hammer back, opening his mouth in an agonized, enraged, bellowing wail, Henry put two bullets into the brigand's chest, six inches below and left of the man's right shoulder from which blood oozed, courtesy Molly's own bullet from Casey's old .44.

Nordstrom triggered his .45 skyward a quarter second before he flopped back into the brush.

Sitting up, the Colt extended straight out before him

in both bound hands, Henry waited for the man to move again. When he did not, Henry dropped the Colt and turned to Molly, relieved to find her now lying on her side, propped on one elbow. Her hair hung down over her left cheek. She looked from the unmoving and likely dead Nordstrom to Henry.

"You all right?" he asked her.

She nodded dully.

"You sure?" Henry reached over to run his thumb through a short line of blood on her left cheek. A shallow burn was all, made by Nordstrom's own bullet.

Molly shifted her gaze to Henry's right. "The teacher," she said softly, slowly sitting up.

Henry turned to Grace.

She lay on her back, writhing slightly. Blood stained her black cape over her chest. The stain grew steadily. She dug her fingers into the ground to both sides of her, and tried to sit up, but couldn't make it. She rested her head back down on the ground.

Henry hurried over to her, knelt beside her on both knees, lifted her head gently, and set it in his lap. "Oh, Grace," he said, smoothing her hair back from her forehead.

"Henry." Her voice was barely a whisper. She lifted her left hand to her shoulder, wrapped it around Henry's own left wrist. "Henry," she said again. Tears shimmered in her eyes. "I'm...sorry..."

"Don't, Grace. Don't try to talk."

"Just one more thing." She smiled as she gazed up at him through pain-racked, tear-bleary eyes.

"What's that?"

"Finish...*Ivanhoe*...for me...will you?"

Henry choked back a sob. "I will."

He didn't know if she'd heard or not, because when

he blinked away the tears from his eyes, her own eyes stared up at him, glazed in death.

Henry sobbed again.

Molly came over and knelt beside him, one arm wrapped around his neck. She leaned her head on his shoulder and sat with him there for a long time while he held Grace's head on his lap.

The wind whispered through the sage and grass and fluttered the dead teacher's hair.

CHAPTER 33

Galloping hell-for-leather, Mannion felt an especially cold and violent rush of wind pass behind him, from his left to his right, only a few feet off Red's arched tail just before an explosion as loud as twenty kegs of ignited dynamite rose behind him.

The concussion of the explosion hurled Red forward so that the bay's stride halted and the stallion fought like hell to keep from dropping to his knees. When the bay got all four hooves set beneath him, Joe glanced over his right shoulder to see that the cabin-sized boulder he'd thought for sure would turn him and Red to cherry jam had narrowly missed them.

It had slammed into the steep ridge forming the side of the pass opposite the disintegrating mountain, which was now a dark-gray cloud of pulverized stone. Stones were hurled toward Mannion and Red; they landed on the trail behind them just as horse and rider galloped down away from the pass that had come too damn close to becoming their sarcophagus in which they'd ride out the ages.

Safe now in the canyon up which they'd climbed to

the pass only a few minutes ago, Mannion drew back on Red's reins, halting the blowing horse and curveting him to gaze back up the narrow trail between steep, forested ridges toward the pass. It was a pass no more.

Now it was a mountain of jumbled rock.

A mountain of rock between Joe and his quarry.

"Think you bested me, do you?" Mannion said, scowling up at that smoking mountain, beyond the howling curtain of wind-driven snow. "We'll see about that!"

He slammed the end of his right fist down hard against his leg.

He swung down from the saddle, leaned his rifle against a tree, then quickly stripped the tack off Red's back. He found a low limb to set it on then went over and ran an affectionate hand down Red's long, sleek, sweat-slick neck as the stallion eyed him dubiously.

"Stay put, boy. Find shelter. Sorry I can't build you a fire."

Mannion grabbed his rifle and set it on his shoulder. "I have to do the rest alone...on foot." He gave the horse a reassuring smile. He knew he was speaking as much to himself as he was to his horse. "I'll be back soon."

He winked and started back up the trail toward the pass, this time on foot.

At the top of this pass—or what had been the pass until only a few minutes ago—Joe stopped and looked at the mountain of rock before him. He blinked against the windblown snow that pricked against his cheeks and eyes like small javelins and shaded his eyes against the glare of the white snow against the low, purple sky.

He could just barely see the top of the mountain, but he thought it was likely about a hundred feet above him. He could hear the rocks still shifting and grinding against each other. Warning himself to go slow and to watch his footing, he drew a deep breath and began the climb the first rocks and boulders and protruding ends of wooden slash with a grunt, holding the Yellowboy down low in his right hand.

The snow was clinging to them—another reason to be sure of his footing. A broken leg or a dislocated shoulder or hip incurred in a fall would only add injury to insult.

He thought he could hear Lodge laughing. Of course, he could not, but the laughter in his head was Lodge's, all right. The crazy man was fairly hysterical with it, even slapping his thigh as he inspected the mountain from his perch high in the rocks above it.

Joe hoped the man believed he'd finally scoured his hunter from his trail. Or had made him *part* of the trail forever, that was. At the moment, Joe needed the upper hand. He'd take whatever he could get.

Even badly wounded from the cat attack, the bear-like bounty man was still a formidable opponent. The most challenging and arduous Mannion had ever come up against.

Upward, he climbed the steep mountain, occasionally having to shove his rifle up onto a ledge above him and then having to hoist himself up and onto that ledge with his arms and legs. Then he picked up his rifle and continued the climb. Sometimes he paused and scrutinized the steep slope for the easiest—or less difficult—route, blinking against the snow, then resumed his slow, plodding, wearying climb.

He gained the top of the mountain of rock roughly a half hour after he'd started. But he still had a hell of a trek ahead of him—over and around fallen slash and rocks and boulders of all shapes and sizes, as he headed for the other side. It was like making your way through a field of giant dominoes sitting at all angles, sometimes standing.

And he had to fight the wind and snow and growing cold, the slippery stone slabs beneath his feet.

He'd fought to maybe a third of the way over that giant dinosaur's mouth of crooked teeth when he stepped through a gap between two cracked, snow-dusted boulders and peered ahead through the snow. It had thickened now so that he could see clearly for maybe thirty feet in front of him. Beyond that was a wavering, heavy curtain of pale gauze contrasting the purple sky above.

A large, vaguely man-shaped figure stepped out from behind a jutting rectangle of broken mountain wall at the extreme edge of Joe's field of vision—roughly thirty-five, forty feet away. Lodge had just turned in Mannion's direction.

He stopped suddenly.

Who else could it be but Ulysses Lodge?

From this distance and in the blowing snow, he appeared a small bear standing upright. He raised his long Winchester in both gloved hands so that it slanted up across his chest. The buffalo hide coat over his left shoulder and down that arm was badly torn.

Mannion could see the redness of blood through the tears.

He could see the redness of blood and exposed meat on the left side of the big man's face.

Yeah, the cat had gotten him good.

Must be in one helluva lot of misery. Still, he'd come to make sure Mannion was not still alive…not still coming for him. He knew he couldn't rest until his hunter was dead, for he knew his hunter would not rest until he, Lodge, was dead.

Something had told him—that sixth, especially keen sense shared by the hunter and hunted—that Joe had not been ground to a fine paste and powder beneath the mountain Lodge had knocked down in his honor. That he was still alive...still hunting...

Mannion took his own Winchester in both hands. He pumped a live cartridge into the chamber.

He gazed toward his prey through the slanting curtains of snow and moaning wind, Lodge's figure obscured now and then by a heavy gust, like a man obscured by an especially heavy windblown curtain of white.

Mannion smiled.

He couldn't tell if Lodge smiled back. He believed he did. The man gave a shallow nod just before he rammed the butt plate of his rifle to his shoulder and aimed down the barrel at his hunter.

Joe sidestepped behind the boulder to his right just as his opponent's Winchester lapped red flames. The bullet slammed into the face of the boulder with a wicked, crackling spang that nearly drowned the roar of Lodge's rifle.

Mannion stepped out from behind his own cover, aimed quickly, and fired...just as Lodge stepped back behind his own covering rock. Joe's bullet clipped the edge of Lodge's rock with a heavy *thunk*! and whine whose echoes were quickly swallowed by the moaning wind.

Lodge snaked his Winchester across the side of his boulder and Joe stepped behind his own rock to avoid the bullet. As the thunder of Lodge's rifle faded on the wind, Mannion saw the man on the run, heading back the way he'd come through a narrow corridor in the jumbled mass of rocks.

Mannion fired twice quickly then strode ahead, picking up his pace despite the perilous footing. He snapped the Yellowboy up and fired again when he saw movement in the murk ahead and to his left. He slipped and slid and stumbled through the debris of broken rock for maybe twenty feet before he spied movement again ahead of him—Lodge extending his Winchester toward him from the right side of two broken trees jutting up from the field of snowy rubble.

Mannion dove forward, struck on a narrow slice of flat rubble to avoid the bullet but felt the shards of stone thrown up by Lodge's rifle pepper his hat, shoulders, back, and the backs of his legs. He cocked another round into the Yellowboy's action but held fire.

Lodge was gone.

All Mannion could see was blowing snow and the hazy, irregular shapes of jutting rubble.

He rose quickly and, huffing and puffing, wincing at the ache and stiffness in his legs, made his way as quickly as he dared through the field of strewn rubble, occasionally glimpsing movement ahead of him, pausing and firing then taking cover to avoid Lodge's return fire. Gradually, he was closing the gap, for the brief glimpses of movement he spied ahead grew clearer and clearer.

The storm disoriented him, but he thought Lodge was leading him east. They were climbing toward the mountain of rock's eastern peak. Mannion was now close enough to his quarry that he was able to follow the growing puddles of fresh blood on the shelving rocks ahead and above him, and the scuffs of the bounty hunter's moccasin-clad feet in the snow.

Occasional lead rained down from above, but Joe could see his quarry well enough now to go to ground, avoiding the lead. He trained his Winchester on his target, ducked quickly to avoid Lodge's own bullets, then returned fire and, missing, continued climbing...until he could climb no more.

He'd come to a broad, cleared area at the eastern top of the rubble heap.

He stopped to bend slightly forward and rake air in and out of his lungs. Every joint ached, but his knees screamed like tortured dogs. He'd come to the point where they were barely bending anymore. He looked down to see that he was holding his second Russian in his hand.

He could only vaguely remember emptying the Winchester, which he'd abandoned against a rock, and then his first, left-side Russian. The second pistol was in his hand now. He frowned down at the weapon, unable to remember how many shots he had fired.

He was exhausted beyond the limits of exhaustion, was now burning only raw hate and the marrow-deep need for revenge. He was a wild thing chasing a wild thing, bent on killing him before he could kill Lodge.

He peered ahead along the ground.

His quarry's blood trail and long scuff marks in the snow trailed on ahead to disappear in the murk. Mannion followed them, looking around, swinging the cocked Russian this way and that, ready for a sudden attack. He stopped when his quarry's tracks curved around to his right.

Joe stared straight ahead and down, realizing with a sudden feeling of vertigo that he was staring out into stormy space and down, down...down toward the gunmetal blue of Treasure Vault Lake set in a deep stone bed several hundred feet below, at the base of the Mountain of the Holy Cross to Mannion's left.

He could just barely see the oblong shape of the bleak

gray jewel set in even grayer stone, beyond the wavering curtains of snow.

He gulped as he looked at his feet planted only inches from that chasm. Shifting them a little, he caused snow and gravel to tumble down over the edge and into the wailing abyss below. He felt his right foot slide a little closer to the edge.

Then the left one...

What was this urge he had—something born of his unconscious mind—to throw himself into nothingness?

Panic rolled through him.

The mountain pitched under his boots. He felt himself lean forward then back then forward again until he dropped the Russian and threw his arms straight out to both sides, either to balance himself or...maybe, suddenly remembering all of his sins, a strong part of him wanted to take wing and fly into the void—into the absence of pain and sorrow, guilt and fury...away from the possibility that Jane had been taken from him forever.

CAW! CAW! CAW!

The crow's cry resounded inside his head, just as it had in the moments before Sarah had stepped out of that tree with the noose around her neck...as it had when Ezekial Storm had somehow healed him with benefit of an energy unseen...possibly from another, even darker world than Joe's.

CAW! CAW! CAW!

He looked down. Both feet overhung the edge of the cliff, dangling him over the void.

CAW! CAW! CAW!

He desperately willed himself back, suddenly realizing that the crow in his head was telling him nothing more complicated than:

LIVE! LIVE! LIVE!

He swung around, took one step forward, and gasped.

Lodge stood before him, not more than three feet away.

Mannion looked up at the man, who had a good six or seven inches on him. The man's left shoulder and arm shone red with fresh blood oozing through the long, deep tears in his coat. Half of the man's face had been clawed off. The left eye dangled down over his left cheek, hanging there by a bloody thread of nerve.

The man's hands hung straight down at his sides. He'd somehow ripped off Mannion's handcuffs.

He, too, had fired off all his ammunition.

As miserable as he must feel, he grinned, showing all those crooked, tobacco-stained knobs of his teeth. The man's breath wafted, warm and sour as a bear's den, into Joe's face as he said in his deep, guttural, bear-like growl:

"You an' me die together, Bloody Joe!"

"I don't think so," Joe said as the big man lunged toward him, raising his paw-like hands intending to wrap them around the lawman's neck and bull him backward off the ledge and into the raging abyss between the top of the mountain and Treasure Vault Lake...between life and nothing.

Joe found his knees working again.

Suddenly, they were a young man's knees.

He stepped quickly to his left, grabbed Lodge's right wrist with his own right hand, stuck his right leg out, and jerked the big man over it and forward, out over the ledge. Joe stared down over the side of the cliff as Lodge turned a somersault in the air and fell straight down, belly up.

His hat was torn away on the wind. His one good eye glared up at Mannion, round as a silver dollar; the other one flopped out in the wind, hanging by the bloody nerve. The man's mouth opened wide, arms and hands outstretched above him as though beseeching Joe to save him.

He gave one last bellowing wail that for several seconds seemed to fill the chasm and drown out the storm.

Then it dwindled to silence and there was nothing but the raging wind again as the bounty hunter's large body grew smaller and smaller as it fell. Quickly, the chasm swallowed the man, and then there was only the chasm gaping at Mannion like the open mouth of a forbidden god.

Joe twisted around and hurled himself back away from the ledge. He struck the ground on his left shoulder and hip. Sitting up, leaning back on the heels of his hands, he raked precious breaths in and out of his lungs as he stared out across the ledge, snow prickling his cheeks, gathering in his brows.

He smiled.

He threw his head back and laughed.

CAW! CAW! CAW!

CODA

When Mannion rode down out of the Sawatch, he was surprised to find it was still autumn down below.

Most of the aspen leaves were on the ground, and there was a penetrating chill in the air—he still wore his buckskin mackinaw—but there was no snow. At least, there was none now, a good month, he realized, since he'd left town in pursuit of his blood enemy, Ulysses Lodge. It had probably snowed, as it usually did this time of the year, a good week or so into October, but it had melted off.

Joe glanced at the mountains behind him. Their high, blunt crests were clad in snow as white as coats of ermine. There had been snow as far down as St. Elmo. He'd ridden out of it two days earlier, and he'd been glad he had. It had been a long, snowy ride down from where he'd consigned Lodge to the void and returned to find Red sheltering under an escarpment partly ringed by tall spruce and balsam trees.

A long ride in which to wonder and worry about Jane...

Was she still alive a whole month now after she'd been shot?

As he rode into Del Norte now in the midafternoon, long shadows slanting out from the buildings on the west side of the street and over the hustling and bustling mine and woodcutters' wagons and businessmen's buggies and horseback ranchmen, he wondered if he'd come home to a woman or to a grave.

Over the long trip back, his guts had tightened steadily in dread at what he would find.

Jane or a grave?

Ahead and on the left side of the street lay Hotel de Mannion. Joe frowned as he rode toward it, remaining on the street's right side. He wanted to check in with Doc Bohannon about Jane first thing. Later, he would inquire about the two U.S. deputy marshals just then heaving a couple pairs of bulging saddlebags into a jail wagon parked in the street just off the jailhouse's porch steps.

Deputies Rio Waite and Cletus Booker, both wielding shotguns, stood out there with the federal men. So did Deputy Henry McCallister and his former girl, Molly Hurdstrom. At least, she *had been* Henry's former girl. Now she was standing so close to Henry and smiling so brightly as she and the tall, lean deputy and Rio chatted affably with the two marshals, that Joe couldn't help acquire the feeling she and his junior deputy were back together again.

Hmmm.

What was in those saddlebags that they deserved the protection of a jail wagon?

None of the men nor the girl gathered around the wagon saw Joe ride past them astride Red. There was too much traffic between him and them. That was just as well. Joe needed to find out about Jane.

He continued riding down Main Street, ignoring the several hails from men and even a few women of the painted variety on both sides of the broad, rutted trace. He wasn't in the mood for chinning. He watched the big, well-appointed San Juan Hotel & Saloon slide up on his right, a half dozen men in business suits and a few of Jane's girls milling on the broad front veranda as they usually did this time of the day, inching on toward happy hour and a night of boisterous frolic ahead.

Joe turned his head quickly away from the San Juan, not wanting to be seen. Even if Jane were well, she wouldn't be there. Not after only a month. Not after the three bullets she'd taken to the chest.

Mannion had to get over to Bohannon's place. He had to see to Jane. He had to find out if that knife in his guts was going to twist around for longer and deeper, or if it was going to suddenly slip away.

His heart thudded.

A dark feeling lay inside him. He tried to ignore it as he rode on past the San Juan.

"Pa!"

The familiar voice, issuing from the left side of the street, brought Mannion up short. He drew back on Red's reins. He turned to see his daughter, Vangie, step out of a feedstore, holding a fifty-pound sack of cracked corn on her right shoulder. The feedstore owner, Burt Kleinsasser—a thick-set German in a green apron—came out behind her, also holding a fifty-pound sack of cracked corn on his shoulder.

"Oh, Joe..." the man said.

Had his eyes set behind small, round, steel-framed spectacles suddenly turned dark?

Vangie walked out to the middle of the loading dock fronting the store and stared, open mouthed with shock, at her father. Her face crumpled a little; tears came to her eyes.

Joe stared back at her in dread. "Oh, God," he heard himself mutter. "Oh, God...no."

"Wait, Pa!" Sniffing and appearing to choke back tears, Vangie moved forward, dropped the feed sack into the bed of her wagon parked in front of the loading dock.

The sack landed with a *bang!*, making the two horses in the traces lurch with starts.

"Follow me, Poppa!" the girl said, beckoning then leaping down off the loading dock and taking long strides up the street's left side, heading in the direction of Bohannon's office.

"Oh, Lordy, Joe," Kleinsasser said, still standing on the dock and holding the corn on his shoulder. His expression was damned hard to read. Was he amazed to see the lawman after all this time, or appalled by the news Joe was about to hear?

Suddenly, Joe found himself surrounded on both sides of the street by mute gawkers.

"Oh, Lord," Mannion said under his breath. "It's bad news. Vangie doesn't know how to break it to me. She's gonna let Bohannon do it."

He booted Red ahead along the street, dread pooling like sour milk in his belly. "At least I got him for you, anyway, honey," he continued to mutter, that knife turning and twisting in his guts. "At least I got him for you..."

He followed Vangie around the next corner to the doctor's office. He tied Red at the hitchrack and followed the girl inside the office. She hadn't bothered to knock but stepped right in and turned to him, backing away.

"Oh, Pa," she said, brushing tears from her cheeks with the sleeves of the cream, fleece-lined denim jacket she wore. "We've been waiting for you! I didn't think...I didn't think...!" She shook her head, sobbing.

Both Bohannon and the handsome, young Dr. Ben Ellison turned to Mannion.

"Oh, God, Joe—you're alive!" Bohannon said, marching up to shake Mannion's hand. He looked up at the taller man, scrutinizing Joe's face and eyes with his medico's gaze. "Are you all right? Good Lord—it looks like frostbite. More than a few cuts and abrasions..." He brushed a thumb across the leathery nubs of both of Joe's cheeks.

Mannion was numb with confusion.

"Doc, please...?"

The doctor looked up at him again, scowling. "I...I'm not sure you're in any condition to hear all that we have to tell you, Joe."

Mannion lunged forward and grabbed the collar of the man's frock coat with both hands. "By God, Bohannon, if you won't tell me—"

"Joe?"

Mannion stopped.

His heart hiccupped.

Still holding Bohannon's collar in his fists, he slid his gaze up and around the shorter man's head. His stomach flip-flopped and his heart leaped into his throat. She stood there in the opening of the doorway that led back to the hospital rooms.

Jane.

In all her glory...

Fair skin returned to its natural cream color with beautiful freckles, her thick, rich red hair flowing across her shoulders clad in a dark-green bathrobe that beautifully contrasted those rust-red locks to which their previous luster had almost fully returned.

Jane regarded Mannion with a wistful little smile, head tilted to one side, amber eyes glinting.

Then, suddenly all business, she jerked her chin toward the hallway behind her and said, "Get back here, you big lug. We have a double wedding to plan!"

She winked at him then turned and walked off down the hall.

You could have knocked Bloody Joe Mannion over with a feather duster.

Lower jaw hanging, he turned to where Vangie stood beside young Dr. Ellison. They were leaning back against the desk. They were smiling at him. They were holding hands.

"Of course," Ellison said, flushing a little as he straightened, clearing his throat. "With your permission, sir."

Mannion just stood there, sliding his shocked, tongue-tied gaze between the two...what?

Lovers.

As a smile began to spread slowly across Joe's craggy face made even craggier by his month-long mountain hunt, Vangie's eyes once more filled with tears and she ran forward and wrapped her arms around her father's waist and buried her face in his chest.

"Welcome home, Bloody Joe!"

A LOOK AT: ONCE A MARSHAL
A SHERIFF BEN STILLMAN WESTERN

FROM THE CURRENT KING OF THE VIOLENT, SEXY, HARD-HITTING WESTERN

The Classic Sheriff Ben Stillman Series Begins…

Playing poker, smoking cigarettes, drinking whiskey—retirement was treacherous business for ex-lawman Ben Stillman. The best of life seemed to be past, but then the past came looking for him…

The son of an old friend rides into Ben's life with a plea for justice and a mind for revenge. Up on the Hi-Line in Montana, a rich Englishman is rustling ranchers out of their livelihoods… and their lives. The boy suspects these rustlers have murdered his father, Milk River Bill Harmon, and the law is too crooked to get any straight answers.

But can the worn-out old lawman live up to the legendary lawman the boy has grown to admire?

For fans of William W. Johnstone and George P. Cosmatos's Tombstone, you'll love this first novel in the epic, fast-paced Sheriff Ben Stillman series.

AVAILABLE NOW

ABOUT THE AUTHOR

Peter Brandvold grew up in the great state of North Dakota in the 1960's and '70s, when television westerns were as popular as shows about hoarders and shark tanks are now, and western paperbacks were as popular as *Game of Thrones*.

Brandvold watched every western series on television at the time. He grew up riding horses and herding cows on the farms of his grandfather and many friends who owned livestock.

Brandvold's imagination has always lived and will always live in the West. He is the author of over a hundred lightning-fast action westerns under his own name and his pen name, Frank Leslie.